THE SCIENCE OF

MARK WOLVERTON

ROGER STERN, EDITOR

SUPERMAN
CREATED BY
JERRY SIEGEL AND JOE SHUSTER

ibooks
NEW YORK
WWW.IBOOKS.NET

DISTRIBUTED BY SIMON & SCHUSTER, INC.

An Original Publication of ibooks, inc.

An ibooks, inc. Book

Distributed by Simon & Schuster, Inc.
1230 Avenue of the Americas, New York, NY 10020

ibooks, inc.
24 West 25th Street
New York, NY 10010

The ibooks World Wide Web site address is:
http://www.ibooks.net

The DC Comics World Wide Web site address is:
www.dccomics.com

ISBN 0-7434-8651-X

PRINTING HISTORY
ibooks, inc. hardcover edition / November 2002
ibooks, inc. trade paperback edition / March 2004
10 9 8 7 6 5 4 3 2 1

Project Coordinator: Howard Zimmerman
Editorial Assistant: Janine Rosado
Cover art by Alex Ross
Cover design by Georg Brewer
Interior design by Gilda Hannah

Printed in the U.S.A.

SUPERMAN ART, pages 14, 43,67,121,203, 241, 254: John Byrne and Dick Giordano;
pages 75 and 213: Jerry Ordway; page 171L John Byrne and Karl Kessel; page 209:
Al Plastino. Text in Superman art by John Byrne, pages 14, 147, 171, 203, 241.

PHOTOS, page 104, 115, 129, 130, 131, 151: courtesy NASA; page 53: courtesy Dr.
Kim Makoi; page 96: courtesy Library of Congress; page 158: courtesy Smithsonian
Air and Space Museum; page 159: courtesy U.S. Department of Defense; page 214:
courtesy DC Comics.

DIAGRAMS, pages 18, 221, 47, 135, 173, 180, 199: Joe Bailey; page 78: courtesy
U.S. Department of Energy.

To the memory of my mother,
Dorothy Wolverton (1932-2001),
definitely a Super-Mom if ever there was one

and to my father, Ronald Wolverton,
a true Super-Dad.

ACKNOWLEDGMENTS

No man is an island, said the poet. Neither is an author. Whatever the name on the cover, every book is a collaborative effort between the person who writes the words and the multitude who bring it to life and to press, whether directly through the publishing process or indirectly by helping the author survive the entire ordeal.

First and foremost, an author needs a supportive and loving family, and I have the best: my father, my mother (who, if there's an afterlife, no doubt had something to do with all this), my sister Linda Chamberlain, her husband Glenn, and my niece Amy and nephew Tim. My love and thanks to all of them.

For friendship above and beyond the call, ceaseless encouragement, unstinting moral support, and general sanity maintenance, much thanks to Jeff Harris, Kristina Blanco, Denise Shubin, and Leila Monaghan, not to mention all the gastronomically-adventurous members of PaSWA, the Philadelphia Area Science Writers Association. And thanks to Nancy Shepherdson for setting me on the path.

For sage scientific counsel, cool ideas, and assistance in running weird notions up the flagpole, thanks to Mark A. Banash, Ph.D. and Dr. Jeff Livingstone. Thanks also to Frank Hoke of the Wistar Institute for telling me about the super-regenerating mice.

I'm also most grateful to the crew at DC Comics: Mike Carlin, John Nee, Charlie Kochman, Sandy Resnick, Eddie Berganza, and Rich Thomas. Thanks are also due to Roger Stern, whose voluminous knowledge of Superman and his history kept me on track; Gilda Hannah, our book designer; Byron Preiss, president of Byron Preiss Visual Publications; and of course, Howard Zimmerman, my patient, good-humored, and highly knowledgeable editor (and fellow *This Island Earth* fan).

My agent, Michael Psaltis of the Ethan Ellenberg Agency, has been both my stalwart guide and my staunch and tireless advocate in the publishing world, and the first person who believed that I could actually do this project. Thanks, Michael . . . let's go have that beer.

Finally, neither this book nor Superman himself would ever have existed without the creativity and energy of Jerry Siegel and Joe Shuster, who started it all when they first dreamed of a Man of Steel.

CONTENTS

Justice and power must be brought together,
so that whatever is just may be powerful,
and whatever is powerful may be just.
—*Blaise Pascal*

Most powerful is he
who has himself in his own power.
—*Seneca*

The superior man is modest
in his speech but exceeds in his actions.
—*Confucius*

INTRODUCTION

I know I have a lot of company, so it's hardly a mark of distinction, but I'll say it anyway: I grew up with Superman. I started out with him back in the Sixties, a decade he began by dealing mostly with rather exotic threats from various alien planets and alternate universes (the Bizarro world springs immediately to mind), and ended by turning his attention more and more to a troubled Earth torn by societal, political, and racial strife.

Being possessed by something of a scientifically minded bent even at that tender age, my friends and I were fascinated by the possibilities inherent in Superman's powers, and how those powers worked. We didn't just accept whatever passing explanations we were offered by the comic writers regarding the origins and nature of X-ray vision, flying, superstrength, and the rest of his superpowers. Maybe the simple declarations of "able to leap tall buildings in a single bound" and "more powerful than a locomotive" were good enough for unimaginative adults, but not for us. We wanted to know more. Just how did "X-ray vision" work, anyway? Did Superman really shoot out rays from his *eyes*? What about the flying thing? How could that work when Superman didn't have wings, and didn't seem to have any kind of exhaust system for propulsion? Okay, we understood about how Superman came from a planet with a red sun, but would relocating to a world with a yellow sun like ours really make that much difference? And so on.

We could speculate, argue, and concoct our own outlandish theories about the mysteries of superbreath and the relative merits of heat vision vs. "superfriction," but unfortunately it was all for naught. We were only kids, after all—extremely smart and precocious ones, perhaps, but still lacking the scientific credentials of, say, an Isaac Asimov, who was usually the guy we relied upon to explain such matters in his books.

Somehow, though, Dr. Asimov had overlooked a detailed evaluation of the residual wind backwash of running at superspeed. Or at least, if he *had* examined the problem, my friends and I had missed that particular book. So, our own vague conceptions aside, we were left wallowing in our superignorance. As we proceeded into adolescence, we began to worry less about comic characters and more about other strange entities, chiefly of the female variety, and soon the *hows* and *whys* of superpowers seemed considerably less interesting.

Some years later, I seem to have come full circle, taking the opportunity to once again consider the nature of those trou-

Introduction

bling superpowers. And science has progressed considerably in the meantime. Now, it's not only possible to seriously examine Superman as a fascinating and scientifically plausible biological phenomenon rather than as simply a fictional being, but also to consider the prospect that human beings may be able to give themselves some of his amazing powers—maybe not today, but within the lifetime of many people who will read this book.

We'll do both in the following chapters: We'll look at each of Superman's major powers in depth, examining how they could work and how they couldn't *possibly* work, their side effects and limitations, and how they complement each other to make Superman more than just the sum of his super abilities. We'll delve into Superman's Kryptonian origins along with that planet's history, science, and its cataclysmic destruction. We'll even consider some of the social and philosophical aspects of superpowers. Just what does it mean to be "invulnerable," anyway? What are some of the emotional and personal concerns faced by someone with such powers? Why should a being who can literally do almost anything imaginable bother himself with helping such ridiculously inferior creatures as human beings? And we'll consider how human beings might someday acquire superpowers of a sort—and what will it mean for us.

Our journey will take us across a broad spectrum of science and through nearly all of its branches: astronomy, geology, chemistry, physics, biology. We'll travel from the very large scale of stars, planets, and spinning interstellar dust clouds down to the microscopic processes of life itself, and beyond into the infinitesimal realm of the atomic nucleus. Along the way, we'll meet some famous and a few not-so-famous people who have opened humanity's eyes to profound mysteries and answered some of its oldest and most important questions. I hope that when we're finished, you'll have not only a better appreciation and understanding of Superman, but of science itself—still the best tool humans have discovered for understanding the universe and their place in it.

Thanks for coming along. Now, as Superman used to say: up, up and away.

CHAPTER ONE

KRYPTON: ELEGY FOR A LOST WORLD

In Western folklore and literature, only the alien worlds of our Moon and Mars are more famous than Krypton, the legendary lost planet of Superman. Yet unlike those worlds, Krypton doesn't exist and never did. Of course, it doesn't exist in Superman's universe either anymore, having completely blown itself apart in a titanic explosion that occurred under rather mysterious circumstances. Superman, Krypton's lone survivor, never lived upon nor even saw his homeworld.

Even now on Superman's adopted planet, Earth, much about Krypton remains shrouded in conjecture and mystery. We know that Krypton orbited a red dwarf star named Rao, located about fifty light years from Earth; it was one of eight planets in its solar system; and it was the closest planet to its sun. Krypton was much like Earth in many ways, with a similar atmosphere and general composition, although Krypton was slightly larger and more massive than Earth with a somewhat greater gravity. And rather than seven large continents widely dispersed over the surface of the planet, Krypton had only one supercontinent and a number of small islands, with a larger proportion of land to sea than Earth.

We also know that Krypton was the home of a highly

advanced scientific civilization, of which Superman—Kryptonian name Kal-El—is the only known survivor. By all outward appearances, Kryptonians were virtually identical to human beings, although there were some substantial differences between the environments of Krypton and Earth.

Those differences are the heart of our investigation. If Krypton had been a more or less precise duplicate of Earth in every way, Kal-El would still be a refugee from another world, but little different physically from any other human being. What accounts for his incredible powers? How did this being from another planet evolve to have so much in common with us in some ways, and yet be so unlike us in others? To find out, we'll have to go back to the beginning—to examine what sort of world could spawn a Superman.

UNDER A RED SUN

With the naked human eye from the surface of Earth, the stars spangled across the night sky look pretty much the same. A sharp-eyed stargazer might notice that some stars seem to be different in color from others, and some are brilliant while others are so faint as to be barely visible, but otherwise there's little to distinguish one from another. It's not hard to imagine how ancient people could believe that the stars were nothing more than holes in a heavenly dome, torches suspended in the sky, or the campfires of the gods.

Until the advent of modern astronomy in the last several hundred years, we had no way of finding out the truth behind the stars. Although it's been called the oldest science, astronomy is also the only one (aside from particle physics) that has never been able to directly touch the object of its study. Biologists can dissect specimens, geologists can hold rocks, chemists

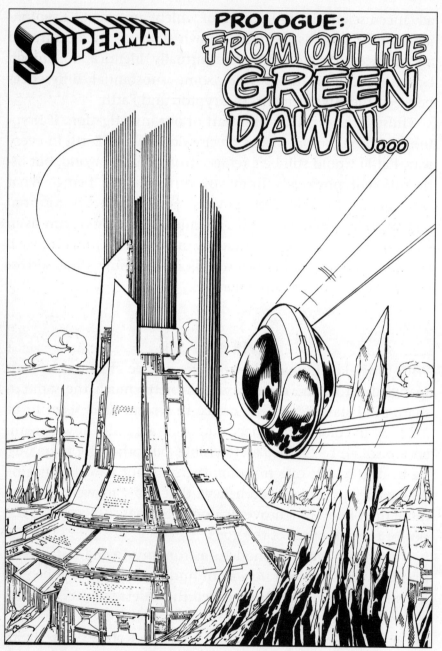

Pre-cataclysmic Krypton, with its sun, Rao, setting in the background.

can mix and analyze chemicals, but astronomers can't examine a piece of a star in a laboratory to find out what it's made of. Instead, astronomers had to find ways of bringing their subjects closer, first through telescopes that collected the light from the stars and planets, then with other instruments that could gather other forms of radiation. Learning how to extract and read the information embedded in the light and other energy produced by these distant objects, astronomers found that they didn't need to be on the scene to do their job. A clear night, a good telescope, and a spectroscope would be quite enough. And astronomers have one big advantage: one star close by that's easy to study and is visible every day from sunrise to sundown. Our own sun, called Sol by astronomers (hence the term "solar"), can tell us a lot about how stars work, and comparing our sun to other stars can tell even more.

Sol and the rest of the stars visible to us with the naked eye seem comfortingly constant and unchanging. The stars and constellations you learned as a child are still there, and they'll be there long after you're gone: the Big Dipper, the North Star, Scorpio, Orion. This appearance of stability is misleading, however, and it's only our short lifespans on this planet that create the illusion. In fact, the universe is in constant change, taking place over vast distances and unimaginably deep expanses of time. Stars are born, live for a finite time, and then die in a grand cycle that repeats endlessly, in much the same way as living creatures. Not that stars are actually alive—not in any definition of the word that we understand—but neither are they peaceful denizens of an eternal universe. And just as with living creatures, stars can be classified in separate "species," not by genetics or body types, but by size, color, temperature, composition, and age.

A typical star begins its life as a cloud of interstellar gas and dust, composed mostly of hydrogen, the most abundant element in the universe. Gravity begins to pull the gas and dust together, and the cloud becomes denser and begins to rotate and flatten, forming an "accretion disk" or "protostar." As gravity continues to collapse the cloud inward, atoms continue to collide at a greater rate, and temperatures rise to the point when nuclear reactions begin to take place as hydrogen atoms fuse to form helium. The heat generated by this process of nuclear fusion begins a self-sustaining reaction, and the star "turns on." The pressure of radiation from the star's interior keeps it from collapsing further, and the star begins the stable period of its life.

The type of star born in this process depends on how much mass the pre-solar cloud contains, which in turn determines the star's size and temperature. First, a certain minimum amount of matter must come together for nuclear fusion to begin and a star to be born. Some protostars can't make it to this level and become "brown dwarfs," failed stars that may give off some heat and light but not enough to qualify as the real thing. Brown dwarfs may shine dimly for a while but will eventually fade out, unable to sustain full-fledged solar existences.

Shortly after most stars are born, they join what's known as the main sequence—the stable period of a star's lifetime. Astronomers visually depict the main sequence through a handy chart called the Hertzsprung-Russell diagram, after the scientists who developed it. It may sound intimidating, but the H-R diagram is simply a graphic representation of stellar evolution. It plots what is called the *absolute luminosity* of a star (a computation of its actual brightness at a particular distance compared to our sun) against its surface temperature. The coolest stars (relatively speaking, of course—even a cool star is still pretty hot by human standards!) are red in color, while the hottest are blue-white. The various temperature/color types are classified by letter in the sequence O, B, A, F, G, K, and M, with O the hottest (blue-white) and M the coolest (red). (The sequence isn't in alphabetical order because of various revisions of the original classification scheme; astronomy students have traditionally used the rather quaint phrase *Oh, Be A Fine Girl, Kiss Me* as a handy mnemonic device to keep the order straight. This was obviously a more amusing joke back in the old days when nearly all astronomers were men who spent all their nights alone on mountaintops peering through telescopes— and perhaps dreaming of more earthly pursuits.)

When star types are graphed in this way, an interesting phenomenon emerges. Rather than a more-or-less random distribution, most average stars tend to fall in a definite band diagonally across the graph, from the hot bright stars in the upper left to the cooler and dimmer stars in the lower right. This band is the main sequence, proving that there's a definite correlation between a star's brightness and its temperature/color. The hotter the star, the brighter it shines.

Why is this so important? The relationship between brightness and color/temperature can tell us a lot about not only how the star was born, but how old it is and how long it's likely to live. As a general rule, the hotter stars tend to burn up their nuclear fuel faster, and thus live shorter lives, while the cooler, slower-burning red and yellow stars enjoy a longer period of stability. Our sun, classified as a G2-type star (each of the letter classes of star type is further divided into subtypes numbered 0 through 9), is only in early middle age and should burn steadily at more or less its current intensity for several billion years more.

But not all of the stars we see fall neatly onto the main

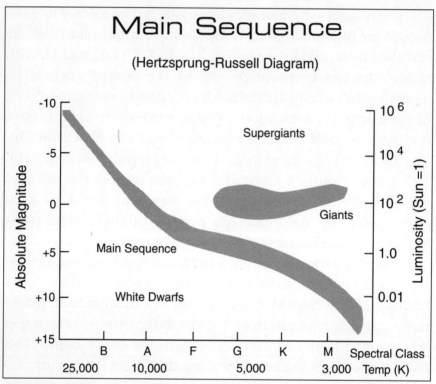

The Hurtsprung-Russell Diagram of main sequence stars. Hot, bright stars appear in the upper left and cooler, dimmer stars in the bottom right. Red dwarfs such as Rao are plentiful, but small, cool, and dim.

sequence of the H-R diagram. There are white dwarf stars, which are still very hot, but also dim. There are red giant stars, which are much brighter and larger than the average red star. Why don't these stars fall onto the main sequence like the rest? Is there something wrong with our diagram?

Not at all. Stars on the main sequence are merely going about their business, living stable and upstanding stellar lives, happily burning hydrogen. But nothing lasts forever, including the supply of hydrogen deep with a star's core. When it's gone, converted into heavier elements, the star has to begin using a different source for fuel to keep burning. It begins to consume the hydrogen and the heavier elements in its outer layers to continue the nuclear fusion that keeps it shining. And this is where a star leaves the main sequence.

The ultimate fate of any particular star depends on its mass and temperature. Some stars expand physically as they burn the fuel in their outer layers; as they do so, their density decreases and their overall temperature drops. An average yellow star swells in size, cools, and changes color as it becomes a red giant. Other stars shrink or become unstable, blowing off vast amounts of stellar material in spectacular outbursts, some of which form colorful nebulae such as the famous Ring Nebula in the constellation Lyra. And some massive stars literally collapse under their own weight, as their diminished nuclear processes can no longer hold back the forces of gravity. These stars face a variety of ultimate fates. They can become white dwarfs or neutron stars, hot and dense bodies no larger than a planet. They may become supernovas, which occur when stars collapse so rapidly that they literally blow themselves apart (the Crab Nebula is the remnant of just such an event). Finally, an extremely massive star may end its life as a black hole, in which the relentless force of gravity causes the star to collapse in on itself to the point that it actually vanishes from the universe, leaving only its intense gravity field behind.

All of these stars were former residents of the main sequence, but just as with human beings, age brings with it inevitable change and deterioration. So, aside from certain types such as brown dwarfs, which were never legitimate stars to begin with, most stars off the main sequence are at later stages in their lives. Astronomers once thought that the main sequence was also a timeline, with most stars beginning hot and blue in the upper left corner and steadily moving to the cool and red lower right corner, but that's not necessarily the case. Stars can enter or leave the main sequence at any point, although usually they enter it soon after birth and leave it later in life. Some, like the hot blue stars, don't stay very long; others may end up being there practically until the end of the universe.

Since stars begin their lives pretty much as pure hydrogen, which they spend their lives converting into heavier elements through nuclear fusion, it follows that, in general, the older the star, the less hydrogen and the more heavy elements it contains. (There are some exceptions, such as red dwarfs, which burn so slowly that they may never exhaust their hydrogen supply.) So the H-R diagram, in telling us about a star's age and temperature, also gives us some broad hints as to its composition. Red giants, for example, have used up most of their hydrogen supply except for deep within their cores, and so are forced to burn other elements farther from their centers. We can detect these elements by analyzing the star's light with a spectroscope, which reveals the telltale wavelengths of light in the star's spectrum emitted or absorbed in characteristic ways by the elements as they burn. Our sun, now about 4.6 billion years old, is about 71 percent hydrogen and 27 percent helium, with a smattering of heavier elements such as calcium, sodium, and magnesium. By the time the sun becomes a red giant, it will contain much more of the heavier elements.

We can now begin to speculate about Krypton's sun, Rao— what kind of star it might be, its probable life cycle, and what this might mean for its family of planets. As we've seen, red stars are always relatively cool, but can be quite huge. Antares, a red giant readily visible as the brightest star in the constellation of Scorpius, is roughly 500 times larger in diameter than the sun; if somehow moved into the center of our solar system, all the inner planets (Mercury, Venus, Earth, and Mars) would

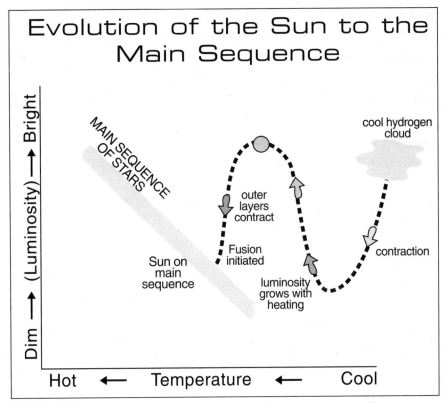

Evolution of the Sun to the Main Sequence

Bright ↑ (Luminosity) →

Dim ↑ (Luminosity) →

MAIN SEQUENCE OF STARS

cool hydrogen cloud

outer layers contract

Fusion initiated

Sun on main sequence

luminosity grows with heating

contraction

Hot ← Temperature ← Cool

The evolution of our own sun, Sol, as plotted on the main sequence diagram.

be consumed in its stellar fires. Yet once upon a time, it was probably a smaller, yellower star, maybe even the heart of another solar system and a source of life—until it expanded to its current monstrous size. Clearly, it's not likely we would find much life native to such a system. Any intelligent beings would have either long ago recognized their imminent danger and moved to another star system, or would have been destroyed when their sun expanded.

So if we want to postulate an intelligent race living under a red sun, we need to look elsewhere: to the red dwarf stars. Red dwarfs are the most common variety of stars in the universe, but because they're fairly small and dim, they're also probably the least conspicuous. The closest star to our sun, Proxima Centauri, is a red dwarf only 4.3 light years[1] away, but is only a faint speck in the skies of the Southern Hemisphere, 20,000 times fainter than the sun. Since life as we know it usually requires both light and heat to exist, a cool and dim red dwarf solar system seems like a fairly unpromising place on first glance.

But there may be hope. We can evaluate planetary systems for the possibility of life using the concept of a "habitable zone" (HZ), which is the region in the system inside of which conditions are suitable for life. The HZ is generally defined in terms of temperature and distance: It's the zone between the closest and farthest distance from the star inside of which it's not too hot or too cold for life to exist. Too close to the star, it's too hot; too far away, it's too cold. A planet has to orbit its sun completely within the HZ for living organisms to arise. A perfect example is our own solar system: Venus, with its surface temperature of 900 degrees, is obviously too hot, and so lies outside the inner limits of the HZ. Mars, on the other hand, is too cold, so it's outside our HZ's outer limit. (Although earlier in our solar system's history, Mars may have indeed fallen within the HZ.) Earth, luckily for us, orbits firmly within the sun's HZ. Its temperature and climate, like Goldilocks' soup, are just right. If our sun were hotter or colder, however, the HZ of our solar system would correspondingly move outward or inward.

Given a cool star such as a red dwarf, the HZ would obvi-

[1] Despite common misuse, "light year" is a measurement of distance, not of time. It's the distance that light travels in one year, slightly less than 6 trillion miles (or about 9.5 million kilometers).

ously be much closer than in our solar system. Krypton, therefore, would have to be much closer to its red sun than the 93 million miles that separate Earth from our sun. This in itself isn't all that outrageous; of the more than 90 extrasolar planets—planets orbiting stars other than our sun—discovered so far in our galaxy, many orbit their parent stars extremely closely. Finding a closely orbiting planet that can also support life, however, isn't as easy. One problem is that the closer a planet orbits a star (or a moon orbits a planet), the more the tidal effects caused by gravity will force the orbiting body into something called *synchronous rotation*. A body in synchronous rotation rotates on its axis in the same time it takes to complete an orbit. Earth's moon is one example: it rotates on its axis in precisely the same time it takes to complete one orbit around Earth. The "day" of a synchronously rotating planet is the same length as its "year," so that the same half faces the star at all times. The hemisphere facing the sun is perpetually in sunlight and scorched by heat, while the hemisphere facing outward is always dark and freezes solid. No liquid water, and thus no life, could exist under such conditions.

Can we somehow get around the problem of synchronous rotation? It's not easy, but there are some possibilities. Krypton might have been located just outside the distance from its sun where synchronous rotation would take hold. Maybe only the inner reaches of the habitable zone would be subject to the effect, and Krypton might orbit in the outer region. Less likely, its mass might be high enough to counteract the effect, at least partly. Finally, if Krypton's atmosphere was dense enough to reflect the worst of the heat, its atmospheric circulation might even-out surface temperatures enough to avoid the bake-and-freeze scenario, even if the planet was in synchronous rotation.

A relatively heavy atmosphere would help to mitigate another problem: high intensity radiation emanating from Krypton's sun. As byproducts from their nuclear fusion reactions, stars emit vast quantities of high-energy subatomic particles—protons, electrons, pieces of atomic nuclei—traveling at nearly the speed of light. There are also X-rays, gamma rays, neutrons—a whole smorgasbord of radiation at various wavelengths and energies, much of it damaging or lethal to living organisms. Our own sun, which we like to think of as benign and friendly, is in fact a deadly source of radiation that can quickly kill any unprotected living creature. Our thick atmosphere, along with Earth's strong magnetic field, keeps the worst of it out. (Being 93 million miles away helps, but not enough.) Krypton's close proximity to its sun makes this a tough problem. It's possible that the weaker, more sedate red dwarf emits a less-intense level of harmful radiation, enough that an Earthlike atmosphere, even without a strong planetary magnetic field, would reduce the surface radiation to acceptable levels. Still, life on Krypton would probably have to learn to adapt to far greater amounts of background radiation than life on Earth. As we'll see later, this has some profound implications regarding the nature of Superman's powers and his near-invulnerability.

One interesting aspect of living under a red sun would be that the nature of light itself would appear different—to Earthly eyes, at least, it would seem "redder." This is not to say that, if you stood on the surface of Krypton, everything would look as though you were wearing a pair of rose-colored sunglasses. But there would be a definite difference between what Earthly eyes and Kryptonian eyes interpret as "normal" light. You're already familiar with this phenomenon, though you might not be consciously aware of it. Consider the difference between the natural sunlight you enjoy sitting out in the park during lunch, and the artificial fluorescent light that surrounds you back inside your office. Both are "white" light, yet somehow they're not the same; the sunlight seems warmer, more yellow or red, more "natural," while the fluorescent light feels cooler, bluer, more "sterile." You're not imagining things. The differences are real, but they exist at the edge of your ability to actually see them. The sunlight contains much more *infrared* radiation (which carries heat), while the fluorescent light is weighted more toward the *ultraviolet*—the blue end of the electromagnetic spectrum. The two light spectra are different because each is being created by different processes, but we can see perfectly well in either type of light because they happen to overlap in the human eye's visible range. If the visible range of our eyes were weighted more toward the infrared, we might still be able to see in the bluer fluorescent light, but much more dimly.

What kind of planets might we expect to find around a red sun? That depends on how the planetary system originally formed, a process that is still not fully understood. We don't know for certain how solar systems, including our own, are born, although there are a number of plausible models. Some of them theorize that planets are created in a number of ways around an already-existing star. A massive star could pass close to another, with the material drawn out from each by gravity, then coalescing and cooling in stable orbits to form planets; two stars could collide, spewing out matter that becomes a planetary system.

Other theories hold that planets and stars form almost simultaneously from the same cloud of rotating gas and interstellar dust. The center of the cloud first becomes a protostar, then a full-fledged star as its nuclear fires turn on. The pressure of radiation from the fledgling sun pushes most of the remaining dust and gas away, but denser areas continue to clump together under gravity, finally forming solid planets revolving around the star. Most astronomers think this is how our own solar system formed, but that doesn't rule out different models for other solar systems; in fact, some of the newly discovered planetary systems in our galaxy are keeping scientists up at night precisely because they can't be explained by our current models.

The way in which a planetary system was formed is a vital issue because it explains why the planets contain some elements and not others. Aside from the elements that are created later in the heart of its sun, everything in a solar system was there to begin with, the ingredients of the original dust cloud or stars that bred the system. All of the elements on Earth—the oxygen we breathe, the iron in our blood, the calcium in our bones, the silicon in our computers—were already here long before even Earth itself was born. And because certain elements can only be created by specific processes, their presence tells us something about the origins of that planet.

All stars create helium from hydrogen through nuclear fusion, and many then fuse the helium atoms to form other heavier elements. But this process only goes so far. Fusing the atoms of heavy elements to create still heavier ones requires temperatures and energies too great even for most stars to achieve. A star such as our sun contains only minute quantities of elements heavier than helium. Yet we have 92 naturally occurring elements on our planet. Even if they were present in the dust cloud from which Earth formed, where did the heavy elements come from if not from the sun?

The not-so-obvious answer is that they were formed in one of the most violent events of the universe: a supernova. Supernovas occur when a massive star suddenly collapses and literally blows itself up, increasing in brightness millions or even billions of times and releasing huge amounts of energy. The last supernova seen in our own galaxy was in 1604 and was described by the famous scientist Johannes Kepler; it was bright enough to be seen in the daytime. Another supernova was seen in 1987, in a small companion galaxy to our own called the Large Magellanic Cloud. Fortunately for us, supernovas don't happen too often (at least, not on a human timescale). If one ever did occur in our part of the galaxy, its vast radiation could quite quickly and efficiently exterminate all life on Earth.

The very heavy elements, including the radioactive elements such as uranium, can only be created in the conditions that occur inside a supernova. The violence of the stellar explosion spreads these heavy elements throughout space, where they drift and eventually collect into dust clouds with other elements, providing the raw material for new stars and solar systems. In effect, the universe is continually recycling itself: when old stars burn out, or destroy themselves as supernovae, new stars are born from their ashes. And the elements within those ashes, created much earlier, also form the planets circling the stars, and everything else in and on the planet. Ever since the late astronomer Carl Sagan first said it, it's become something of a new-age cliché, yet it's also an accurate and sober scientific reality: "we're all made of star stuff."

All of this means that in order to be a place capable of forming life, a star and its planets have to contain a certain amount of heavier elements. Just hydrogen and helium won't do it, because life needs more than that: carbon, silicon, oxygen, nitrogen, and so on. The oldest stars in the universe would have nothing more than hydrogen and helium, because that's all that existed when they formed. So although many red dwarfs are thought to be quite old, perhaps even dating back to the very early universe, Krypton's sun probably couldn't be one of those. It's certainly possible for a star born without planets of its own to capture some that happened to be wandering alone through space, but the odds against such a random occurrence make it unlikely.

So Rao, although it might be extremely old, would still be a product of at least several previous generations of star formation and death. Assuming that it formed through the accretion of a rotating disk of gas and dust, as our solar system probably did, enough heavy elements were present to form a system of eight planets. When Rao began to shine, its solar wind blew off the lighter hydrogen gases from the inner planets, leaving the heavier, denser cores, while the larger outer planets remained less-dense gas giants, such as Jupiter in our own system. Settled into a comfortable orbit well within the narrow habitable zone of Rao, perhaps only several million miles away from the small sun, the Kryptonian biosphere began the process that would lead to the evolution of living creatures.

SPINNING THE EVOLUTIONARY WHEEL

From the time humans finally realized that the lights in the night sky were other suns, they've dreamed and wondered about the possibility of new worlds circling those suns—and whether other creatures might live on them. Would they be radically different from human beings, perhaps even horrifyingly so? Or would the laws of evolution produce intelligent beings much like humans?

Although evolution itself is a well established biological fact, many of the specific details about just how it works are still subjects of scientific debate. Scientific knowledge is always undergoing its own sort of evolution, as new discoveries fill in holes in old theories while raising fresh questions to be answered. There's never a final answer in science, because there are always more details to find, more "whys" to ask to follow the "whats." In evolutionary biology, one question concerns how much variation is possible in the process of evolution. Does it always follow a predictable path, a more-or-less straight arrow from the simple to the more complex? If the clock could somehow be turned back on Earth, and evolution begun all over again, would it turn out pretty much the same way, or would radically different forms of life now rule the planet?

Most scientists agree that over the four-billion-year history of Earth, evolution was shaped by far too many completely random factors—climactic change, meteor and comet impacts, geological upheavals—to allow it to occur in precisely the same way if it could somehow be repeated. On a second spin of the evolutionary wheel, new numbers would come up: perhaps a race of intelligent dinosaurs would have arisen, dominating the weaker and smaller mammals that shared the land. Maybe Earth would suffer greater and more frequent cosmic catastrophes that would so disrupt the planetary environment that nothing more complex than microorganisms could survive. Perhaps animal life would never have left the sea to establish a beachhead on dry land. Or maybe a nearby supernova explosion in our galaxy would scorch Earth with such intense radiation that any life would be completely eradicated, never to form again.

Since there's no way to literally run such an experiment, any discussion of alternative evolutionary pathways on Earth remains a matter of pure speculation. But given the innumerable variables, one thing is clear: human beings as we know them are definitely not preordained by evolution. Even the development of intelligence may not be a foregone conclusion. We like to believe that our great intelligence makes us superior to all other species, but this may be an illusion. Some evolutionary biologists theorize that the evolution of sentient, self-aware creatures may be nothing more than a fluke, a mere aberration in the tableau of life. In fact, it might even be more of a detriment than a benefit in the long run. Bacteria, coral, ladybugs, and sea otters may not be intelligent, but they also don't invent hydrogen weapons, irreparably damage their own environments, or slaughter each other wholesale. If the success of a species is judged on the basis of how many individuals exist on Earth and how quickly they can reproduce in different conditions, then amoebae and cockroaches beat humans—pseudopods, antennae, and hands down.

If we extend the question to include evolution on other planets, matters become even more complex and the odds even trickier. While many planets like Earth may exist in the universe (although nothing close has been discovered thus far), the operative part of that phrase is "like"—the chances of another world precisely matching all the characteristics of our own in size, mass, temperature, atmospheric composition, geological activity, and all of the other myriad factors that define a planet are nil. A single tiny, seemingly insignificant variation can have a huge impact on the forms of life that might exist on that world. In our own solar system, Venus and Mars are quite Earthlike in many respects, yet no earthly creatures could survive in the 900-degree poisonous atmosphere of Venus, or on the barren, radiation-bathed surface of Mars. Our Earth may be an oasis of life now, but for most of its long history almost every modern-day Earth inhabitant would have considered it worse than hell.

Obviously, if evolution on Earth wouldn't turn out the same way twice, it's practically impossible that it would follow precisely the same path on another planet, which by definition is a wholly different environment. So we won't find more examples of *Homo sapiens* living in another solar system, beings that would match ourselves chromosome for chromosome, gene for gene, amino acid for amino acid.

Just how different might they be? Here again, we move into an area of pure speculation. And because we can speculate, we also have a fair amount of wiggle room if we want to postulate humanlike beings from another planet. While evolution on different planets at different times would undoubtedly produce organisms that were genetically dissimilar, it's possible that the solutions to functional problems might result in physical similarities. The need to pick up and hold an object, for example, is the same problem for an organism whether it's on Earth, Krypton, or any other planet, assuming roughly the same gravity. Basically, some kind of appendage must be extended from the body and be capable of moving freely and grasping onto an object. (We'll disregard the other necessary attributes, such as sensory and nervous systems able to locate, identify, and track an object, although the same principles apply.) On Earth, we see many ways of solving the problem and performing the task: claws, tentacles, paws, mouths, hands. But all of these various answers share common mechanical factors, and within a particular related group of animals—mammals, for example—the strategy tends to be more or less the same. No mammals use tentacles or crablike claws to manipulate objects; all, including humans, use a combination of some sort of articulated appendages and their mouths. The form and exact characteristics of the appendages might vary—some cats can handle objects with their two front paws, while dogs use their mouths—but in both cases, a mouth is a mouth and the front paws are front paws. When humans first stood upright, they developed sophisticated abilities to manipulate objects with their "front paws," i.e., hands—but they can still "walk" on all fours if desired, and actually start out that way soon after birth.

Despite different solutions to the same problem among various animals, physical similarities are still easily recognizable. This is a phenomenon known in biology as "convergent" or "parallel" evolution: different species evolving similar traits to deal with similar environmental challenges. (Note the body shapes of tuna, sharks, dolphins, and the extinct marine reptiles known as ichthyosaurs. All four different species approached the problem of moving quickly through the medium of water by evolving similarly streamlined body shapes.)

If form follows function in an evolutionary sense on Earth, it is reasonable to postulate that the principle of convergent evolution would extend to life on other planets. If the ability to handle objects with fine detailed movements is needed to build tools and eventually develop and use technology, some kind of hand is required. It might have ten fingers rather than five; it may lack fingernails or have some kind of adhesive pads on the fingers; yet it will still be recognizable as a hand. If a large brain and sophisticated sensory apparatus are necessary to operate the hands, they will share certain things in common with other brains and sensory organs. A species lacking in one or more of these attributes might be much like Earth's whales and dolphins—obviously intelligent creatures able to communicate and form social groups, but unable to develop tools and technology because they lack the necessary physical appendages.

We don't know if the basic human form—two arms, two legs, one head containing the brain and the major sense organs, etc.—is the most efficient evolutionary solution to the problems of being an intelligent, tool-using animal. On Earth at this time, it appears to be, since we have no other major competition, no non-human animals trying to establish their own rival civilization. As previously mentioned, however, evolution might have engineered something much different, given another chance. But it's hard to imagine how any sort of technological civilization could develop without sharing a lot of things with humans on a large-scale physical level.

In the universe of Superman, on the planet Krypton, this is precisely what happened. A race of intelligent beings evolved that by all outward appearances was virtually indistinguishable from humans. Yet because their environment was different from Earth in some important respects, the similarities would be largely on the visible, physical scale. Kryptonians would need some unique abilities in order to evolve and thrive in their own environment. The differences between Krypton and Earth would shape the evolution of the Kryptonian race in important ways.

ONLY THE TOUGH (AND THE LUCKY) SURVIVE

From space, Krypton would probably appear much as Earth does, a blue planet enveloped by white clouds. Assuming an axial tilt similar to Earth's 23.5 degrees, the planet would experience seasonal variations. At somewhat closer range, however, some distinctive differences would emerge. One major contrast between Krypton and Earth is in the distribution of land mass. Although early in its history almost all of Earth's land area was concentrated in a supercontinent called Pangaea, this land mass broke apart over the ensuing millions of years and separated into the seven (or six, if Europe and Asia are counted together as Eurasia) continents we know today. On the slightly larger planet Krypton, however, the initial supercontinent that existed after the formation of the planet's oceans never broke apart, and was much larger in proportion to the planet's full surface area than Pangaea. While Earth's surface is over 70 percent water-covered, Krypton's surface would be nearly the opposite: only 25 percent ocean. The persistence of a supercontinent implies little or no plate tectonic activity on the planet. Despite outward appearances, Earth's surface isn't all in one piece: it's actually composed of a number of huge plates of rock that "float" on deeper layers of the planet. Plate tectonics, the movement and interaction of these plates, has been a vitally important process driving Earth's geological history. Collisions between plates or slippage along the borders of adjacent plates create mountain ranges and cause earthquakes. Much of the west coast of the United States lies on just such a plate boundary, explaining the frequent shakiness of California and the occasional volcanic eruptions in the Northwest such as Mount St. Helens. Although its exact mechanism is still unclear, plate tectonics is believed to be driven by heat generated by radioactive elements deep inside the Earth, and carried to the upper layers through convection currents that make rock expand and move.

Aside from the obvious danger of earthquakes and volcanoes, the fact that a planet's surface is moving about in pieces like an eggshell doesn't sound like something that would make much difference to living creatures, especially since tectonic plates might move no faster than a few inches per century. To the individual creature living out its relatively short lifespan on a planet's surface, this is basically true. But from the long-term perspective of the evolution of life, plate tectonics turns out to be extremely important—and so is its absence.

It's hard to say why a planet such as Krypton would lack plate tectonics. Maybe temperatures within its core weren't hot enough to drive the process. The physical composition of the planet might also have been a factor. And without a large natural satellite such as Earth's moon, Krypton would have been free of the gravitational and tidal effects caused by such a body, which might also have contributed to the phenomenon. So far, however, Earth is the only planet we know of to display the process of plate tectonics—we've yet to observe it on any other world in our solar system, although that doesn't mean that a planet such as Mars didn't also undergo tectonic changes in its geological past.

Whatever the reasons, what are the implications for Krypton and Kryptonian life? How would the lack of continents widely separated by oceans influence the evolution of life and an advanced civilization? Evolutionary biologists and geologists have discovered that speciation—the process by which organisms evolve from a common ancestor and "split" into separate and distinct species—is greatly dependent on geography. Long mountain ranges create widely separated habitats and climates that promote diverse forms of life. Separation of continents by other natural barriers such as oceans has the same effect. Earth owes its dizzying biologic wealth of between three to 30 million distinct species of plants and animals to these phenomena.

Even with a huge supercontinent, there would be variations in climate arising from differences in latitude (closer or farther from the equator). These would provide for some degree of biodiversity: some creatures would evolve better suited for life in the colder polar regions, while others would thrive in the warmer equatorial habitat. Still, given a single landmass and a lack of natural barriers such as mountain ranges, interbreeding, and genetic mixing would be far more prevalent on Krypton than on Earth. This would result in life on Krypton which was far more homogeneous, both genetically and on a visible scale, than life on Earth.

But there's a big problem here. A lack of biodiversity is generally considered to be a grave threat to the continued survival of life on a planet. Throughout the millions or billions of years of its existence, every planet inevitably faces disasters of all kinds from both outside and inside: bombardment by asteroids and comets, geological upheavals, gravitational stresses from passing bodies, intense radiation from its sun and elsewhere in the galaxy. Events on this scale nearly always completely disrupt and destroy a planet's climate, wiping out the complex balance of factors necessary for life to survive. Although life evolved fairly soon in Earth's early history, it was almost completely exterminated on several occasions. Geologists have documented at least fifteen "mass extinction events" on Earth, in which at least 50 percent of all living species were destroyed. The most famous of these, of course, is the cometary impact 65 million years ago that led to the extinction of the dinosaurs and the rise of mammals and human beings.

With a wide variety of species there may be at least a few for which a planetwide catastrophe doesn't prove fatal. If enough of these survive, life hangs on to again spread across the planet. Fortunately for us, this has happened time and again on Earth. (Which is not to say, however, that we'll continue to be so lucky!)

Kryptonian life would also need to be lucky, but in a different and more basic way. Its lack of diversity would make it extremely vulnerable to any of a vast catalog of catastrophes—for example, if a large asteroid struck the heart of the Kryptonian supercontinent early in the planet's history, it would almost certainly turn it into yet another dead world spinning its way through space. To become and to stay a living world, then, Krypton would have to dodge these cosmic bullets by sheer chance. It may not be as unlikely as it sounds. Just because our own solar system is filled with literal cosmic debris such as asteroids and comets (even more so early in its history, when Earth endured near-constant bombardment from space), the

Kryptonian system might be relatively "clean." Krypton's close proximity to its sun might also help, as Rao's much greater gravity could divert incoming, planet-killing rocks.

Whatever works—as long as Krypton cheated the grim reaper of cosmic disaster, life would be in good shape. Multicellular, complex organisms could arise fairly soon, with intelligent humanoid life evolving not long after. Without the mass extinction events that impede and slow the spread of life, Kryptonian civilization wouldn't have to await the false starts and dead ends of repeated evolution before establishing itself on the planet. With only a single, albeit huge, continent to explore, and without the obstacles of impassable mountains, canyons, and other barriers, early Kryptonians could spread quickly across their world's habitable regions, establishing thriving settlements throughout the main continent.

Moving and interbreeding freely throughout the Kryptonian supercontinent during the whole of their evolution, the Kryptonian people might not develop the marked differences in external physiognomy that could be defined as various "races." External similarities among Kryptonians resulting from genetic homogeneity could have helped to promote social cohesiveness and discourage conflict based on racial, cultural, or religious grounds. City-states might have been the major defining social unit of early Kryptonian civilization, ultimately supplanted by large extended families as technological improvements in transportation and communication brought people from widely separated parts of the continent closer together. A strong and resilient world government could develop naturally under such conditions. While the whims of evolution may have laid the foundations for millennia of violence, war, divisiveness, and unreasoning hatreds among humans, the Kryptonian people would likely have developed a natural tendency toward unity and cooperation, allowing both the advance of technology and the establishment of a stable civilization to occur much earlier than has proven possible on Earth.

KRYPTON'S END

Whatever the glories of the Kryptonian civilization, however, all were destroyed when Krypton blew apart. Astronomers on Earth would be able to detect the shattered remains of the planet as an immense cloud of debris orbiting Rao; over many years, this cloud might form into a ring, although like our asteroid belt, such a ring would probably be too diffuse to be seen from a distance. The gravitational effects of Krypton's destruction would also affect the orbits of the remaining planets in its solar system, and these effects would also be detectable from Earth. Even without a surviving native such as Superman to tell us the story, it would be clear that something terrible had happened in the system of Rao.

What kind of force could so completely devastate a planet? Aside from the obvious, such as a direct collision with another huge massive body (as depicted in the classic 1950s science-fiction film *When Worlds Collide*), gravitational and tidal forces from outside can easily tear a planet asunder. Tides are created by the interaction of gravity from different sources and varying directions (in Earth's case, from the Sun and Moon); if these forces are strong enough, they can weaken and eventually rip apart the structure of a planet. At least some of the magnificent rings we see in our solar system may be the result of such processes, as a moon's orbit happened to shift just a little too close to its parent planet and the moon was torn apart.

The planetary death sentence can also be imposed from within, as heat and internal stresses deep within the core build up to the breaking point. This may be especially likely in a planet without active plate tectonics to relieve the pressures. As internal tensions reached critical levels, earthquakes, volcanoes, and other geological upheavals would break out across the surface of the planet. These would release some of the pressures, but if the core processes were building too rapidly, matters could escalate into total devastation.

Exploding planets, exploding stars, colliding celestial bodies—the universe is hardly the tranquil place it seems. Yet life seems to display a remarkable resilience, continually coming back for more after it's been repeatedly almost wiped out. (At least, this is true on Earth, which is the only case we have to study so far.) And living creatures who manage to escape one cosmic catastrophe and attempt to set up stakes elsewhere would have much to contend with. What would the evolutionary differences between humans and Kryptonians mean for a Kryptonian refugee on Earth? We'll look at those questions—and some answers—next.

The Science of Superman

CHAPTER TWO

A KRYPTONIAN ON EARTH: LIFE AS A REFUGEE

S uppose we took a being that was conceived on another planet and brought it to Earth before it was actually born. It would be a collection of cells, a fetus (or the alien equivalent), a mass of biological potential waiting to enter a new world. It would be a product of millions of years of evolution in a different environment, a place much different from Earth, with all of the strengths, weaknesses, abilities, vulnerabilities, and traits acquired by its ancestors over those millions of years. Yet it would be born not on the world where all those qualities were slowly, laboriously selected and weeded out from others and honed through natural selection, but in a wholly new place in which the factors and chances that shaped living creatures were much different. How would our newborn guest fare?

In most cases, probably not well. Even if our guest's home world was much like Earth, the inevitable variations in its evolutionary history would leave it vulnerable to a host of hazards. It might be susceptible to Earthly bacteria, finding deadly the same organisms with which humans can coexist quite contentedly. The entire science of ecology is based on the extremely sensitive factors that attune organisms to a particular environment, and how changes in that environment affect them—usu-

The Kents discover the infant Superman.

ally for the worse. Pluck an organism out of the intricate web of intertwined conditions for which it's perfectly adapted and drop it into a completely different place, and it's unlikely that its individual characteristics will permit it to thrive as well as a native creature, much less better.

But unlikely doesn't mean impossible. For a Kryptonian, evolved and formed for a world much like Earth yet with some vital differences, Earth would be a challenge of a different sort. Instead of being weighed down by greater gravity, a Kryptonian would feel somewhat more buoyant. The greater brightness and warmth from our sun would be offset by a feeling of greater energy and vitality.

Assuming that Krypton's atmosphere had a lower oxygen content than our own, Kryptonian lungs would be larger and able to extract oxygen from the air more efficiently. Our Kryptonian might tend to hyperventilate a bit at first, but as he or she became more accustomed to the richer air, the higher oxygen levels would contribute to greater endurance and strength. Although this all sounds very positive for our Kryptonian, adapting to and becoming comfortable with the different conditions would take some time. And the longer our Kryptonian remained in Earth's environment, the more pronounced these differences would become.

The most important differences, however, would probably stem from life under our yellow sun. A Kryptonian being would have to deal not only with different types of radiation, but with levels and intensities much varied from those under a red sun. Before we get down to Kryptonian cases, we'll examine the electromagnetic spectrum and find out just how much ground the word "radiation" covers.

FROM ONE END OF THE SPECTRUM TO THE OTHER

Most people think of atomic bombs and nuclear reactors when they hear about radiation, but those sources are only a small slice of the pie. The electromagnetic (EM) spectrum includes everything from light to radio and television waves to energies so powerful that they're not naturally seen on Earth.

Radiation is simply defined as the transmission of energy from one place to another, either in the form of waves, similar to those that occur in water when you throw a stone into a lake, or particles of energy (sometimes called quanta) moving through space. Nuclear radiation consists of high-energy pieces of atoms (usually protons, neutrons, and combinations thereof) that are generated as atoms are fused together (as in stars), torn apart (as in an atomic fission bomb), or decay into simpler elements (as radioactive elements all naturally do). Some of these particles or groups of particles have an electrical charge (positive or negative). Since they are charged, they can be affected by outside charges and magnetic fields, and are called "charged particles." Heat is nothing more than the random motion of atoms and molecules in a substance, transmitted when some literally bump up against others and set them moving at the same rate. Electromagnetic radiation such as light or radio or X-rays is something of a special case: it acts like waves at some times and like particles at other times, a property with the fancy name of wave-particle duality. In general, EM radiation behaves like waves when moving from one place to another, and like particles when interacting with matter. But unlike sound, which also travels in waves, EM radiation can move through a vacuum—it doesn't need a medium such as air or water to transmit it. And electromagnetic radiation always travels at a constant speed. In a vacuum, it moves at about 186,282 miles, or slightly under 300,000 kilometers, per second—light speed. In air, water, or other media, it moves at a somewhat slower speed.

The wave characteristics of electromagnetic radiation provide a way of distinguishing different types from one another. The number of waves per second is called the frequency; the distance from one point of a wave to the identical point on another wave is the wavelength. Pictured this way, it's easy to see that if more waves are going to fit in the same length of time, i.e., a higher frequency, they have to be shorter, i.e. a smaller wavelength. So frequency is inversely proportional to wavelength—the higher the frequency, the shorter the wavelength, and vice versa.

If you've ever held a prism in sunlight to project a rainbow onto paper, or for that matter, if you've ever seen a rainbow after a spring rain, you're familiar with the concept of a spectrum. The prism breaks visible white light down into its component parts, from red at one end to violet at the other. The red light is the lowest frequency and longest wavelength, while the violet is the highest and shortest. It works precisely the same way when the idea is expanded to encompass the other forms of electromagnetic radiation. We have radio and TV waves at the low-frequency/long-wavelength end, followed by microwaves, infrared radiation, visible light, ultraviolet, and on into X-rays and gamma rays at the high-frequency/short-wavelength end.

We humans can detect only a fairly narrow band of the entire EM spectrum. We can see light, and we can feel (but not see) some infrared radiation in the form of heat. We're completely blind to everything else. Of course, the fact that we can't see it or feel it doesn't mean the other forms of electromagnetic radiation aren't there. We're constantly bathed in a sea of EM radiation, some of it human-generated, some of it naturally produced. Much of it, such as the radio and television waves now passing through your body, doesn't affect you at all; the wavelengths are too long and the energy too low. Other invisible forms of EM radiation can have a profound effect. Try lounging about in a bathing suit under the midday July sun without any sunscreen for several hours, and you'll quickly discover the painful effects of too much ultraviolet radiation. Or expose yourself to an intense source of gamma radiation such as an unshielded nuclear reactor, and you likely won't survive long enough to worry about your sunburn.

A Kryptonian on Earth: Life as a Refugee

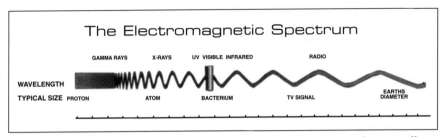

A simple graphic representation of the electromagnetic spectrum. What we call "visible light" is represented by a vertical band near the center of the spectrum.

While all electromagnetic radiation is part of the same spectrum and is produced by electromagnetic processes, its properties—and its effects on living organisms—can vary greatly depending on its wavelength and frequency. And since different types of stars emit different types and amounts of electromagnetic radiation, the type of sun under which life evolves is of paramount importance to its existence and development.

SUNSCREEN AND SOLAR CELLS

We've already examined the implications of a single large super-continent on Krypton's biodiversity and the development of its civilization. But all of this would be moot if Kryptonian life were unable to adapt to the high radiation flux emanating from its sun. Without the protection of a dense atmosphere to absorb, divert, or attenuate gamma rays, X-rays, and other particle radiation, our own sun would make the surface of Earth as barren and sterile as that of the Moon, at least to any form of life as we now know it. Hurtling subatomic charged particles and intensely powerful quanta of high-energy radiation are as destructive to the complex molecules of carbon-based life as a speeding rifle bullet is to an ice sculpture, destroying their intricate organization and tearing apart their very structure. Earth is fortunate

47

enough to possess a strong magnetic field, which acts as a shield against harmful charged particles. Unfortunately, the same internal processes that drive Earth's plate tectonics are also thought to create its magnetic field—and as we've determined, Krypton probably wouldn't have plate tectonics. No plate tectonics, no protective planetary magnetic shield—and a great deal more charged-particle radiation reaching the planet's surface and affecting the creatures living there.

This is all made worse by the fact that Krypton's red sun would be relatively cool, meaning its habitable zone would be much closer to it than the habitable zone in our own solar system in which Earth happily resides. But in order to be close enough to its sun and thus warm enough to harbor life, Krypton would also be subjected to much heavier radiation than a planet farther away. If Krypton also lacked a protective ozone layer in its upper atmosphere to screen out and attenuate short-wavelength ultraviolet and other high-energy radiation, some form of natural defenses, resistance, or sheer invulnerability to radiation would be even more essential for life to evolve. Creatures that lacked natural defenses against the constant onslaught of energy would be rapidly eliminated. It might take hundreds of thousands, perhaps millions of years before an organism emerged that could withstand the harsh environment. Once such a life form emerged, however, it would quickly become dominant over any other organisms with lesser defenses. In the ceaseless evolutionary struggle for living space and food, the more hardy animals that can produce more offspring will always win out over those less well adapted to the prevailing environment.

On Earth, organisms exist that have evolved an amazing resistance to environmental conditions that would annihilate other species. Some varieties of cockroaches, for example, are remarkably resistant to nuclear radiation, thriving in the waste of recently detonated atomic weapons. And as city dwellers know all too well, roaches can thrive in many other types of environments. Other, more exotic creatures, known to biologists as "extremophiles," have been discovered living near deep-ocean volcanic vents in the absence of sunlight and under intense pressure and heat. Microorganisms have even been reported quite happily inhabiting pools of radioactive waste water from reactors! Given time and perhaps a bit of luck, life has displayed a formidable ability to scratch out a foothold in the most unlikely places.

The intricate biochemical processes of living organisms require complex molecules such as carbon that are capable of joining together with other elements in myriad ways. It's unlikely that life of any reasonable definition could be based on simpler (and thus more radiation-resistant) molecules, so any form of resistance or invulnerability to radiation would require the evolution of natural defenses—a "radiation immune system." Such a system could take a variety of forms. It could be as simple as a dense shell or other covering that radiation cannot penetrate, shielding an organism's innards just as a lead apron protects an X-ray technician. Or it could be an adaptation on a molecular level: the ability to rapidly repair and regenerate radiation-induced cellular damage. In fact, all Earth creatures already have such an ability to a certain degree, since all evolved in an environment with some natural background radiation. (Otherwise a sunburn would never heal, and a few chest X-rays would probably kill you.) It's only when radiation disrupts the process of cellular division, causing mutations to arise, or is so intense as to overwhelm an organism's natural regenerative capabilities, that unfortunate consequences occur.

An even more sophisticated evolutionary protection against

hard radiation might be the generation of a biologically produced electrical field that would ward off harmful charged particles on the individual organism scale exactly as Earth's magnetic field does on a planetary scale. Earth's magnetic field is
caused by the electromagnetic currents created by the movement of molten iron and radioactive elements deep inside its
core, so obviously another process would have to account for a
similar effect in living beings. An organism with a high amount
of heavy metallic elements in its cell walls and other electrically conducting metals in its blood cells could conceivably generate electromagnetic fields through the circulation of its
blood. All complex animals, including human beings, are gen-
erators of electromagnetic fields that arise from the biochemical activities of their nervous system and muscular system. The
tiny contractions that are moving the muscles of your eyes as
you read this line across the page are caused by minute electrical charges coursing through nerve fibers carrying messages
from your brain. Electrical current, whether moving through a
wire, a piece of metal or a nerve fiber, generates a magnetic
field. The strength of the magnetic field is directly proportional to the strength of the electrical current: the stronger the current, the stronger the magnetic field, and vice versa. On Earth,
although the electrical activity in the nervous systems of
humans and other animals can be measured by instruments
such as an electroencephalograph, which displays the electrical
currents of the brain, such activity is much too weak to affect
anything outside of the body. "Psychic healers" may claim to
see the "auras" of people or manipulate their "energy fields" to
cure what ails them; "remote viewers" believe they can see
events occurring far removed from them physically; and other
psychic people may claim they can read minds or even move
solid objects with the power of thought. But the energy that

such powers would require is far greater than can be generated or manipulated by the human nervous system. And even if a person were capable of generating such power biologically, he or she wouldn't escape detection; they'd be instantly recognizable by the electromagnetic interference and disruption they'd cause whenever they used their powers. Of course, maybe it was your psychic neighbor in the next apartment who inadvertently caused your cable service to go out or your cell phone call to break apart into static, but it's unlikely your neighbor will be sympathetic enough toward your theory to pay you back for your lost service.

Consider, however, humanoid life that evolved under much different electromagnetic circumstances, such as Kryptonians living on a planet bathed with radiation from their red sun. Just as those who possessed a denser, more radiation-resistant skin or an increased ability to repair cellular damage would be at a distinct evolutionary advantage compared to others, so too would individuals who by chance had a nervous system operating at higher levels of electrical activity, thus generating a more powerful "bioelectrical field." The individuals who possessed two of these attributes would be hardier and more likely to survive than those who had only one, and the Kryptonians enjoying all three protective traits would be hardier still, more likely to live longer and breed more offspring with the same beneficial traits. They would be less susceptible to cancers, leukemias, and other radiation-induced illnesses, and their genes would be less likely to suffer the damaging mutations that would cause debilitating disease or death in their children. The naturally generated bioelectrical fields around their bodies would probably still not be strong enough to affect their surroundings to any great degree, but it would be sufficient to deflect or neutralize certain types of charged-particle radiation.

So a Kryptonian life form might have evolved with a three-fold defense system against radiation. The bioelectrical field would be the first line of defense; some radiation that managed to penetrate the field would be stopped by dense, resistant skin layers; and any damage caused by harmful particles not stopped by the first two layers would be rapidly reversed by a highly sophisticated cellular-repair system. In fact, human beings already possess such a three-fold defense mechanism, although the bioelectrical field component is by far its weakest and most insignificant part and can thus be ignored. Alpha and beta particles, for example, are stopped by nothing more than your own skin; it's only when they get inside the body through breaks in the skin or by inhalation that they cause mischief. The Kryptonian resistance to radiation, evolved under a more intense level of natural background radiation, would simply be much stronger than that of an Earth native.

Along with the ability to resist the deleterious effects of various forms of solar radiation, Kryptonian organisms might have arisen that were capable of directly using certain wavelengths of radiation. All living creatures use and convert energy of some form in order to live, and most do so in a variety of ways. Human beings and all other mammals consume bulk matter—food—and extract energy from it through chemical conversion processes. Yet just as humans need food in order to survive, we also need certain types of radiation: visible light, in order to see; infrared radiation (heat) in order to maintain the environmental temperatures required for life. Another familiar form of life uses radiation to literally create its own food: green plants, through the process of photosynthesis. On Earth, only plants and certain species of bacteria are autotrophs—organisms capable of creating their own food from inorganic material. The rest of us are heterotrophs—we need to ingest organic material from

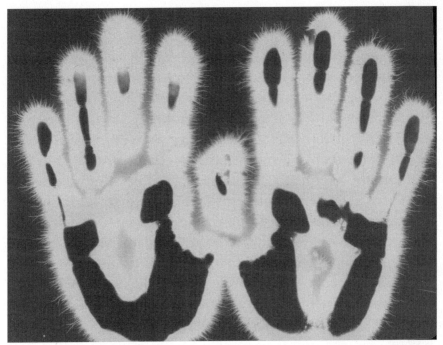

Place an object on an unexposed photographic plate, expose it to a high-frequency, high-voltage EM field, and the resulting image is what is known as a "corona discharge." The process, known as Kirlian photography (after its discoverer, Seymour Kirlian), is also said by many to picture a living object's bioelectric aura.

outside our bodies to provide the raw material necessary for our digestive systems to synthesize the nutrients that keep us functioning.

Why is it that on Earth, it's mostly only plants that are autotrophs? Why can't we supposedly more advanced animal types derive nutrition directly from sunlight, instead of relying on the sensually pleasant but rather cumbersome method of consuming bulk material? (For one thing, it would make dieting much easier—just stay out of the sun for a few weeks and watch the pounds melt away!)

The most likely reason is that on Earth, at least, autotrophs appeared first. The earliest entities that could be called "living" by any reasonable definition[1] were not plants as we know them, but they did have the ability to survive solely by using inorganic elements. The reason is simple—nothing else existed. Obviously, if the very first living organisms could survive only by consuming others of their kind, sooner or later only a single individual (the hungriest and most aggressive, probably) would be left—and then it would starve to death. Instead, the first examples of life on Earth were capable of deriving sustenance from materials immediately available in their environment, such as carbon dioxide, sunlight, and nitrogen, among others.

As more complex multicellular animals appeared, so did the ability to derive energy from organic molecules outside the body—in the bodies of other creatures. Thus was born what's commonly known as the "food chain": plants create energy from the sun using photosynthesis; plant-eating animals (herbivores) eat the plants and make use of their stored energy; other animals (carnivores) eat the herbivores. And when the higher animals die, carbon dioxide is released during decomposition, which is used by plants during photosynthesis, and the cycle continues. The essential truth of life on Earth is that all animals, even those who never touch plants, are ultimately dependent on photosynthesis for food.

It's possible to imagine a different scenario, however. Another adaptation that would help animals to cope with life under strong radiation is the ability to use that radiation directly. Humans have some capability along these lines, creating vitamin D in their bodies by direct exposure of the skin to sunlight. Kryptonians would be able to synthesize a greater variety of

1. The meaning of the word "living" can become extremely ambiguous when dealing with the very small—by most definitions, viruses are not actually alive on an individual level, yet are capable of invading living organisms.

essential nutrients in larger amounts by exposure to their red sun. In effect, they might evolve to become living solar cells. It's doubtful that such a process would provide enough energy to serve as the sole source of nutrition for something as sophisticated and energy-intensive as humanoid life, but it would be a useful supplemental source of food and energy. An added benefit would be that Kryptonians could survive on smaller amounts of solid food if necessary, a handy ability in times of drought and poor harvests. This scenario presents another example of how a particular evolutionary adaptation can have a direct effect on the social development of an intelligent species: Kryptonians would be less likely to fight over limited resources, and thus their society might develop in a less ruthlessly competitive and more openly cooperative way than one plagued by constant shortages.

The capability to derive nutrition, and thus energy, from more than one source would also be extremely useful for beings needing the strength and endurance to withstand high gravity—especially if they walk upright. Even if Krypton was only slighly greater in mass than Earth, its surface gravity would be correspondingly higher. A native of Earth on Krypton would definitely notice the difference, tiring more easily and moving with greater difficulty; but a normally fit person would eventually adapt to the higher gravity. (Conversely, a Kryptonian would enjoy greater strength and stamina in Earth's weaker gravity, which in small part accounts for Superman's abilities.) The back troubles of millions of present-day Americans testify to the hazards of being a large animal trying to function in an upright position in a gravity field, and that's only on Earth. Kryptonians under higher gravity would need not only stronger and denser bones and muscles to get along, but also the strength to move those heavier parts under a greater gravity load. Storing the required energy could be done by eating huge amounts of food almost continuously, as do many species of Earthly birds and other animals. A more efficient strategy would be to have a way to supplement food intake with another energy source, as with the "solar cell" process mentioned above. Again, evolution would favor the animals who didn't need a constant intake of food: they would sit and watch as the non-solar-powered types desperately fought each other for limited food and ultimately died off, starving and exhausted from struggling under the gravity load.

How would such an ability—deriving energy directly from sunlight—work? Strange as it may sound, probably through some variation of photosynthesis. Kryptonians would probably not use chlorophyll (although perhaps other alien beings—the legendary "little green men"—might). But chlorophyll is similar in structure to the hemoglobin found in blood. Perhaps Kryptonian hemoglobin (unlike that of humans) would be capable of functioning much as Earthly chlorophyll. Or other substances contained in Kryptonian skin might function in much the same way. We're in the realm of speculation here, but such a biochemistry, while unknown on Earth, isn't entirely inconceivable.

With these various adaptations to life under their rather harsher variety of an Earthlike environment, it's clear that Kryptonians would be pretty tough customers, biologically speaking. An average Kryptonian would find Earth a much more congenial place than a human would find Krypton. In fact, a human on Krypton would be in dire straits indeed. Fettered by stronger gravity that would make it hard to move, a human would tire easily and also probably have trouble breathing, especially assuming a somewhat denser Kryptonian atmosphere. And while our human ambassadors might not notice any great difference in temperature, they would notice something else: a very quick sunburn, followed by nausea, vomiting, and internal bleeding—the classic symptoms of radiation sickness. If our humans stayed very long, they'd probably end up being buried on Krypton. Not an auspicious beginning to opening up diplomatic relations, to say the least.

LIGHT AS A FEATHER

Even considering the importance of the radiation environment to an organism removed from its home planet to another, the most immediate phenomenon it would notice would be the difference in gravity. As animals who evolved in a gravity field, we tend to take gravity for granted. We understand the basic rules from a very early age: if we let go of something, it falls to the ground, and if we trip over a crack in the sidewalk or lose our balance on a bike, so do we. We learn to adapt and allow for the inevitable effects to the point where it becomes essentially automatic. When someone tosses a ball to you, you can judge its movement and can (usually) catch it. You don't have to think about how much effort is required to pick up a book, walk up a flight of stairs, or stand on one foot; your body has absorbed the lessons of a lifetime in Earth gravity, and compensates instinctively as it moves.

It's a whole different ballgame—literally—under a different gravity, or with no gravity at all. ("Weightlessness" or "zero gravity" are actually not technically accurate terms, because even in orbit, a small degree of gravity is present. In fact, there's probably no place in the universe *completely* free of gravity. The precise term used by scientists and engineers is "microgravity"—but we'll stick with the common term here.) For the first human space travelers in the early 1960s, strapped firmly into their capsules on flights lasting no longer than a day or two, weightlessness was little more than an amusing curiosity. As spacesuit gloves and pens spun freely in the cramped spacecraft, the major concerns were medical and very basic: How would humans fare without gravity? Would they become disoriented and confused? Would they be able to breathe and swallow? Would the shape of their eyeballs become distorted, affecting their vision? When astronauts and cosmonauts reported feeling just fine both while in flight and after returning home, their worried doctors decided that their initial concerns were unfounded and that weightlessness posed no ill effects on human beings, at least in the short term. The human body functioned quite well without gravity, and in fact, the astronauts even enjoyed its absence, especially when they popped the hatch and dangled outside in the void for a few minutes. Surely there was nothing to worry about as mission planners devised longer and more demanding space missions.

That confidence didn't last long. During the American Gemini program of the mid-1960s, a chief goal was the development of EVA skills: the ability of a spacesuit-clad astronaut to do useful work outside of his spacecraft. Floating aimlessly at the end of a tether attached to the ship might be fun and picturesque, but it wasn't very useful. Astronauts had to learn to *work* in space: how to use tools, how to move from one craft to another in case of emergency, how to assemble equipment, even how to do simple repairs if necessary. It didn't appear to be a difficult proposition. After all, shouldn't it be easier to work and move around without the constraint of weight?

Astronauts quickly learned otherwise. Something as simple as turning a bolt with a wrench became a frustrating exercise— if you try it floating in zero gravity, not anchored to anything, the bolt turns *you* as you turn it, and you go spinning. It was an aggravating display of Isaac Newton's Third Law of Motion: For every action, there's an equal and opposite reaction. Trying to move only a few yards from one side of the capsule to another on the outside could be like climbing on glass. Without anything to hang onto, without anything to push against (or more properly, to push back on them), and without the natural resistance of gravity to help them control movement, the first astronauts trying to work in space found it an incredibly exhausting and nearly futile endeavor. Techniques and tools were soon developed that made it possible, and now extremely complex work is routinely done floating in zero G—but only by highly trained men and women who've spent hundreds of hours mastering the tricks of the trade.

It was somewhat easier for the Apollo astronauts who walked on the Moon. Even one-sixth Earth gravity is much better than none at all. Still, the moonwalkers had to adapt themselves to the difference. On the Moon they were "supermen" of a sort—an astronaut could lift and move objects he couldn't budge on Earth and, though safety rules prevented it, he could have jumped higher and run farther and faster than he could back home. But to move about safely, set up equipment, and perform scientific experiments on the surface of the Moon required years of training on Earth in conditions of simulated one-sixth gravity (using special harnesses and other equipment). Without such preparation, the astronauts could have easily damaged valuable instruments, or injured or even killed themselves.

Working in space is one thing; spending a great deal of time there is quite another. In the Apollo era, astronauts were in space for only a couple of weeks at most, but with the advent of orbital space stations, human beings now live and work in zero gravity for months at a time, even a year or more. The men and women who have lived on the Mir space station, and the

International Space Station that replaced it, have provided scientists with the first real data concerning what happens to human beings taken out of their native environment for much longer periods. The data are somewhat discouraging for the planners of long-term space missions, but also confirm that definite physical changes occur when complex organisms such as human beings stay in a different gravity environment—and some of them may be permanent.

It's been known for decades that humans in low or zero gravity experienced some loss of muscle mass, loss of calcium in bones, and gastrointestinal symptoms (i.e., space sickness). Other problems included insomnia and general disorientation. Most space travelers adapted quickly and recovered their normal well-being soon after returning to Earth. As flights grew longer and more intensive research was done, including longer-term medical follow-up of astronauts after their time in space, scientists realized that these effects and the physical changes that induced them weren't as benign or as transient as they seemed. Human beings and other animals have undergone various environmental changes in their evolutionary careers as Earth's climate has fluctuated and as life has moved from one part of the planet to another. Our bodies have consequently evolved ways to deal with some environmental changes: we shiver when we're cold to keep the body warmer, and sweat in hot weather to cool the body. However, the strength of Earth's gravity has remained virtually the same throughout the evolution of life on our planet. Put us in a different gravity and our bodies don't "know" how to adapt. Muscles, bones, and joints are designed to move under gravitational stress. Remove that stress, and like any other unused complex mechanism, the mechanical equipment of the body starts to fall apart. Some studies show a permanent 15 to 20 percent loss of skeletal bone mass in human beings returning home after a fair amount of time in space. Maintaining a rigid exercise schedule in space helps a little, but doesn't stop these processes. Though it's hardly widely publicized, most astronauts—who are, of course, already exceptional physical specimens—face weeks or months of recovery from long periods in space.

These physiological effects of prolonged weightlessness are a major hurdle that will have to be addressed if truly long-duration spaceflight to Mars or elsewhere is to become a practical reality. But what about humans living in a lower but constant gravity, such as on the Moon? Would they experience the same negative effects? Or would even one-sixth Earth gravity, coupled with the fact that humans could probably work harder and longer without tiring, be enough to forestall permanent physiological damage? Unfortunately, we don't know yet. If people are able to move and work in an environmentally controlled Moonbase without being encumbered by bulky spacesuits, perhaps they can enjoy all the benefits of lower gravity without the ill effects. Until humans return to the Moon to stay for more than just a few days, we can't tell for sure. And until the first Earth child is born and raised in such an environment, we won't know how a being that evolved on one world, yet first opens its eyes on another, will develop.

The one thing that *is* certain is that gravity has a profound effect on life. It might even be impossible for life to exist and evolve without it. So far, though, all the life we know about has evolved in one particular gravity field—ours. Before we can answer all the questions about gravity's ultimate importance to living creatures, we'll need to find some examples of life that evolved under a gravity field other than our own.

UNDER A YELLOW SUN

Let's return to the individual we met at the beginning of the chapter—one of Kryptonian evolutionary and genetic origin yet born and raised on Earth. For convenience's sake, we'll assume a male, and call him Kal-El. Would he literally be a superman?

Probably not at first. Aside from all the usual problems that any newborn animal must face, Kal-El would have to deal with a certain period of adaptation to the alien environment, a sort of biological shakedown phase. This might last even as long as several years, as he grew and matured. He would find himself subjected to conflicting pressures: While his Kryptonian genetic heritage would allow him to develop greater strength, endurance, and speed in Earth's lesser gravity, his natural defenses against radiation might be sorely tested by Earth's more intense yellow sun. On the other hand, Earth's protective magnetic field, ozone layer, and atmosphere might be enough to mitigate the greater solar intensity, while Kal-El's Kryptonian capacities to absorb and convert solar energies for biological use would enjoy a more energetic source in our sun.

Given time, Kal-El's Kryptonian body would find an equilibrium in this strange environment, and new capabilities would begin to manifest themselves. He would begin to exhibit unusual strength, speed, and resistance to injury. In games and other physical play, he would tire much less quickly than his peers; he'd never have trouble finding his "second wind," because his more capacious and efficient lungs and respiratory system would enjoy air much richer in oxygen than that of his native world. He wouldn't be impervious to injury as yet, but he certainly wouldn't bruise, skin his knees, or cut his finger as easily as other children, and would heal faster when he did. Kal-El would probably think nothing of this at first. He would simply be using his natural abilities much as any other child. Since, at least in his early years, those abilities would probably be only slightly superior to other children, it's unlikely that anyone else, including his foster parents, would consider him as anything more than perhaps a very strong and athletic boy.

But eventually his Kryptonian nature would assert itself in ways that would be impossible to ignore or discount: lifting the back of a car off the ground to retrieve a ball that had rolled underneath, for example, or apparently seeing through solid objects. The reactions of his parents and others to such feats, and their inability to do the same things, would soon make it clear to Kal-El that he was profoundly different. As his body became more acclimatized to Earth, more efficient in its ability to store and use the sun's solar energy, and as Kal-El became naturally stronger and more agile with age, those differences would become even more marked. He would have to learn to control his superior abilities in certain situations: For example, if one has the ability to kill someone with a single punch, it's wise to avoid being goaded into confrontations where angry passions can get out of hand. And if one wins every race, hits a home run every at-bat, and scores a touchdown every time he catches the ball, he's going to find himself the object of serious resentment from his peers. So just as Kal-El was discovering and exploring his amazing powers and abilities, he would also be forced to consider and deal with their social implications.

There would also be psychological considerations. Kal-El would have to guard against allowing himself to begin feeling too superior, too dominant over others. Such an attitude would be difficult to avoid, because in Kal-El's case, the feelings wouldn't stem from adolescent insecurity or wish-fulfillment, but would be based on reality: in many ways, Kal-El *would* be superior physically to humans. He would have to temper that knowledge with a strong sense of humility and a moral awareness. His foster parents would be a crucial influence in this regard. When a being with such powers realized his full potential, there would be little or no force on Earth capable of controlling him. Instead, he would have to learn to control *himself*, and make a conscious choice to use his unique gifts for positive rather than negative purposes.

Having explored the general reasons a Kryptonian like Superman would enjoy abilities and powers on Earth far beyond those of its natives, we'll now consider some specifics: just what those powers would be, and how they might work.

CHAPTER THREE

INVULNERABILITY: A MAN OF STEEL

One of the classic images displaying Superman's amazing powers is bullets spattering harmlessly off his chest in all directions as a dazed gunman stares in amazement, his useless weapon dangling in his trembling hand as he realizes his criminal career is about to come to an abrupt, ignominious end. Superman's invulnerability to bullets, fire, explosions, and pretty much every other sort of Earthly misfortune is an enviable advantage in his never-ending fight against evil, and one that we relatively puny humans would love to possess ourselves. It seems magical, even supernatural.

But is it possible? Could a humanoid being—even a uniquely enhanced one such as Superman—literally be indestructible? Probably not, in the absolute sense. It's hard to imagine how any living being could survive the millions of degrees and the intense pressure of a stellar core, for example, or the heart of a nuclear explosion. Such forces aren't just inimical to life—they literally tear matter apart at the most basic level. But these are the extremes of the universe, and a living creature, even a Superman, would be unlikely to ever encounter them. So, while

complete invulnerability probably isn't possible, we could have the next best thing: *near*-invulnerability for all practical purposes. (We'll use the term "invulnerability" from here on, while acknowledging that we're speaking only in relative, not absolute, terms.)

If such a being existed on Earth, how would he be put together? Would his cells be different from ours, or would he possess some kind of impenetrable "force field"? Wouldn't he have at least some weaknesses, some limits to his invulnerability? What would they be? And perhaps most intriguing of all: what would be the implications of Superman's invulnerability on his mortality? Would he also possess a "super immune system"? And if so, how long would he live? Would he literally be immortal?

To answer these questions, we'll first have to consider what it means to be vulnerable biological beings. We will discover that, just as there are many things that can harm living creatures, there are many natural strategies for protection against those harmful forces. If we want to be invulnerable (or nearly so), there's more than one way to pull it off.

A SHIELD AGAINST HARM

The most obvious and basic mechanism to protect anything from something else is a barrier: a wall, shield, or obstruction that stands between the protected object and whatever might threaten it. Walled cities and forts are as old as the first human settlements, and it's easy to understand why. A nice thick wall keeps your enemies out, your own people together, and remains on duty twenty-four hours a day. Once you've built it, your work is done, except maybe for a little routine maintenance now and again. You're safe and secure, and needn't worry about threats from outside. Or if you have something valuable you want to hold onto, you simply seal it inside a safe, vault, or crypt that only you know how to open. Since no one else can get inside, your property can't be taken away from you.

Forts, walls, shields, vaults, safes—any protective barriers for people and property—are all passive devices. Once built, they're just *there* all the time, being barriers. They keep out anything that needs to be kept out, and conversely, keep in whatever needs to be kept inside. But the passivity of barriers is also their greatest weakness. When something or someone tries to get through, over, or under a wall, the wall can't do anything. It can't respond, can't fight back, can't make itself thicker or higher or stronger. If whatever is challenging the barrier is stronger, the contest is over. As defenders from time immemorial have learned to their dismay, there's simply no such thing as an impenetrable barrier. And once the wall is breached, anything and anyone on the other side is at the mercy of the invaders—unless they have some other type of defense on tap.

What's true in military history, safecracking, and burglary is just as true in biology. Barriers are basic, the first line of defense for nearly all animals, whether consisting of skin, scales, hide, shells, or exoskeletons, all the way to the microscopic scale, where the barriers are cell membranes thousandths of an inch thick. Most animals have evolved further defenses for when their skin, shells, scales, and hide aren't enough. These defenses work on both the large scale, in the form of claws, horns, great speed, and so on, and the smallest, in the cell walls that keep out poisons and harmful organisms, and the tactics of immune systems that seek out and destroy microscopic invaders.

Superman's invulnerability, then, would be based on more than just thick skin. Still, just as for human beings and other creatures, a protective barrier would be Superman's initial defense. And as a Kryptonian on Earth, Superman has a few decided advantages over the natives in this department.

Doctors sometimes call the skin the largest organ of the body, and there's much to support that assertion. It's much more than a passive barrier: It's a living, constantly growing and changing thing, and unlike a stone wall or steel vault, it can respond in a number of ways when outside forces attempt to break through.

Human skin consists of the epidermis on the outside, which is a layering of cells that are constantly shed and replaced, and an inner dermis, which contains hair follicles, the sweat glands that help to regulate the body temperature by cooling its exterior, and sebaceous glands that generate oil to keep the skin soft and pliable. There's also a dense network of nerve endings, blood vessels, connective and lymph tissue, and muscle fibers. All this in a single package roughly twenty square feet in size and weighing around six pounds for an average human being.

It may all seem pretty fragile when you get a paper cut or stick yourself with a pin, but your skin protects you from many potential dangers that likely never enter your mind—and thanks to the skin, never enter your body either. Chief among these are harmful microorganisms. We live in a virtual sea of bacteria—all around us, everything we touch, everything we wear, everything we walk on, sit on, lie on, everything we own—it's all bathed in millions and millions of live bacteria, not to mention other microscopic creatures such as viruses, protozoans, fungi, mites, and so on. Creepy it may be, but it's a fact of life on this planet, and there's no way around it. Fortunately for us, much of this microscopic menagerie is harmless, and we've evolved a defense against many of those organisms that are not—our skin. Aside from being a purely physical barrier to prevent dangerous microbes from entering the body and wreaking havoc, the skin is equipped with glands that excrete natural oils and fluids—substances which, not incidentally, are deadly to a wide range of bacteria and other microbes. Before you take a shower following your next heavy workout at the gym, take a moment or two to bask in the heady aromas emanating from your sweat-drenched body: Those smells are the final testament of millions of dead bacteria, drowned in the poison soaking your T-shirt, shorts, and sneakers. Your skin is on the job.

Nasty microbes aren't the only things trying to invade your body, though. Our environment is also rife with noxious substances: chemicals that could damage or poison us if they somehow got inside our bodies. The skin keeps these out quite well. Some of the more dangerous substances might exact a toll on the skin, burning or otherwise damaging it, but usually the skin (with some help from the reflexes of your neuromuscular system pulling you away from the source of sudden discomfort) prevents the bad stuff from getting too deep.

Various forms of radiation also constantly assault your body, including charged particles, ultraviolet, X-rays, and nuclear radiation. If these penetrate your vital organs, they can literally tear apart the DNA in your cells, disrupting their growth and division and causing mutations that can lead to cancer and other diseases. The skin is up against a tougher foe here than with microbes, but it still puts up a good fight. Gamma radiation and X-rays are just too powerful to be warded off by the skin, so the body has to rely on other tactics against these agents, which we'll examine later. But the skin is an effective shield against other forms of radiation: alpha particles generated by radioactive decay, for example, which have little penetrative power. A skin tan is the result of the battle between your skin and certain wavelengths of ultraviolet radiation: It's an increase in the production of melanin, a dark pigment, as the skin tries to protect itself. If this defense mechanism is overcome by too much ultraviolet radiation—too many unprotected hours in the sun—the skin can burn and ultimately develop cancer. Again, we're encountering the inevitable limits of barrier defenses: no matter how good they are, there's always something out there that can overcome them. Still, if the body is a temple as some say, then the skin is the protective wall around it.

These are the limitations of human skin, but what about Superman's skin? Just how impenetrable a barrier would it be? If Superman, as a Kryptonian, is the result of evolution under a dimmer, weaker sun, wouldn't his skin be even less resistant to radiation than ours?

The answer to the latter question is yes in some ways, no in others. As we've already seen, Kryptonians would have the ability to use sunlight directly as a food source, through a process closely related to plant photosynthesis. To do this, Kryptonian skin would have to be at least somewhat photosynthetic, able to receive and absorb sunlight just like the leaves of plants. So it couldn't be too resistant, warding off everything; instead, Superman's skin would have to be near-transparent to those wavelengths of solar radiation his body used for energy, while barring other harmful wavelengths. This phenomenon of being opaque to some forms of radiation while transparent to others is quite familiar in everyday life. If you wear glasses or contacts, for example, they probably feature UV protection—they allow visible light into your eye, but block ultraviolet wavelengths that can cause cataracts and other eye damage over time. Since Superman's skin would have evolved to serve as a collector of energy rather than just a protective covering, it would be even more efficient in this department.

Under Earth's yellow sun, of course, Superman's skin would be subjected to a different spectrum of more intense solar radiation. But as long as the wavelengths of sunlight that Superman needed were also contained in the sun's spectrum, he'd get along just fine. In fact, Superman's body might even find itself able to use other wavelengths not found in Rao's sunlight, and this along with the greater intensity of sunlight on Earth would provide him with a vast source of energy.

What does this have to do with Superman's physical invulnerability? As we've seen, Kryptonians might have evolved a fairly strong bioelectric field surrounding their bodies, created and possibly even manipulated by biological processes of some sort. If the processes that generate the field are strengthened by a greater intake of energy, the field itself would be correspondingly stronger. This would not only enhance the ability of Superman's body to fend off harmful radiation (the original function of the bioelectric field in the Kryptonian environment), but possibly have the effect of "hardening" his cells and making them literally more resistant to physical assault. It would not be the actual "force field" so popular in science fiction—an invisible barrier that behaves just like a physical wall—but it would intensify and reinforce the natural resistive forces of all matter that produce the macroscopic effect of a physical surface.[1]

Still, resistance to subatomic particles and microscopic organisms is one thing; resistance to much larger threats such as bullets is something else. Human skin can't stop a speeding bullet or the thrust of a knife, because the physical force propelling those objects is far greater than skin can resist and easily tears apart the bonds that hold the cells together. (Not surprising, since humans didn't evolve with pelting bullets or slashing knives as an integral condition of their natural environment. Nor did Kryptonians.) Why wouldn't Superman's skin, enhanced bioelectric field or not, be just as vulnerable to damage as our own?

Possibly because of an adaptation that would arise as a natural defensive response to the more intense Earthly radiation environment: an outer layer of skin (the epidermis) that was denser and thicker than Kryptonian skin under its natural sun. As mentioned earlier, most materials—including skin—are opaque to some energies and transparent to others, and Superman's skin is no exception. It would be able to absorb and use certain frequencies of sunlight for conversion into biological

---

1. In a very real (though subatomic) sense, you never really "touch" anything; instead, the outer electron shells of the atoms of your hand interact with the electron shells of the atoms of outer objects, temporarily attracting or repelling. You're not presently touching the atoms of this book—subatomic forces operating between your hands and the book are keeping it in place.

energy, and keep out those frequencies that couldn't be converted or were directly harmful. How best to keep out that unwanted energy? Simple—a barrier to shield and deflect it away. Human skin tries to protect itself from radiation by darkening, as in a skin tan, and from repeated, prolonged physical stress by growing thicker, as the calluses on the fingertips of a guitarist, the hands of a manual worker, or the soles of anyone who spends a lot of time barefoot will attest. This works fine for us, since we don't use our skin as a primary means of collecting energy. Organisms whose skin provided a vital source of food, such as Kryptonians, couldn't survive if that skin became too much of a barrier. If sunglasses are too dark, you're essentially blinded; if they're just dark *enough*, you can still see perfectly well without being dazzled by brilliant sunlight. In the same vein, some sort of biological compromise would be necessary for Kryptonian skin. It might darken somewhat under Earth's sun, akin to a permanent tan. But the mechanism to do so would already have to be present, such as human skin's ability to produce melanin. With beings who evolved to absorb and use light energy, this seems to be a fairly counterproductive evolutionary tactic. A more likely and efficient response would be for the skin merely to become thicker, denser, and stronger, while still retaining its transparency to the energies necessary to maintain life. This might involve the absorption and retention of heavy elements—iron, silicon, or even titanium, for example—and storing them in the cell walls, making them physically more resistant. The process would be limited to the epidermis, the skin layers at greatest risk of exterior damage. In effect, Superman's skin would develop a body-wide layer of "callus"—and if dense enough, this could also serve as a physical shield against other dangers, like pesky bullets, knives, and explosions.

Lightning strikes Superman but causes no lasting harmful effect.

Even this, however, wouldn't be foolproof. Superman might be able to withstand pretty much the worst that crooks and other evildoers could throw at him, but there would be limits. He might be able to resist a force under some circumstances but not in others. If someone merely throws a bullet at you by hand, it'll bounce off you just as if you were Superman. But if someone puts that bullet in a gun and fires it at you at a speed of many feet per second, you'd better make sure you get out of the way. By the same token, Superman might shrug off the explosive force of a 2000-pound conventional bomb tossed at him, but a 20-megaton nuclear blast might ruin his whole day.

So once in a while, at least, Superman's going to get hurt. What happens then? To use a military analogy once more: If the enemy breaches the outer defenses of your fortress, then you need to take action both to drive them back and to limit the damage they can cause. This brings us to the second aspect of invulnerability: the ability to rapidly repair and heal the damage done.

THE BODY UNDER REPAIR

Even without the wonders of modern medical science, the human body possesses a remarkable power to heal itself and fix the slings and arrows of physical injury. In fact, much of modern medicine is simply the effort to strengthen, encourage, and otherwise help along the body's inbuilt repair mechanisms. Sometimes, of course, we receive injuries or contract diseases that cause greater damage or spread more quickly than our natural defenses can react, and this is where surgery and drugs take over. Our healing powers are remarkable, but they take time— sometimes too much time. And there's much they can't cope with. If a main artery is punctured by a bullet or knife blade, the damage may well be too extensive for the body to repair—and even if it weren't, the injured person would bleed to death long before the body could do the job.

Since the body's defenses work mainly on the small scale, they can be overcome by sudden, large-scale attack. They do much better work in preventing little problems from becoming big ones—a job that goes on every moment of your life. Consider what happens when the barrier of your skin is overcome by the edge of a piece of paper and you get a nasty cut on your finger. Immediately you start to bleed, which is only to be expected since quite a few tiny blood-filled capillaries have just been sliced through. Losing a drop or two of blood is no big deal, but many drops over a long time can add up to an ocean. And you can't live without blood. So the first defensive response of your body is to stop the bleeding. Minuscule cells called platelets are dispatched to the site, speeding through the blood. Reaching the cut, the platelets begin to collect, creating a substance that makes them stick together. The platelets build a wall across the abyss, stemming the flow as other chemicals begin to thicken the blood, causing it to clot. Fibers form a web across the open area as platelets continue to seal the opening, and a scab forms. Meanwhile, white blood cells called phagocytes (literally, "cell eaters") flood the area, gobbling up foreign assailants such as bacteria and other germs that used the cut as an opportunity to invade. Eventually new cells reform, the scab dissolves and disappears, and all is as it was before. Despite this simplified description, it's a complex biochemical process, and all completely automatic.

When damage occurs on a smaller scale—to individual cells—matters are even more efficient. Cells in your body are continually being born, growing, dividing, dying, and being replaced by new ones. The activity is regulated by the genetic code contained in the DNA of each and every cell, which is precisely duplicated in a new cell during the process of cell division. If the DNA is damaged in some way, however, so that some of the genes are defective, cell division can be disrupted, and the damage can be reproduced in new cells. This is called mutation, and it's not necessarily a bad thing. Some mutations survive that are beneficial to the organism, so much so that they end up being incorporated into new generations. This is basically how new varieties of life and new species come into being.

Most mutations cause no trouble, but some are harmful, and it's here that cellular defenses come into play. Aside from the

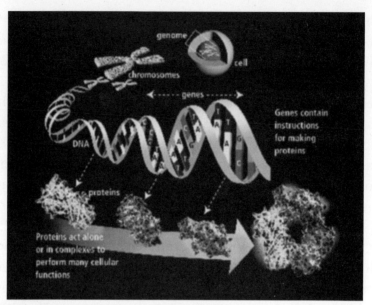

A graphic representation of human DNA.

genes contained in a cell's chromosomes that determine its basic characteristics and function—muscle cell, nerve cell, and so on—there are genes that help the process of cell growth and reproduction. Some genes "turn on" the process, telling the cell when to divide; these are called *oncogenes*. Others turn off the process, so the cell divides only when necessary and doesn't keep reproducing indefinitely; these are called *tumor suppressor genes*, because when they don't do their job, cell division runs wildly out of control in the abnormal condition known as cancer. Some genes can repair broken strands of DNA, preventing them from causing further mutations. And some can actually cause an irreparably damaged cell to self-destruct before it can create other copies of itself.

What causes the cellular damage that results in mutations? Some defective genes are inherited, passed on through generations, in innocuous cases cursing individuals with annoyances such as an allergy to cats or eating shellfish, or in more serious cases, a predilection toward various diseases such as diabetes or breast cancer. Until and unless true genetic engineering becomes a scientific and social reality, there's little we can do about these inherited flaws, although they can sometimes be detected beforehand. Other genes are damaged by radiation, as a spinning subatomic particle or energetic quantum passing through the body scores a direct hit on a strand of DNA. Harmful substances absorbed into the body can also wreck some genes in various ways.

Our cellular defense systems save our bodies from myriad threats we never see and that never enter our awareness. But just as a bullet can overcome our skin, other forces can overwhelm the small-scale line of defense. If too many cells are damaged at once, perhaps by a large dose of radiation, the body has to resort to desperate measures. Resources and energy are diverted from other bodily functions in an attempt to shore up the damage, affecting the organism as a whole—the person becomes sick, weak, and stricken with debilitating symptoms. Sometimes the situation is just too dire and requires more resources to reverse it than the body has available, and the person dies—although outside intervention in the form of medical treatment can pick up the slack and reinforce the body's own healing powers.

Superman would possess the same healing and regenerative powers as we do, both on the large and small scale. However, his capacities, spiked with the greater energies he derives from solar radiation, would dwarf those of humans. As we've seen, his denser skin would provide a great deal of protection from run-of-the-mill threats such as guns, bombs, and projectiles. If a fair degree of elasticity were combined with structural toughness, his skin might bounce back with near-equal force, deflecting bullets. Even if a bullet managed to penetrate his skin, it probably wouldn't get too far; it would have lost so much energy going through Superman's tough epidermal layers (not to mention his bioelectric field) that it would stop or even disintegrate before hitting any major organs. And assuming that Superman's body is capable of incorporating various elements directly into the cell walls and tissue planes, the remnants of the bullet would actually be dissolved and absorbed, just as the stomach does with food. Whatever the external threat, the greater vitality of all of Superman's life processes would allow his body to respond faster and with more energy than a human could muster. Instantaneous regeneration and healing aren't possible—there will always be at least some time lag between cause and effect—but in Superman's case, that time lag would be inconsequential on a human scale. If it takes Superman's body several milliseconds to recuperate after a crook slams an iron bar against his head, but the crook needs twenty minutes to recover after one right cross from Superman's fist, it's not hard to see who will win the fight.

This is the key to Superman's practical invulnerability, at least vis-a-vis humans and most other foes he encounters. He's not impervious to their attacks for the most part; he simply recovers from them much faster than his opponents. He doesn't necessarily escape injury, but he's able to heal it and regenerate damaged cells much more efficiently and quickly than humans. He's not alone in this ability on Earth. There are a number of animals capable of regenerating entire lost limbs or damaged organs: starfish can regrow completely, as long as their vital central axis remains intact. Some reptiles and amphibians can regenerate lost tails or limbs, and if nothing else, many shed and regrow their skin.

Until recently, scientists thought that lizards and snakes

were the highest forms of life capable of such extensive regen- eration—it was beyond the capacities of humans or other mam- mals. In 2001, though, scientists at Philadelphia's Wistar Insti- tute, one of the world's leading centers of biomedical research, discovered a strain of laboratory mice, known as MRL mice, with the startling ability to regenerate damaged heart tissue, something formerly unheard of in mammalian life. The same variety of mice show other interesting recuperative powers, completely healing wounds that would normally be perma- nent, such as holes punched through the ears, with no scarring or signs of damage. Researchers are currently searching for cru- cial genetic and molecular differences between the MRL mice and other varieties to isolate the reasons for these regenerative abilities, work that may ultimately lead to drugs and other treatments to produce similar effects in human beings.

Although they may seem to be the stuff of miracles, sophis- ticated regenerative and healing powers are quite possible. Superman's abilities in this area would simply operate at a much higher level than those of Earthly creatures. He would probably be most vulnerable to a sudden shock to his entire body at once, since there would be no unaffected areas able to marshal energies to restore and repair a single site of attack— but even so, Superman would only be stunned, knocked out of action for a few moments at most. The inner cellular fires that energize Superman might dim and flicker under a particularly heavy blow, but are too powerful to be snuffed out by nearly anything on Earth.

Still, no living creature, however strong it may be and how- ever fortunate in avoiding illness or injury, can escape the rav- ages of time. Everything gets old, everything gets weaker, and sooner or later, everything dies. Why? It hardly seems fair that even if we spend our lives eating the right foods, exercising regularly, and avoiding major accidents, it's all for naught in the end. Why can't we live forever? And if we can't, then would a being like Superman enjoy virtual immortality, or would he too be unable finally to elude the grasp of the Grim Reaper?

NOBODY LIVES FOREVER

Some biologists argue, perhaps half-jokingly, that there's no real reason for life to end. It's a self-perpetuating process, given the basic requirements of food and a congenial environment. Theoretically, if a creature avoids its enemies, doesn't fall to fatal diseases or accidents, and doesn't run out of food, it should live indefinitely.

Other scientists contend the opposite. Even in the extremely unlikely event that a living organism can evade all the dangers of the world, eventually its time runs out. Its systems will wear out, its cells lose the ability to repair and reproduce themselves, toxins and other harmful substances will build up, and the organism finally succumbs to the inevitable. All living cells may be programmed genetically to self-destruct after a certain time, whether damaged by outside agents or not, in a phenomenon called senescence. Or death may be due to the fallout of natural processes that literally create the seeds of life's eventual destruction, producing molecular by-products that harm healthy cells, or mutations in DNA replication that multiply into long-term disease. Naturally, with all the hazards afoot in our world, very few creatures face this sort of predetermined end: Something else usually beats them to it. But no matter how insanely lucky one may be, there's no escaping the Damoclean sword of death that hangs over our heads from the moment we take our first breath in this world.

Although they may debate the specifics—the proliferation of

free radicals vs. programmed cell senescence, the loss of telomerase vs. the buildup of molecular toxins—most biologists agree that death is unavoidable. Not only that, but in the larger sense, it's actually a positive thing. Evolution can't proceed without the continual births and deaths of individual organisms, because that's how DNA is passed along and recombined into the seemingly infinite variations that have given the world everything from sea slugs to supermodels. Death clears the decks and provides a clean slate for the next generation's improvements, change, and evolutionary experiments. And it keeps the place from getting too crowded. If nobody ever died, where would we put all the new ones who come along?

Even if we accept the inevitability of death, including our own, it's still understandable that we strain our minds by thinking about ways to delay it as long as possible. Humans spend an awful lot of time thinking about death, or trying *not* to think about it; some anthropologists think that the fear and denial of death is the primal motivating force behind the human religious impulse. We are certainly unique in the kingdom of the living in the awareness of our own eventual death. As far as we know, no other living creature is cursed with such knowledge. You are not likely to see a paramecium, frog, squirrel, or even your cat sitting about, darkly worried about death. But human philosophers from Socrates to Woody Allen have spent years doing just that.

Such fears are worsened by the phenomenon of aging, which provides a graphic, slow-motion picture of the decline and loss of our strength, vitality, and appearance. As we age, we find that we can't do the things we used to do, we don't look the same, we don't feel the same, and we know that we're getting closer to the end than we are to the beginning of our lives. And as the advances of medical science in the past two centuries have steadily increased the human lifespan, we age for longer periods than in the past. As recently as several thousand years ago, an average human was lucky to make it to age thirty; now many routinely live to eighty and beyond. The sting of death is only forestalled, not banished, by an extended lifespan. In a sense, it may be made worse, because it actually grants you far more time to contemplate your impending extinction.

The battle against aging, then, isn't being fought just for biological reasons; there are profound psychological and social implications as well. Much has been discovered in recent years about why we (and all other living things) age and die, and while no "fountain of youth" has yet been discovered (or is likely to be), we're learning some things that give cause for comfort, if not hope—knowledge that may extend life further while making the deterioration of age less of a burden.

Many scientists believe that a chief instigator of aging is the proliferation of "free radicals" in the body. These are atoms or molecules with an unpaired electron—in other words, they're missing a piece (an electron) that makes them search out another atom to bond to and thus complete themselves. Free radicals are a common byproduct of many chemical reactions and are naturally produced by cell chemistry, but they can be troublesome. They're not very picky about the hapless, innocent atoms they latch onto to share an electron, and when they hook up with some molecules in the cells, they can disrupt and derail vital functions, killing the cell, preventing it from dividing, or interfering with DNA replication and perhaps laying the groundwork for cancer. Since free radicals are a normally occurring phenomenon in the body, the longer you live, the more time they have to do their damage, and inevitably their effects build up. More and more cells are damaged or stop dividing, systems don't work as well as before, things dry up, loosen up or tighten up—basically, you get older. Research shows that the effects of free radicals may be mitigated somewhat by various means, mainly the use of antioxidants, which are chemicals that bond safely with the free radicals and prevent them from harming other molecules. Still, while some companies and health gurus loudly proclaim the wonders of megadoses of antioxidants such as vitamin C, the final scientific verdict isn't in yet. Free radicals can definitely be harmful, but antioxidants aren't necessarily a magic bullet against them and may have other negative effects.

Another theory is the notion that all cells come with a built-in "clock" of one sort or another that causes a cell to destroy itself after a certain time. We've already seen that cells have mechanisms that make them self-destruct if they're too badly damaged in some way, and the process of cell senescence is similar. While there are probably several different mechanisms at work, one that has received a great deal of attention in recent years involves *telomeres*. Telomeres are sections of DNA that cap the ends of chromosomes and keep them intact, acting like the plastic tips of shoelaces. When a strand of DNA divides during cell reproduction, a tiny bit of the telomere is lost. More is lost with each later division in the lifetime of the cell and the chromosome becomes shorter and shorter, eventually reaching the point where further division is impossible. The cell's activity slows, it stops dividing, and eventually dies, a process that may contribute to common aging traits such as arteriosclerosis and skin wrinkling. In this way, telomere shortening acts as a biological clock that literally tells the cell when to end its life.

But there's another interesting wrinkle (so to speak). Researchers discovered that in some types of cells, the telomeres didn't seem to shorten even with repeated cell divisions. These cells contain telomerase, an enzyme that works as a telomere repair system. The telomeres in these cells still lose a piece during cell division, but the telomerase enzyme replaces what's lost, maintaining the telomere in fighting form. Cells with sufficient telomerase are virtually immortal, capable of dividing indefinitely. Does this mean we've found the fabled fountain of youth? Can we live forever just by taking megadoses of telomerase?

Not so fast. (You didn't think it could be that easy, did you?) It turns out there are some nasty catches hidden in the apparent miracle of cell immortality. For one, the longer a cell lives, the greater chance it has of acquiring and accumulating harmful mutations from radiation, free radicals, mistakes in DNA replication, and so on. As we've seen, in most cases these problems don't get too far, because the cell repairs or destroys itself before it can reproduce other defective cells. Normal control mechanisms restrain and shut down cells when they're not working right. An "immortal" cell, however, will keep reproducing, creating more and more copies of itself with the same problems. If you think this sounds a lot like cancer, you're right. A fair number of studies have shown that most malignant tumors harbor large amounts of telomerase, which removes the brakes on normal cell division and lets cancer cells multiply at a furious rate. Based on this discovery, scientists are currently studying the idea of telomerase-inhibiting drugs that could slow or even stop tumor growth. Since most normal cells contain little or no telomerase, one advantage of such a drug is that, unlike conventional chemotherapy drugs, an anti-telomerase drug would target only cancer cells and leave other cells unscathed. (Except, unfortunately, human sperm and egg cells, which do contain telomerase. Still, sterility might be an acceptable trade-off for a cancer cure, particularly for older patients past their reproductive prime.)

While telomerase is unlikely to help us live forever, it's possible that its judicious application could have significant benefits. It could speed up regeneration and rejuvenation in tissue grafts and transplants, and help restore the ravaged immune systems of bone marrow transplant or AIDS patients. And yes, in the not-too-distant future, telomerase therapy might slow or even reverse the curses of wrinkling, creaky joints, and even arteriosclerosis.

An actual "cure" for aging may never be possible. If it truly is a natural, programmed part of life in this universe, we may be able to delay it or soften its impact, but not eliminate it entirely. And if we do find a way to stop the process of biological decay and death, a new realm of social, psychological, and possibly unimagined medical problems will face humanity. In the meantime, we can take some comfort in the fact that science is hard at work finding ways for us to live longer and happier lives.

And Superman? No matter how powerful he may be, he remains a biological being, a living creature, and as such, ultimately not exempt from the immutable laws that govern the rest of us. Free radicals prowl Superman's cellular pathways just as they do ours, and his chromosomes are probably also capped by telomeres. The same biological processes that allowed him to grow from a baby to an adult in Earth's environment would go on throughout his life.

So Superman would definitely age, eventually weaken, and die of natural causes. Yet he's also stronger, able to store and use more energy, and possessed of more efficient natural defenses both on the macro and the micro levels, than human beings. These qualities would definitely help his body better withstand

and weather the steady ravages of age, although not escape them. In the end, what is true for all living creatures is true also for Superman: Nobody lives forever.

FLIGHT: no WINGS, no STRINGS

CHAPTER FOUR

FLIGHT:
no wings,
no strings

Human beings have dreamed of flying for thousands of years, giving life to those reveries in countless songs, stories, and legends. But it's only been within the last two hundred years that human beings have been able to take to the skies in reality instead of just fantasy. First there was the balloon, a wondrous creation that lets you drift on the breeze—but you're also pretty much at the mercy of the wind. Then, a hundred years ago, the Wright brothers gave us the airplane, with which humans can fly anywhere with complete control. But the airplane is still subject to the whims of the weather, and it's still a mechanical device which needs fuel and maintenance, and can break down for many reasons.

The dream of flight in its purest form has always been free of any such encumbrances. It's the idea of standing on a high cliff, stepping off, and not falling: flying with absolutely nothing between your body and the air, just like a bird, soaring and coasting on the breeze, under nothing but your own power.

Of course, this isn't possible for humans. It used to be said that if God had meant man to fly, he'd have given him wings.

Flight: No Wings, No Strings

There's something to that sentiment, even if you don't agree with its implied religious determinism: if humans had *needed* to fly, evolution would have given them wings. Since neither God nor evolution saw fit to include that particular accessory, we've learned to build our own wings to at least partly fulfill our desire to fly. Still, the fantasy in its pure form persists, in our nighttime dreams, our myths, our stories—and in Superman.

What could be more awe-inspiring, more magical and powerful, than a being who can fly all by himself, without any of the devices we puny humans need to do the same? A man who can fly—more than anything else, this defines Superman and sets him apart, because it's so inherently mysterious. Superman doesn't have wings, nor does he have rockets or any other sort of obvious propulsion mechanism. So how does he do it? No strings, no wings—it must be magic.

Not necessarily. As it happens, there are perfectly natural phenomena afoot in our universe that just might provide an explanation. We may not yet be able to exploit them for ourselves, but Superman, as a refugee from a far-off world, just might be. These phenomena have little to do with flight as we know it or as it's practiced on Earth, but involve principles at the very frontier of current scientific knowledge. First, though, let's take a look at exactly what it means to fly, and how it's done in its more familiar forms.

TAKING WING

Birds do it, bees do it, even some species of fish and mammal do it. They all fly, at least after a fashion. They are capable of movement through the air above the ground, the basic definition of flight. True flight requires two things: *lift*, which counteracts the constant downward pull of gravity; and *thrust*, which propels the flying object forward. Everything that flies, living or nonliving, has to contend with these two basic requirements, but there's a variety of ways to achieve them.

Air, like liquid, is a fluid—it flows, instead of maintaining a

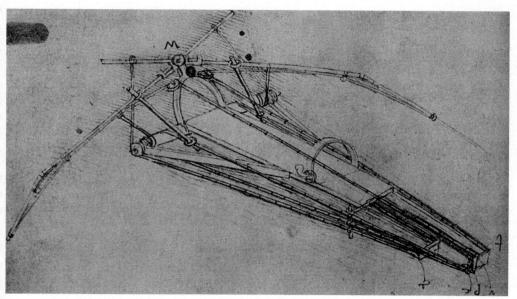

A drawing from one of Leonardo da Vinci's notebooks, circa 1486, illustrates one of his many ideas for a flying machine.

constant shape. Just as living creatures can swim in water, they can "swim" through the air, using parts of their bodies to provide buoyancy (or lift) and thrust. Fish use their fins for propulsion, while the shape of their bodies and an internal air bladder provide buoyancy to keep them from sinking to the bottom. Similarly, birds are built for flying. Physically, they're very light and delicate, which helps (the heavier you are, the more thrust is needed to counteract gravity). They're also streamlined to permit the flow of air around their bodies with a minimum of resistance. Most of all, they have wings: specially designed limbs that not only provide thrust by moving in ways that push air backward, but are also shaped to provide lift.

In cross section, most wings have the same basic shape, whether they're on a bird or a 747. The wing is fairly flat on the bottom surface, but curved in an arc on its top surface. As air flows across the wing, it takes slightly longer to travel over the top surface, since the curve creates a longer path, than it does to flow over the bottom surface. This creates lower pressure on the top surface of the wing than on the bottom. The higher pressure against the bottom of the wing pushes it up, and the wing rises. We have lift. And we'll continue to have it as long as air flows over the wing. Lose the flow of air and the pressure evens out between the top and bottom of the wing, and lift vanishes.

How do we maintain the steady movement of air over and under the wing? Simply by pushing it forward through the air—in other words, by creating thrust. With airplanes, thrust is provided by engines; with birds, it's the complex movements of the wings themselves.

Insects do things slightly differently. Their wings aren't true airfoils, but they're light enough and strong enough that rapidly beating them against the air actually pushes the insect through the air. The fact that insect bodies are extremely light also helps the insect to glide and maneuver simply by moving against air resistance or with the wind. You've witnessed this if you've ever watched a dragonfly drifting on a summer breeze. The disadvantage, of course, is that the insect is essentially at the mercy of a strong wind.

Of course, the actual physics of flight are considerably more complicated, involving such matters as the elasticity of the air, variations in shape of the wings, air resistance, temperature, and so on. Understanding and finding ways to balance among these various factors and use them to best advantage are how aeronautical engineers and aircraft designers earn a living. Any aeronauticist worth his wings would consider you hopelessly naive if you told him or her that all you need to fly is higher pressure against the bottom of an airfoil. Still, whatever equations you want to use to describe the phenomenon of winged flight, it all comes down to lift and thrust. Even helicopters, though they may lack conventional wings, use the same principles of lift and thrust to achieve flight.[1]

Sometimes, it's possible to achieve a limited sort of flight relying mostly on only one of these factors. Some so-called "flying" animals, such as certain species of fish or squirrels, don't really fly; they just literally jump into the air and manage to glide a little on their way back down. The lift provided by the modified parts of their bodies isn't enough to allow true sustained flight—it only allows them to fall back to Earth a little more gracefully and with slightly more control. Once the energy of the initial leap into the air is expended, there's not enough thrust to overcome gravity, and down the animal comes. It's the same reason a paper airplane usually doesn't stay aloft for more than a few seconds. (The world record, set in 1998, is 27.6 seconds.) The small amount of energy imparted to it by your wrist in launching it is rapidly overcome by air resistance and the pull of gravity, and there's no other energy source on board to keep it going.

What about flight *without* wings? A rocket, for example, has no wings, yet it definitely flies. In this case, we have nearly all thrust and little if any lift—or more properly, we're dealing with both in the same package. But the powerful thrust of a rocket engine is quite capable of making a mockery out of gravity—at least for a short time. Gravity eventually wins, either by pulling the rocket back down to earth, or into a state of perpetual falling, i.e., an orbit. Only if the rocket has enough

---

1. The "wings" of a helicopter are actually the rotor blades, which are just as much airfoils as the wings of an airplane. The rotors provide both lift and thrust, and also maneuver the craft by controlling each force.

thrust to achieve escape velocity (on Earth, around seven miles per second!) can it break the pull of gravity forever.

Flight is all about reaching some kind of temporary accommodation with the force of gravity. Because of the way in which wings accomplish this (i.e., providing lift), they require thrust to maintain that accommodation, along with the flow of air (or some other fluid). Other craft such as rockets do it through sheer brute strength, so they don't need wings or the flow of air. What if there were some other way to counteract gravity, coupled with some means of controlled movement? Could we—or Superman—then fly both without wings and without some form of built-in propulsion? The answer is yes—if we can find a way of *using* gravity instead of fighting it.

Kitty Hawk, North Carolina, 1903. Wilbur and Orville Wright successfully test their first heavier-than-air, self-powered flying machine. Thus was born the airplane, and the world was changed forever.

FORCES OF NATURE

If flying is all about defying gravity, it would help to have a clearer idea of just what gravity is. Know your enemy, as the old saying goes. We talk about it in all sorts of contexts, we can calculate its effects, we deal with it all the time, we live with it, we live in it—so what is gravity, anyway?

Asked this question point blank, a physicist will usually either burst forth with a stream of nearly indecipherable equations, or shake his head, shuffle his feet, and say, well, actually, we just don't know. Or if the physicist has a rather mischievous sense of humor, he might tell you to step off the top of a skyscraper, and you'll not only gain an instantaneous and intimate understanding of the phenomenon, you also won't be asking any further irritating questions.

Thanks to people such as Isaac Newton and Albert Einstein, however, we can make a stab at an admittedly incomplete definition. *Gravity* is one of the four fundamental forces at the heart of everything that happens in the universe. The other three are the *electromagnetic force,* which deals with the behavior of charged particles, the *strong nuclear force,* and the *weak force,* both of which concern the interactions of subatomic particles. Of the four, the electromagnetic force and gravity are the only two we routinely and directly encounter in everyday life; the strong and weak forces, while just as essential to the existence of our universe, rule only in the domain of the subatomic and thus don't generally come up in normal conversation, except among physicists. As the names imply, the electromagnetic force governs all phenomena dealing with electricity and magnetism, and the gravitational force deals with—well, step off that skyscraper and you'll find out.

Aside from operating in different realms, the four fundamental forces also greatly differ from one another in strength and range. The weak and the strong nuclear force exert their influence over an incredibly short distance, about a millionth of a millionth of a centimeter, but the strong nuclear force is, as its name implies, the strongest of all four forces. The electromagnetic force wields itself over a much greater distance, but falls off rapidly in strength the farther it travels from its source.[2] And despite overt appearances, gravity is actually the weakest of all four—yet it makes up for this by having the greatest range.

Gravity is odd for some other reasons. We understand quite a lot about the electromagnetic force, and how particles known as photons carry electromagnetic energy from one place to another; it's the harnessing of these phenomena that's given us TV, cell phones, and radar detectors, among many other wonders and annoyances of modern life. But how does gravity affect objects over a distance? Some current theories postulate the existence of "gravitons," minute particles that carry gravity waves across space just as photons carry electromagnetic waves. Unfortunately, no one has yet detected a graviton, and we're not even sure we'd recognize one if they did. Scientists are also searching for gravitational waves, but none have been detected so far.

In his general theory of relativity, Albert Einstein explained that gravity is best understood as a curvature of space and time—not in a metaphorical or poetic sense, but in a real, physically measurable manner. The reason a moon orbits a planet, for example, is that the mass of the planet literally creates a

---

2. This may seem odd, since we all know that light or radio waves can travel for billions of miles. But the fundamental electromagnetic force shouldn't be confused with electromagnetic radiation. EM radiation is produced by processes that involve the electromagnetic force, but the force itself directly concerns only the attraction or repulsion of charged particles.

gravitational depression or well in space-time, inside of which the moon circles. It's almost like a speck of dirt in water, circling around a drain, but not being sucked in. The distortion in space-time created by the mass of the planet alters the path of anything else nearby that encounters it.

Einstein also predicted that because of the curvature in space-time caused by gravity, light and other forms of electromagnetic radiation could also be affected by intense gravitational fields. He proposed some experiments to test this hypothesis. One of the most famous, conducted during a total solar eclipse in 1919, measured the degree by which the position of a distant star seemed to shift as the sun passed near it in the sky: the gravitational mass of the sun actually bent the starlight, making the star seem to be in a different part of the sky than it actually was. Another experiment measured the perturbations in the orbit of Mercury caused by its closeness to the sun. Many such experiments have been conducted since Einstein first published the General Theory in 1915, and in every single case, the results have tallied precisely with his predictions.

So we know that gravity curves (or warps, or bends, if you prefer) space and light. We can precisely calculate orbits around the Earth or any other body, as long as we know the mass of the body. We can see how an extremely massive object such as a galaxy can literally act as a lens, gravitationally producing multiple images of other objects behind it on images from the Hubble Space Telescope. In short, we can observe and calculate the effects of gravity to the last decimal point—but we still can't truly define gravity itself.

Such a definition, and finding a way to integrate it with the other three fundamental forces, has been the Holy Grail of theoretical physics since Einstein. The Grail is known by different names, chiefly the Unified Field Theory or the Theory of Everything. Whatever it's called, such a theory would prove that all the fundamental forces are really just different manifestations of a single force. All would be united in one elegant set of equations, from which all the rest of physics could be derived.

It sounds straightforward, but it's a problem that has stumped the most brilliant minds of humanity for most of the past half a century. It's been partially accomplished; experiments with powerful particle accelerators have led to the unification of the electromagnetic and weak forces into the electroweak force. But connecting the rest of the dots has proven elusive. Einstein spent the last years of his life in search of a unified theory, without success. Since then a number of candidates for a Theory of Everything have been proposed, most recently an odd construction called *superstring theory*. But there's always a nagging piece left hanging, something that won't fit in, a gap that can't be filled. Sometimes, as with superstring theory, the problem is that no one knows how to construct an experiment to test the theory. Or if an experiment can be proposed, it's not practical for reasons of expense or sheer difficulty. (The giant Superconducting Supercollider that was to have been built in Texas but was killed by Congress about ten years ago might have solved some big questions and maybe even led to a testable unified theory by now, but as is usually the case, politics trumps science.)

Gravity causes other problems that keep physicists up at night. Another of its unexplained characteristics is that it seems to be strictly an attractive force—it only pulls objects together. Unlike the electromagnetic force, which can be either positive or negative, gravity has always been thought to work in only one way. But if gravity pervades the universe, and it pulls everything together, why hasn't everything collapsed into a single glob of matter by now? Einstein came up with something called the cosmological constant, a kind of negative force or pressure throughout space that offsets gravity. But he was never very happy with this idea, considering it a kind of mathematical fudge, and when astronomer Edwin Hubble later proved that the universe was actually expanding, Einstein abandoned the notion, calling it the "biggest mistake" of his career.

He may have been too hard on himself. In the past several years, astrophysicists have made observations that have revived and expanded Einstein's cosmological constant explanation. An enduring question in cosmology for decades has concerned the fate of the universe. It began in a massive explosion called the Big Bang, but how will it end? Will it expand forever, will the expansion slow down and stop, or will gravity eventually cause the universe to reverse itself and begin contracting? Cases could be made for each possibility. But the debate was ended for all practical purposes by the Hubble telescope and other new powerful instruments, which have shown that the expansion of the universe is not only continuing—it's actually speeding up.

How is that possible? If the universe was born in a Big Bang, it makes sense that its expansion might slow down and stop. Given the force of gravity, it even makes sense that it might eventually pull itself back together. But to *expand faster*? That has scientists puzzled, to say the least.

The only possible explanation is the existence of something driving that acceleration—another force pushing everything apart. Scientists are calling it by a variety of names: negative gravity, dark force, even quintessence. The exact nature of this force, how it works, and how it originated are topics of hot debate in astrophysical circles, but the evidence of its existence is mounting. Unlike "positive" gravity, which can be felt from small distances all the way up to billions of light years, this negative gravity or dark force might manifest itself only over the immense distances between galaxies. Another possibility is that gravity itself has changed since the birth of the universe. Whatever the answers, many scientists think that the discovery of "dark force" may herald the beginning of an entirely new type of physics. We may find our Grand Unified Theory—only to learn that rather than explaining everything, it merely opens up an entirely new realm of mystery.

How does all this get Superman "up, up and away"? Gravity—specifically, the possible existence of gravitons and negative gravity—gives us a mechanism that Superman might be able to use to achieve flight without encumbrances like wings and engines.

THE ATTRACTIONS OF GRAVITY

The idea of using gravity for propulsion isn't new. In fact, NASA has been using gravity to propel spacecraft for years. In December 1973, when *Pioneer 10* became the first spacecraft to visit Jupiter, it followed a trajectory set months earlier that caused it to slingshot around Jupiter and hurtle out of the solar system, becoming humanity's first emissary to the stars.[3] In 1974, *Mariner 10* made a similar maneuver around Venus to set itself on course for Mercury, and later in the same year, *Pioneer 11* used this "gravity assist" technique at Jupiter to speed itself onward

---

3. *Pioneer 10*, over seven billion miles from Earth and still alive at this writing over thirty years after its launch, may also have provided a small hint of the existence of "dark force" or "negative gravity." Several years ago, flight controllers noted that the craft seemed to be mysteriously speeding up slightly, as if some unknown force were tugging (or pushing) it along through space—despite the fact that *Pioneer* is millions of miles from any planet or other source of gravity. The effect remains unexplained.

for the first Saturn encounter. The incredible journeys of later Voyager probes to the planets of the outer solar system were made feasible by gravity-assisted trajectories. NASA's mission planners have developed the technique to a high level of sophistication: to send the *Cassini-Huygens* spacecraft on its way for a Saturn rendezvous in 2004, flight controllers looped it around Venus twice, then around the Earth, and finally Jupiter!

What's the point in sending spacecraft careening about the solar system looping drunkenly around various planets? Simple: it's one of the few ways in the universe to pick up a nearly free ride. When a spacecraft is approaching a planet, it speeds up somewhat, because the planet's gravity starts to pull it in. Makes sense, and is certainly consistent with everything we know about gravity and how it behaves. If the craft moves close enough to the planet, it will be captured by gravity and enter into an orbit about the planet. Again, sounds logical. But what if the spacecraft passes by the planet close enough to be affected by its gravity but not close enough to be captured in orbit? Shouldn't the craft slow down a little after it passes by, since the planet's gravity is still pulling on it until it's far enough away?

The answer is that it depends on how the craft passes around the planet. (Encountering the gravity field of a planet will alter the course of a spacecraft in any case.) If it swings by the planet's leading edge—i.e., the forward side of the planet as it travels in its orbit around the sun—then the spacecraft will indeed be slowed down. But if the spacecraft passes around the planet's trailing edge—the side in the opposite direction of the planet's orbital velocity—it will speed up. The planet actually pulls the craft along with it for a brief time in its path around the sun, also imparting a bit of its momentum to the spacecraft. So the spacecraft literally hitches a short free ride, and leaves not only traveling faster, but in a different direction. Because there

Pioneer 3 was one of the early planetary probes. They were built small to reduce the cost of the missions by keeping down the weight of the payloads. Less weight means less fuel needed to launch a vehicle beyond the gravitational pull of Earth. A later effort in the program, *Pioneer 10*, became the first manmade object to travel beyond the solar system.

truly is no such thing as a free lunch in the universe, the planet actually slows down in its own orbit around the sun. The passing spacecraft has stolen just a bit of its momentum. Of course, because of the huge difference in mass between the planet and the spacecraft, the planet is affected much less than the spacecraft, and the slow-down is barely detectable.

With clever planning, we can use this technique to send space probes to distant planets for much less fuel and energy than would be needed for a more direct course. To send *Cassini* directly to Saturn from Earth, for example, would have required a huge, powerful rocket, much bigger than even the giant Saturn V that launched men to the moon. Bigger rockets cost more money and burn more fuel. With the gravity assist trick, though, Cassini only needed enough energy to get to Venus—gravity and a lot of savvy trajectory calculations did the rest.

Deep space missions simply wouldn't be practical or affordable without the gravity-assist technique. Plans are currently underway for a mission to Pluto, the most distant planet in the solar system and the only one not yet visited by a spacecraft. Without the ability and know-how to use Jupiter and other planets to boost the Pluto probe on its way, such a mission would be beyond the means of NASA or any other space agency.

The gravity assist phenomenon demonstrates that gravity—or rather, differences in gravitational fields among various bodies—can be used to alter the course and speed of a moving body. In effect, it's possible to "surf" on gravitational "waves" (though this is a very inexact analogy, and as discussed, no one's detected gravitational waves yet!).

Let's indulge in some fanciful (some physicists might even say wild) speculation. Suppose that gravitons do exist as theorized—some kind of elementary particle that carries or embodies gravity, much as photons do with electromagnetic energy. What if it were possible to generate and control the flow of gravitons as easily as we do photons whenever we turn on a light or use a cell phone? To put it another way: what if Superman could either alter the level of gravitons in his body, or modulate and control their gravitational strength in some way?

There's a famous classic TV commercial for superstrong glue in which a hardhat worker hangs gleefully in midair, his helmet glued to a high steel girder. (Of course, you might have noticed that even though he's wearing the helmet, he's also holding onto it for dear life with both hands—otherwise, the weight of his own body would probably decapitate him!) The strength of the superglue is enough to resist gravity pulling on it with the approximately 200-pound weight of the worker's body. We've also all seen the giant electromagnets in scrap yards that can lift tons of metal into the air. In both cases, gravity is being outmatched by another force, whether the adhesive properties of superglue or magnetism. A strong enough magnet can even cause a piece of metal to "jump" into the air against gravity. The capacity to increase gravity levels in a highly localized area would have the same effect. If somehow the gravity embodied in a steel ball, for example, could be reduced, it would rise from the ground; manipulating the gravitational fields could cause it to be pulled toward another object. Rapidly changing the strength and direction of the gravity of the ball could allow us to actually maneuver it with great precision. We might be making some use of "negative gravity" to repel the ball from objects, or simply manipulating the attractive force of gravity.

To emphasize, we have absolutely no idea of how this sort of thing might be done, or even if it's possible. But we're engaging in wild speculation, remember?

And we're about to get even wilder. If Superman could control the gravitational content of his own body, whether by altering graviton levels or flow, or by blocking them, he could not only levitate but also propel himself by attracting or repelling his body against variations in the gravitational fields of everything around him.

Consider how this might operate if Superman wanted to launch himself from the window of the Daily Planet Building, for example. If he were high enough from the ground, he could simply let himself drop from the window. As he fell, his body would isolate and focus on the gravitational fields of matter above him, perhaps while emanating an increased flow of gravitons. This would have the effect of slowing his fall and attracting him upward on the gravitational waves between his body and objects above. As the waves, or graviton flow, grew more intense, Superman would overcome the downward pull of Earth's gravity and move through the air, almost as though pulled by magnetic attraction. His control over the process would be much more sensitive, however. By minute and rapid alterations in graviton flow between other matter and different parts of his body, he could maneuver with precise control over direction, speed, and acceleration. Assuming that "negative gravity" or "dark force" exists, Superman may also be able to use it to augment his ability to fly.

Superman could also get himself airborne by simply standing and focusing on gravitational fields in the direction he wanted to go. He wouldn't have to leap upward, although a modest jump might help the gravity in his target direction grab hold a little easier, not to mention looking more dramatic than just standing still and being yanked away. In fact, the use of gravitational fields for propulsion avoids one major problem that would constantly plague Superman if he did literally launch himself by the power of his legs: the force he would exert in the *opposite* direction. If Superman leaped off from the Daily Planet Building with enough force to propel himself into flight, the strength of his back-kick would probably wreck the building!

Since gravitational fields also pervade all of space, Superman could also fly outside of the Earth's atmosphere. Unlike that of an aircraft, his power of flight isn't dependent on aerodynamics, so an atmosphere isn't necessary. His abilities to control and maneuver would be most effective within a fairly strong gravitational environment, in the vicinity of planets and stars; if Superman were in interstellar space, far from strong gravity fields, he might be unable to do much more than drift on the weak gravitational waves he encountered. (Of course, because even Superman needs air to breathe and eventually has to take a breath, this would be the least of his concerns!) However, it's possible that Superman might be able to generate and emit a stream of charged particles in a focused direction; if this were the case, even a tiny amount of thrust would be enough, because it would increase as long as he continued to generate the particles. Such an ability would only work in the void of outer space, however; it would be far too weak to overcome air resistance and gravity on Earth.

How would this kind of gravitational flying power work? What mechanism would make it possible? We won't be able to answer those questions until we learn a whole lot more about gravity itself and verify that gravitons and/or gravitational waves actually exist. Even then, the question of how a biological creature could generate and manipulate such an ability at will may be far from explained. Obviously, though, Superman would need to be able to control this power. Otherwise, if he were subject to random fluctuations in the gravitational force of his own body, he'd be hard pressed to walk, much less fly. Imagine walking down the street, for example, and suddenly finding yourself gravitationally attracted by a passing bus!

Control would also be necessary for Superman to avoid unintentionally affecting other people and objects around him. The consequences of unrestrained gravity fluctuations from his body would be dangerous both to others and to the preservation of his secret identity. If Lois Lane one day became gravitationally stuck to Clark Kent, the gossip around the Daily Planet offices would be most embarrassing! In midair, however, Superman would generally be far enough away from other people and objects that he wouldn't affect them. Most likely, such a power would require the development of some kind of highly specialized internal organ inside Superman's body, one that would grow as the rest of his body matured. It would probably be a byproduct of the increased amounts of energy being absorbed and converted by his body, and would have to be closely associated with his brain and central nervous system. It might be an extension or mutation of some natural Kryptonian organ, or one unique to Superman as a result of his birth and growth in an alien environment.

One possible mechanism involves a fascinating phenomenon that was discovered by a Dutch physicist, Heike Kamerlingh-Onnes, about a hundred years ago. Experimenting with liquid helium, a form of the element that exists only at extremely low temperatures, specifically 7 degrees above absolute zero,[4] Kamerlingh-Onnes discovered that mercury lost all resistance to electricity. Under normal temperatures, electrons moving through a conducting material encounter resistance as they bump into other molecules. The energy of these collisions produces heat, and even light at very high levels, as in the filament of an incandescent light bulb. The usefulness of light bulbs notwithstanding, electrical resistance can be a big problem, because it not only reduces the flow of current, but the heat it generates can damage and wear out components. If resistance can be removed, current can flow more efficiently without any wasted heat energy. This is called superconductivity.

Since Onnes's original Nobel Prize-winning work, many other materials have been found that could display superconductivity. In fact, practically anything that conducts electricity can, in theory, be made superconductive—it's the practical

---

4. Absolute zero is the lowest temperature possible, at which all molecular motion stops. It's -459.67 degrees Fahrenheit, or -273.15 degrees Centigrade.

aspects that cause problems. The chief difficulty is that super-conductivity tends to occur only at extremely cold temperatures. The -452 F° chill of liquid helium isn't easy to achieve, and liquid helium is hardly a common substance and is difficult to make. Eventually other materials and alloys were devised that could exhibit superconductivity at higher (though still extremely cold) temperatures that were somewhat easier to achieve with more common substances such as liquid nitrogen. This opened the door for the practical use of superconductivity in applications including supercomputers, in which the lack of electrical resistance leads to much faster processing, and MRI medical scanners, which use superconductivity to generate intense magnetic fields.

Still, the difficulty of creating and maintaining the extremely low temperatures needed to achieve superconductivity makes such machines exorbitantly expensive. The dream of superconductivity researchers is to find a way to induce the phenomenon at room temperature. It would be a breakthrough that would be as revolutionary as the development of the computer or the discovery of the DNA molecule.

How does superconductivity provide a way for Superman to control gravity and get into the air? Superconductivity is related to electromagnetism, and this relationship may also extend to gravity as well. About twenty years after Onnes discovered superconductivity, Walter Meissner and Robert Ochsenfeld found that superconducting material repelled magnetic fields, a phenomenon that became known as the Meissner-Ochsenfeld effect, or more commonly (to Ochsenfeld's great annoyance, one imagines) as the Meissner effect. This can be easily demonstrated in the laboratory: In a classic experiment, a magnet hangs in midair, levitating above a superconductor, defying gravity. This is such a well-known effect that mail-order kits are available for home experimenters to demonstrate it.

Flight: No Wings, No Strings

Recently, some scientists have proposed the idea that super-conductive matter may have a similar effect on gravity, specifically in the form of gravitational waves. Some experiments have also suggested an anti-Meissner effect which could increase magnetic fields rather than negate or repel them. In the same way the Meissner effect negates magnetic fields in the presence of a superconductor, a sort of gravitational Meissner effect might negate gravity (or increase it, as with an anti-Meissner effect). If such gravitational (or "gravitomagnetic") effects do exist and can extend over large distances and be controlled, they would give us a mechanism to explain Superman's manipulation of gravity in order to fly. Some people believe we've already found it.

For the past decade, the possibility of a connection between gravity and superconductivity has been fueling a mad rush to isolate the phenomenon and invent a literal "antigravity" device. Wild ideas have always been a staple of the fringes of science, usually frantically espoused by eccentric home inventors toiling in their basement workshops in the quest for "perpetual motion" machines and other supposedly earth-shattering miracle discoveries. Not since the cold fusion furor of the 1980s, however, has an exotic scientific notion raised such a stir as antigravity.[5] Aside from sending multitudes of supposed undiscovered Einsteins back to their workshops in the hopes of changing the course of history (and, not incidentally, becoming billionaires in the process), the prospect of neutralizing

---

5. In 1989, two University of Utah chemists claimed to have discovered "cold fusion," a means of generating energy by nuclear fusion at room temperature instead of the million-degree temperatures of the sun or hydrogen bombs. If real, cold fusion would have meant a cheap source of limitless energy. Unfortunately, the claims didn't hold up to scrutiny, and no one has yet found a way to make room-temperature nuclear fusion work—assuming it's even possible.

gravity has attracted the attention—and the money—of some of the pillars of the mainstream scientific and technological establishment, including NASA and Boeing Aircraft Company.

It began in 1992 with an obscure Russian materials scientist, Eugene Podkletnov, studying superconductivity at a Finnish university. Experimenting with a spinning 12-inch superconducting disc in an electromagnetic field, Podkletnov found that objects suspended over the disc seemed to lose about 2 percent of their weight, as if gravity was being partially negated. The finding was completely accidental and unexpected—Podkletnov wasn't trying to build an antigravity gizmo—but seemed to occur in all types of materials, whether metal, plastic, or ceramic. Had Podkletnov inadvertently invented a "gravity shield"?

As Podkletnov prepared a scientific paper for publication in a respected physics journal, someone at the journal leaked the paper to a British journalist, who published a sensationalistic newspaper story about the invention of an "antigravity machine." Although Podkletnov had carefully avoided making such a claim, he found his credibility damaged and his work dismissed by most of his peers, particularly when no one else seemed to be able to repeat his experiment and confirm the effect. Most physicists considered Podkletnov's experiment as little more than an over-hyped curiosity, probably the result of flawed technique or misinterpreted data, and certainly not to be taken seriously. The scientific community at large was content to yield the antigravity playing field to the fringe experimenters and wishful-thinking inventors of all stripes trying to duplicate Podkletnov's work, usually claiming to achieve even more amazing results.

Not everyone dismissed Podkletnov so easily, however. In 1996, scientists at NASA's Marshall Space Flight Center were intrigued enough that they funded experiments to search for

the effect. When those failed, NASA hired an Ohio superconductor company to build a duplicate of Podkletnov's apparatus.
Tests of that device were also unsuccessful, but NASA continues
to investigate antigravity on a modest level. Meanwhile, Boeing
and several other aerospace and defense companies have been
conducting their own discreet investigations into the subject.
Various experimenters, some legitimate scientists and others
not, continue to claim to have reproduced Podkletnov's discovery, but truly substantial and reliable verification has yet to
be made.

Is Podkletnov's work a true breakthrough? Will it someday
result in antigravity technology that could slip the surly bonds
of Earth in everything from elevators to spaceships? According
to physics as we now understand it, probably not. But if other
scientists are eventually able to detect and repeat whatever it is
that Podkletnov observed, and a verifiable new theory—or a
revision of present theory—is found to explain it, an entirely
new frontier of science may be opened. Perhaps Podkletnov's
"antigravity" is somehow related to the "negative gravity" or
"dark force" we discussed earlier. Perhaps it's all nonsense, and
scientists fifty years from now will laugh at our ignorance and
gullibility for entertaining such far-fetched notions. In science,
as with so many other things, only time—and careful, pain-stak-
ing work that results in conclusive proof—will tell. For our purposes, however, we'll assume that the manipulation of gravity in
some form—whether blocking it *a la* Podkletnov, strengthening
it, or counteracting it with another force such as negative gravity—is possible. Even so, a fly still remains in our speculative
physics ointment. If such phenomena require superconductivity, and superconductivity happens only at temperatures hundreds of degrees below zero, how could this work at normal temperatures for Superman? Either some part of his body would

have to be cold enough to become superconductive, or it would have the ability to become superconductive at normal temperatures. This may be where the specialized internal organ mentioned earlier comes into the picture. Perhaps such an organ could vary greatly in its internal temperature, under Superman's conscious (or partially conscious) control. At very low temperatures, this organ could then be the source of the Meissner-like effect that Superman would use to alter and control gravitational fields. Its effects might also interact with his bioelectric field in such a way as to augment the ability.

If Superman lacks the ability to internally generate low temperatures to induce superconductivity, then he must possess at least some tissues that are superconductive at high temperatures. The most advantageous might be nerve tissue, for several reasons. First, like normal human nerves, superconducting nerves would be tied into Superman's brain, which would give him full conscious control over his flying power. They would extend to all parts of his body, facilitating the projection of his bioelectric field in any direction. A superconducting nervous system would also allow very fast nerve impulses and neuromuscular responses, which would come in very handy for superreflexes and a supersensory system. It might even have interesting implications for super fast and efficient mental processes.

Whatever Superman's abilities to use gravity for propulsion, as opposed to the less exotic principles used by birds and airplanes, he couldn't ignore aerodynamics entirely, not as long as he stayed within Earth's atmosphere. Aerodynamics is a factor

Opposite: *Voyager 1* blasts off in 1977 for a rendezvous with Jupiter and Saturn. The explosive combustion of the rocket fuel, vented through exhaust tubes, provides both lift and thrust for the launch vehicle.

when anything moves through the air, whether a rock or a Boeing 777, and Superman would have to contend with forces such as aerodynamic drag. Adopting his familiar posture of arms outstretched in front and legs straight behind him, Superman would reduce the drag on his non-streamlined body as much as possible. At high speeds, he would experience aerodynamic heating of the surface of his body—not that this would trouble him much as a nearly invulnerable being. He would also be able to use his body to "surf" the airflow to some degree, and perhaps even provide some amount of lift. Finally, his cape, while mostly worn for looks, could also be useful for some low-speed maneuvering, similar to the way a parachutist can guide his descent.

There may come a time when human beings will be able to fly without wings or any other artificial aid other than a wearable device that manipulates gravity. Or perhaps some people will even choose to be genetically modified with wings or some other kind of physical structure that allows them free flight. Meanwhile, we have our sophisticated aircraft and a century of powered flight. Yet flying hasn't lost all of its magic. Dreaming and speculating about flight will be a part of our culture and our science for the foreseeable future. And Superman will continue to be one of the most intriguing manifestations of our age-old desire to take to the skies.

SUPERSTRENGTH: MORE POWERFUL THAN . . .

CHAPTER FIVE

SUPERSTRENGTH:
MORE POWERFUL
THAN...

The idea of a superstrong being is certainly nothing new: it's been around ever since Samson, Hercules, and countless other figures from mythology. But whereas those muscle-bound types were never really much more than an exaggeration of normal human capabilities, Superman is something else entirely. His abilities consist of much more than simply being able to bench press an unusual amount of weight. Superman can apparently defy the laws of physics: He can not only lift tons of weight, he can hold it, move it around, manipulate it. He can throw and catch objects at great speeds, with reflexes far superior to any human being. His superbreath can create hurricane-force winds, either while inhaling or exhaling. Obviously, he's far more than just another strong man.

Such abilities can't be explained simply by asserting that Superman is stronger than human beings, because sheer strength only gets you so far. The strongest human being in the world may be able to lift hundreds of pounds, but still requires the proper leverage to do so. He might be able to lift the end of a car off the ground, but not with one hand, and not without properly positioning his body to exert the necessary force.

Superstrength: More Powerful Than . . .

Watch a weightlifter on TV: you'll notice how he (or she) spends quite some time positioning the feet properly, breathing in, breathing out, placing the hands carefully on the bar, and *then* lifting—or more properly, pushing from underneath, against gravity. No weightlifter alive could just walk up to a set of weights and pick it up by the end. To move the amount of mass against the pull of gravity, precisely the right force must be applied in the proper way.

Superman, however, doesn't seem to be bound by such constraints. He can lift and carry an ocean liner or a locomotive across the sky with nary a care, and doesn't have to worry about proper placement of his hands or finding the correct leverage. Before we consider such feats, let's take a look at strength in general. What does it mean, and what creates it?

HOW STRONG IS STRONG?

Strength, like beauty, is a relative concept. Some insects, for example, can lift objects such as a leaf or twig that are much larger and heavier than themselves, but they can't lift a phone book like we can. So in that sense, a human being is stronger than an ant. On the other hand, that same human being couldn't budge an object larger and heavier than himself, in the same proportion as the twig to the ant. Proportionally speaking, the ant is stronger than the human. Why is it that an ant can lift a twig, but a human being can't lift a car?

It's because strength is more than simply the ability to exert force on something else—it's also the capacity to resist an equivalent force. Take gravity, for example. Every second of your life (unless you're an astronaut), the Earth's gravity has been pulling on your body, trying to draw you toward the center of the Earth. Why hasn't it crushed you into a puddle by now? Simple: the human body evolved to resist the force, with bones and muscles strong enough to counteract gravity's constant pull. If you were to stand on the surface of a more massive planet with much greater gravity, however, your ears would be wearing your shoes. And even on Earth, as we age and grow weaker, it becomes more difficult for our bodies to withstand gravity, and we begin to experience various musculoskeletal ailments.

In previous chapters, we've explored how Superman's body is nearly invulnerable in Earth's environment, thanks to factors including a denser, thicker skin; a highly efficient ability to resist and repair cellular damage; and a self-generated bioelectric field that wards off harmful radiation. His ability to directly convert and use solar energy further enhances these factors. Superstrength, in fact, wouldn't be much use without a good deal of invulnerability, because when Superman exerts force on an object, the object exerts force on him. Without the ability to resist that force, Superman could be seriously hurt or killed. He might have the ability to smash through a brick wall, but what good would that be if he sustained multiple traumatic injuries in doing so? For a painful demonstration, you might try running at full speed headfirst into drywall. You'll probably put an impressive hole in it, but at the price of a concussion or worse! Or punch through a glass window, something well within the power of anyone with normal human strength. You'll wreck the window, but make a bloody mess doing so. These rather outlandish (and—must we say it?—definitely *not* to be tried at home, or anywhere else!) scenarios prove that the theoretical ability to do something isn't always accompanied by the practical ability to exercise that power.

So the first requirement for superstrength is near-invulnerability, or at least bones, joints, and muscles able to hold their

In an impressive display of his powers, Superman spots Lois Lane's car going under via supervision, flies to the river, holds his superbreath, dives in, and lifts the car out of danger with his superstrength, once again using his power of flight.

own against great force. If Superman is going to lift a ten-ton weight, his spine has to be able to resist that ten tons of force without collapsing like a straw underneath a brick. (This is why, even if you had a superstrong "bionic" arm, you'd never be able to lift a locomotive: if you tried, you'd rip that magnificent artificial limb right off of your shoulder!) As we've seen, Superman's skin is remarkably tough and resilient partly due to the incorporation of heavier and denser elements such as silicon and iron; it's logical to assume that similar processes would be at work in other tissues of his body, including the bones, muscles, joints, and connective tissues.

Up to a certain level that we'll examine shortly, super-strength is less a unique "power" than an enhancement of natural abilities that are already present in a normal Kryptonian. We've already discussed the Kryptonian capacity for using energy directly from solar radiation—which may be exotic from a human perspective, but is perfectly normal for a native of Krypton. The greater energy Superman would derive from this ability may not be enough to make him "super" in itself, but it would supplement his other more conventional source of biological energy: the metabolic processes of breaking down and synthesizing various molecules from food, just as humans and all other animals do.

The precise mechanisms by which the substances derived from food are converted to energy to power the functions of life are fiendishly complex and far beyond the scope of this book. Such biochemical alchemy not only keeps us alive, it also helps to maintain and repair our bodies and stores energy for later use. For our discussion, though, it's enough to realize that in all living creatures, the energy of life depends on a complex organic molecule, a nucleic acid called *adenosine triphosphate*, or ATP for short. Cells, of course, are much more than simple lumps of protoplasm—they contain smaller structures, called *organelles*, that perform various functions. Just as your body contains different organs, every cell contains various organelles. Among the many organelles found inside cells are *mitochondria*—minuscule rod-shaped compartments that serve as cellular power plants. It's inside the mitochondria that ATP serves as the middleman for chemical processes that generate energy from the respiration of oxygen. Using oxygen—aerobic metabolism—generates much more ATP and thus more energy than anaerobic (without oxygen) metabolism, which is why animals need to breathe to stay alive. Certain enzymes (molecules that trigger other reactions) break down ATP into another molecule called ADP (adenosine diphosphate), releasing a lot of energy in the process. This energy from the mitochondria powers other processes in the cell, and consequently the cell itself as it goes about its particular cellular business. If the organism is resting and doesn't need much power at the moment, the mitochondria can turn ADP back into ATP, storing the energy as if in a battery until it's needed later.

This is a terribly simplified explanation of a much more complicated process, but basically ATP can be thought of as "energy money"—it's the means by which energy is created, stored, and moved about within the cell. ATP is absolutely essential to life—all life, even plants. Animals create ATP by breathing oxygen, and plants do it through photosynthesis, but both types of organism use it in the same way and for the same purposes. As far as life is concerned, ATP is a molecule as indispensable as DNA—maybe more so. It's certainly important enough that studying it won three scientists (John Walker, Paul Boyer, and Jens Skou) the 1997 Nobel Prize in chemistry. Aside from its crucial role in energy production, ATP has a few other useful functions in animals. When cells suffer damage, the release of ATP can trigger pain, informing the animal that something is wrong. And on a more mundane but no less important level, you'd have trouble deciding when to visit the bathroom without ATP. As urine fills and stretches out your bladder, ATP is released in the bladder walls to signal the brain and inform you of the impending crisis!

If superstrength means greater energy, then, and greater energy means more ATP and a higher rate of processing it, it's logical to deduce that Superman's body both creates and uses more ATP. This makes sense given his ability to extract energy both from food and from sunlight, because it means that he's producing ATP in two different ways rather than just one, as we do. Superman would also enjoy greater stores of energy that would come in handy when he needed an extra boost—when his body was transitioning from the upper limits of his normal strength to superstrength, for example—and when other bodily systems were under stress and needed some reinforcement.

Each of Superman's cells might also contain more mitochondria to provide more energy-generating capacity. The only problem with this idea is that, while the cells of all Earth creatures contain mitochondria, this may not be true of life originating elsewhere in the universe. Among the many interesting attributes of mitochondria is the fact that, unlike all the other organelles found in the cell (except, of course, for the nucleus), they actually contain DNA. This isn't to be confused with the DNA of the individual animal that provides its special genetic blueprint and dwells in the cell nucleus—it's a separate DNA strand that controls the internal workings of the mitochondrion itself. It's almost as if the mitochondria aren't merely parts of the cell, but complete cells in themselves, living inside of larger cells. Expanding on this idea, biologist Lynn Margulis of the University of Massachusetts has speculated that, during the

early development of Earthly life in the dim past, mitochondria may actually have been separate organisms that either invaded or were consumed by other cells. Instead of taking over or being digested, however, the mitochondria eventually adopted a symbiotic relationship with the host cells, performing jobs that the host couldn't do for itself—energy production through ATP, for example. Margulis concludes that the reason present-day mitochondria contain their own DNA like a separate independent cell is that, millions of years ago on Earth, they *were* separate cells.

If this theory is true, it's possible that extraterrestrial life might not have mitochondria. Their presence in our cells might be nothing more than the result of an evolutionary fluke, and cells born on other planets may have developed other organelles that perform a similar energy-generating function through different processes. On the other hand, if the primordial symbiosis that Margulis describes is essential for the evolution of complex life, and if it fails to occur and thus create mitochondria for energy production, life wouldn't progress past the primitive stage on another planet. This is simply one of the multitude of questions that can't be answered until and unless we're some day able to examine a living sample of extraterrestrial life.

Still, we can say with reasonable certainly that, ATP-processing mitochondria or not, any conceivable complex living organism has to have the ability to generate and use a lot of energy to keep itself going. If Kryptonian life evolved without mitochondria, it would still require other structures on the cellular level to perform the same tasks—perhaps a great number of them in order to compensate for those times when the Kryptonian solar-energy biological processes weren't enough. Again, a biological characteristic that would be merely normal on Krypton would be much enhanced on Earth: Superman's "solar-powered" metabolic functions along with his more intense and efficient aerobic metabolism would be the cornerstones of his vast muscular strength, endurance, and recuperative powers.

Another element contributing to Superman's strength is the possibility that before their own destruction, Kryptonians had been engaged in the process of enhancing and perfecting themselves through genetic engineering. By altering their genome, Kryptonian biologists may have all but eliminated disease and banished their genetic flaws, and then gone beyond those achievements to increase their natural abilities and create new ones. And if a "normal" Kryptonian would already be super on Earth, a genetically enhanced Kryptonian would be still more powerful. He would be much stronger than normal on their home planet, but on Earth, his powers would be magnified by several orders of magnitude.

Given the fact that Krypton's civilization was highly advanced scientifically, such technology would be almost a certainty. The only barriers to its use would be social and ethical. Humans have already learned genetic engineering on a small level, and we're learning more every year. In 2002, researchers at the University of Pennsylvania, funded by the National Institutes of Health, created a synthetic gene that when injected into lab mice, makes them "super." The mice are up to 60 percent stronger than normal mice, with bigger muscles, more stamina, and greater ability to heal from injury—and they don't weaken with age. The scientists are trying to find a way to slow down or reverse muscle weakening in elderly people and those afflicted with muscle diseases, but their gene could also be used to enhance athletic abilities far beyond the limits of today's greatest athletes. Just as the use of steroids and other performance-enhancing drugs has become a hot issue in both professional and amateur sports, gene manipulation is set to become the next controversy born of the marriage of sports and science. In the next decade or so, you might see your favorite baseball player suspended for the season or your favorite ice skater stripped of a gold medal not because of drug use, but because of illegal synthetic gene injections. If humankind is on the verge of creating athletes who never tire and never age (imagine a 60-year-old NFL linebacker!), a civilization as scientifically sophisticated as Krypton could do much more.

As you might expect, gravity would also be an important factor in Superman's strength. Just as a human astronaut on the Moon can move objects he'd never be able to budge on Earth, Superman and his Kryptonian muscles can manipulate great weights on Earth. There's a catch, however. It's true that, for example, a 180-pound human weighs only 30 pounds on the Moon. But weight isn't the whole story. While the weight of an object changes in different gravitational fields, the mass of the object—the actual amount of matter it comprises—remains the same. Here we return to Isaac Newton, whose first law of motion states that objects at rest tend to remain at rest unless acted upon by an outside force. This property is called inertia, and it depends on mass, not weight. Astronauts working in zero G have to keep this in mind constantly. They might be able to push around a two-ton satellite in the cargo bay of the space shuttle, but if that moving satellite happens to hit something, it will do so with two tons of mass.

This fundamental difference between weight and mass would be a concern even for Superman. Perhaps he can pick up a hundred-ton locomotive as if it weighed only a hundred pounds—but he's still dealing with a hundred tons of mass, with all the inertia of those hundred tons. If he wanted to throw the locomotive up into the air, he'd still have to do so with enough force to move a hundred tons. (And if he neglects to catch the locomotive when it comes back down, it's going to make whatever it lands on awfully flat.)

But when we're talking about this much mass (or weight, in Earth gravity), it's hard to imagine how Superman would be able to toss it about so easily, superstrength and invulnerability

Repairing the Hubble Space Telescope. An astronaut moves carefully from the Shuttle's movable arm to a handhold on the Hubble. He must not make any sudden moves, or Newton's Third Law will send him flying off into space.

notwithstanding. Whatever his strength, Superman still weighs only about 225 pounds; without proper leverage, he's not going to be able to lift something of much greater mass than himself. So if he can lift, move, and manipulate massive objects while disregarding basic physical laws, he's somehow circumventing those laws, employing some other kind of power that makes them irrelevant, or both. In other words: there's more to Superman's superstrength than big muscles.

An astronaut cavorts on the surface of the Moon. He carries only one-sixth the weight he has on Earth, but his mass remains constant.

Opposite: The dangers of microgravity make it necessary for astronauts aboard the Space Shuttle to exercise daily to reduce loss of bone density. Notice the straps across his feet to keep him from drifting up and away.

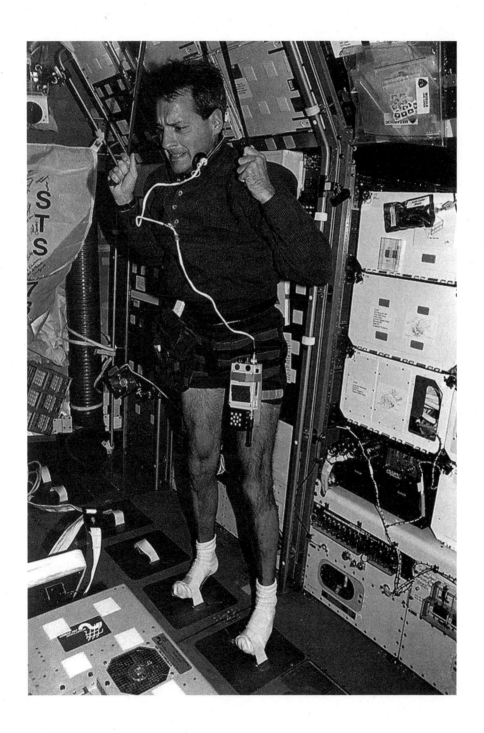

KEEPING IT CONSTANT

It's common to think of Superman's powers as separate and dis-crete phenomena, but actually they're all interrelated and com-plementary. His Kryptonian ability to take in energy directly from the sun increases his strength, endurance, and invulnera-bility, because the spectrum of electromagnetic energy from our sun is more intense in particular wavelengths. His body's greater powers of regeneration and self-repair contribute to his invul-nerability. In effect, one power or ability derives from another. The same applies to humans and other animals: Your abilities to avoid danger, find food, and so on, are a direct result of a high-ly sophisticated and sensitive sensory system.

For most purposes—"everyday use," as far as that term can apply to a superbeing—Superman's superstrength would derive solely from his greater Kryptonian energies, Earth's weaker gravity, and simply greater physical strength. This would be enough for punching out crooks, smashing through walls, stop-ping getaway cars, and so forth. But when greater feats were demanded of him—those which required more than "normal" superstrength, such as holding up collapsing buildings, moving a ship out of an iceberg's path, or guiding a crippled airliner to a safe landing—Superman would require a boost from another power. It's one we've already examined, and perhaps the most mysterious in terms of present-day physics: his ability to manipulate and control the force of gravity.

As we've seen, Superman is able to focus on gravitational fields external to his body, somehow adjusting the flow of graviton particles or gravitational waves and thus pulling or pushing his body toward or away from other objects, using this ability to fly. He also possesses a bioelectrical field that serves to protect his body in various ways. Obviously, this field doesn't impede the flow of gravitational energies; otherwise, Superman wouldn't be able to fly. Suppose that Superman, when in direct physical contact with an object, can extend his bioelectric field around the object to some degree. Suppose further that in doing so, Superman's capacities to adjust gravity can then be imposed on the object he's touching. He would be able to extend his power to control gravity to any other object merely by touching it, much in the same way as you can transfer heat to something (or someone) cold by physical contact.

What effect might this have? Once again, we're in the realm of pure speculation, but let's go with it. If Superman could somehow temporarily alter the gravitational constant in a confined area of space-time, namely the area contained within his extended bioelectric field, he could literally change the gravitational laws of the universe to his liking—but only in that confined area. He would change the amount of gravity contained in the object, making it possible to move the object with less force than would normally be required. Recall our discussion of Eugene Podkletnov's controversial work in the last chapter. In essence, Superman would be generating a localized effect similar to that which Podkletnov claimed to observe, but with much greater intensity and full control.

How might this work? As we've seen, no one knows exactly, and not everyone believes it's even possible—not yet. But we can provide a metaphorical illustration. In our discussion of gravity in the previous chapter, we mentioned Einstein's theory of general relativity and its idea that the presence of gravity literally curves the space around it. Think of a bed sheet held tightly against a wooden frame, parallel to the ground. If you place a ball on the sheet, its weight creates a depression in the cloth. Gravity curves space-time just as the ball curves the surface of the sheet. Although it's the weight of the ball that's creating the depression in the sheet, the mass of a planet (or any other matter) curves space in the same way.[1] Roll another ball nearby and its course will be diverted by the depression, just as an object passing near a planet is pulled in by gravity (remember the gravity-assist technique used to send spacecraft on distant flights?). If you want to move the ball out of its depression to another place on the sheet, you'll have to push it hard enough to move it out of its original spot—the sheet will resist the movement somewhat. What happens if you pull the sheet tighter against the frame? The depression caused by the ball becomes shallower and the ball rises—although (unless maybe you're using a ping-pong ball!) the sheet will never become completely flat under the ball, no matter how tight the sheet is pulled against the frame. The "gravity" of the "planet" is lessened, but never completely disappears. Roll a second ball past the first, and its course will be less affected than before. And it will take less force to move the first ball than before, because you'll be pushing it out of a shallower depression.

In this example, pulling the sheet tighter and thus raising the ball and shallowing the depression it makes is the equivalent of changing the gravity of a planet (or whatever object we want the ball to represent). We could also alter its gravity by reducing or adding to the mass, but the only way to maintain the same mass yet reduce gravity is to alter the gravitational constant, which is what pulling the bed sheet tighter represents.

This is how Superman might deal with handling something like a locomotive, jet airliner, cruise ship, or anything else really massive. He would simply use a variation of the same mechanism that enables him to fly, altering the gravitational constant in a narrowly-confined area within his bioelectric field. The

1. The unimaginably intense gravity of a black hole would be the equivalent of a hole in the sheet—anything coming too close would fall through and disappear completely.

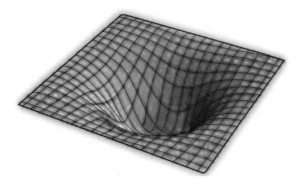

A graphic representation of how gravity affects spacetime. The grid represents spacetime, and the center depression represents the presence an object of significant mass, such as a star. The curving of spacetime around the massive object would make another, smaller object (such as a planet) tend to curve in its direction. In essence, this is how the sun's gravity keeps the Earth in solar orbit.

mass of the airliner, office building, or asteroid would be unchanged, but in effect, it would be in a slightly different space-time temporarily, in which the force required to move it would be much less. As soon as Superman finished whatever task was necessary with the object, he would retract his field and the gravity of the object would return to its normal value in our universe.

LAYING DOWN THE LAWS

If all of this sounds pretty fanciful, well, it is. So we'll digress briefly to clarify the terms of our discussion. Many of the concepts we're throwing about involve ideas on the very frontiers of science, and in some cases, far beyond. But however far we may stray from the familiar shores of established knowledge, we are endeavoring to maintain at least a tenuous lifeline with it. Although physicists can't yet tell us how to alter the gravitational constant or extend a bioelectrical field (or even if it's possible), such ideas are based on current science. Gravity itself was once considered a rather spooky concept, and even Sir Isaac Newton, the man who originally devised the principles by which it operates, was criticized for thinking that "action at a distance," as he called it, was possible.

In fact, this notion of Superman lifting and moving around huge objects not by his muscles but through some innate power sounds practically supernatural, like the claims made by purported psychics of bending spoons, moving coins, or influencing dice by psychokinesis. Why is Superman changing the gravitational constant any different?

For one thing, it's based on a demonstrably real phenomenon, namely, gravity. Although we may not yet understand all its subtleties, we know the laws by which it operates, and thus can calculate and predict the behavior of gravity, or more properly, the behavior of objects in gravity, with enormous precision. Because of this, we can also speculate on what would happen if some of the laws were altered—which is what Superman would be doing in changing an object's gravitational constant.

On the other hand, reports of psychokinesis (or telekinesis, if you prefer), are based on nothing more than anecdotal evidence—one person's story about what happened. Even more important, while gravity is a repeatable phenomenon—i.e., it always behaves precisely the same way, time after time—psychokinesis isn't dependable. Even those who support its existence admit that sometimes it works, sometimes it doesn't. And when it does work, it's not always in the same way. This frustrating problem makes psychokinesis, telepathy, and various other psychic phenomena impossible to test reliably. If they can't be tested, we can't pin down an explanation of the underlying processes at work.

Of course not, say the psychics—they're phenomena that follow different laws than the ones we know. Yet even if that's the case, we should be able to discover those laws, just as we've discovered so many of the others by which the universe operates. The existence of a universal law[2] implies predictability and repeatability. If you hold a cinder block over your foot and drop it, the law of gravity states that it will always result in a trip to the emergency room. Any phenomenon that can't be repeatedly observed, defined, and understood in this way is suspect, because even if it's something hitherto unknown, if it occurs in this universe it must ultimately conform with the laws of this universe. And if a new law is discovered derived from the phenomenon, it will also fit in with other established laws—although it might cause considerable alteration along the way.

Albert Einstein caused just such a shake-up. Before he came along with relativity theory, the universe was thought to operate much like clockwork, according to the laws of gravitation and motion devised by Isaac Newton. Newton's laws seemed to work perfectly well and could be verified by experiment, although they did leave a few annoying holes in the picture here and there. Then Einstein turned everything upside down with his apparently crazy ideas of curved space and warped time and relative speed and motion, much of which seemed to directly contradict Sir Isaac. Who was right, Isaac or Albert? Did 250 years of elegant science have to be completely thrown out and torn down, merely on the word of an obscure Swiss patent clerk?

Not at all. As it turned out, and as has been verified by experiment, both Newton and Einstein are correct. Einstein provided the bigger picture into which Newton fit most neatly, and in

2. The term "law" in this context, of course, is descriptive, not proscriptive (as is human-made law). Scientific laws describe how things work and are determined through observation and experiment; human-made law is created by people based on their own morality, ethics, and needs.

so doing helped to clear up some of the problems Newton couldn't resolve. Rather than discarding Newton, scientists found out how to fit him into the new framework. Now, almost one hundred years after Einstein, young scientists are stretching the limits of his theories, trying to fill in the empty spaces he couldn't complete, expanding and complementing his picture of the universe with new discoveries and theories.

This is why the common idea of "paradigm shifts" in science that completely set the clock back to zero and refute all that came before is inaccurate. Theories and ideas get thrown out and tossed away all the time in science, of course. But when something's been around for hundreds of years and has been put to the test, like Newton's laws, it's rarely if ever completely overturned by the new. Instead it's modified, expanded, altered, and ultimately incorporated into a better, more complete and precise model.

But this isn't the way things have gone with psychokinesis and other psychic phenomena. Nothing is ever actually proven, repeatable, pinned down. There's no there there. Nothing is established that can be built upon later. The work of Podkletnov and other antigravity theorists faces the same difficulties, although perhaps not to the same degree; there's some credible science behind it. Until the supposed antigravity effects are independently repeated and verified, however, scientists aren't going to toss away or completely revise over one hundred years of physics merely to accommodate a promising possibility. However cool the theory and however magnificent the implications for humankind, new ideas in science have to survive the crucible of experimental verification before being accepted. As the late Carl Sagan was fond of saying, extraordinary claims require extraordinary evidence. And there are few ideas more extraordinary in physics than the possibility of shielding, negating, or otherwise manipulating gravity.

Okay, but putting your hands on an aircraft carrier and changing its gravity so you can lift it up like styrofoam still sounds pretty magical. And if Superman really has such an ability, it has to conform with some kind of physical laws, even if we don't yet completely understand them, right?

Absolutely. The existence of laws means the existence of limitations. What constraints on his strength might Superman face?

HOW SUPER IS SUPER?

Just as Superman's body would develop and grow physically from his birth to adulthood on Earth, his various abilities and powers would mature and increase. There's nothing unusual about this—it's the same for every other animal, including human beings. In general, an adult human being is stronger, faster, more agile, and more precise in movements than a child. How strong, fast, etc. an individual person may be depends on many factors; some adults are obviously stronger than others, for example. But human physical abilities largely increase from childhood to maturity, reach a particular individual limit, and then slowly decline as the person ages.

Superman's invulnerability and ability to regenerate damaged cells would no doubt greatly retard his aging process, but he's probably not actually immortal. His powers in his adult life are most likely at their peak, but eventually they will decline, just as with any other living creature. What are their limits?

To find out definitively, Superman would have to be tested under strictly controlled conditions, and he's far too busy for that sort of thing. So we'll have to make some educated guesses.

Superman's strength, defined as his ability to manipulate objects, is comprised of two elements: his natural muscular strength, greatly magnified by the Earth environment and his double-edged capacity to use and store vast amounts of energy derived from solar radiation and food; and his ability to manipulate gravity in a limited way. These elements supplement each other directly—the second picks up where the first leaves off. If Superman is lifting an object slightly over the limits of his muscular superstrength, the gravitational ability kicks in and picks up the slack. The proportion of one to the other would vary as the mass of the object increased, to the point where Superman would hardly be using his muscular strength at all. Therefore, the ultimate limits of Superman's superstrength would be determined by his gravitational abilities. And since this is dependent on the use of his bioelectric field to contain and intensify the gravitational effect, it comes down to how far and how strongly he could extend that field.

Superman's bioelectric field is essentially electromagnetic in nature. Although electromagnetic energy can travel great distances, it tends to fall off very rapidly in strength as the distance from its source increases, as anyone who's ever tried to pick up a distant television signal with an antenna knows. Therefore, the farther Superman attempted to project his field—in other words, the larger an object around which he tries to extend it—the weaker the field will become, particularly in the area farthest from him.

We know that Superman can call on great stores of energy when needed, and no doubt this is what happens when he's using his strength on a very massive object. And he's going to feel the strain, the same way you do when lifting a heavy suitcase as opposed to a lighter one. Sooner or later, Superman is going to encounter something that's so massive and so large in volume that moving it would require more energy than he has available, perhaps even more energy than he's capable of taking in and using in any circumstances. He'll have met his match, at least in terms of sheer superstrength.

Without that time-consuming controlled testing mentioned earlier, it's not possible to calculate Superman's match. But a good guess might be any average-sized planet. The Earth, for example, has a mass calculated at roughly 6.6 billion trillion trillion trillion tons. That, to put it mildly, is an awful lot of rock. It's hard to conceive of how any being of near-human mass could possibly muster enough force to budge such a huge amount of matter.[3] There's also the problem of extending his bioelectric field around a globe almost 25,000 miles in circumference.

Of course, even for Superman, shoving planets around isn't a task that comes up very often in everyday life. Moving mountains, buildings, and aircraft carriers are feats more than adequate to earn Superman his name. As we noted at the beginning of the chapter, strength is relative, and Superman is much stronger than any human—indeed, any creature—that has ever lived on Earth. It's unlikely that he would run into situations completely beyond his powers in the course of his usual duties, because for most of those, his greater basic muscular strength would be more than adequate.

There are other byproducts of that muscular strength that even qualify as powers in themselves. Superbreath, for example, is simply a manifestation both of Superman's greater lung capacity and his ability to expel air with extreme force thanks to powerful diaphragmatic musculature. Related to this is Superman's ability to hold his breath for extended periods of time. Not only

---

3. This doesn't mean that Superman wouldn't be able to move the Earth indirectly, through some other means than actually trying to push it. After all, few people can lift up the end of a car with their bare hands, but almost everybody is strong enough to use a jack.

are his lungs able to extract oxygen from much thinner air under lower pressure than human lungs, but the muscles that control his breathing can hold that air inside for hours.

Superstrength, then, is a great deal more than a talent for juggling ocean liners, playing catch with locomotives, or carving a tunnel through a mountain of granite. In conjunction with invulnerability, it's the foundation of all of Superman's other powers. All of those powers involve the use and control of energy—energy provided by the enhanced biological processes that are the very essence of Superman's life itself. Superman's muscular physique bespeaks power, but that power isn't due so much to the size and tone of his muscles as it is to the biochemical processes that happen at the level of the cell, and more deeply, among the molecules that make up those cells. It's here, in the realm of the very small, that the true key to superstrength and all the rest of Superman's abilities is found. ATP, ADP, DNA, RNA, and all of the other odd letter combinations that sound like a mysterious secret code are actually the cryptography of life, not just for Superman but for all living things, and it's a code that is wondrously subtle in its complexity and importance. As creatures built to live on a larger scale, we may not be consciously aware of all of the constant froth of activity in the biomolecular world, but everything that we do and everything we are ultimately rests on that infinitesimal foundation.

Readjusting our perspective from the microscopic back to the macroscopic, we'll turn our gaze to another example of the interconnected relationships of Superman's powers. Closely related to superstrength is superspeed—because, just as invulnerability is needed for superstrength, superstrength is a requirement for superspeed. Our examination of superstrength has set the stage for a look at the hows and whys of superspeed.

CHAPTER SIX

SUPERSPEED: NO LIMITS?

To move with great speed has always been an attribute admired by humans. Our ancestors conceived of it as a godlike quality and bestowed it upon such immortals as Mercury, the messenger of the gods. Other ancient peoples formed cults or religions based on those animals that were the embodiment of superswift movement, such as the great cats and birds of prey. Today, we celebrate the fastest in sports, transportation, even computers, and are constantly striving to achieve greater and greater speed. Limits are an annoyance: Pilots and engineers balked at the belief that airplanes couldn't fly faster than sound, and stubbornly (and sometimes fatally) pushed at that barrier until it was broken. And although science has proclaimed that the speed of light is the ultimate universal speed limit, there are still those who refuse to accept it.

Perhaps one reason we're so enamored of speed is that it's hard to achieve and maintain. Whether with automobiles, aircraft, or sneakers, going fast is an expensive proposition— or, more properly, we should say going faster than *normal* speed. For those animals and vehicles specifically designed for blazing speeds, it's no trouble at all, although it can still be costly.

What makes some things faster than others? Why do some

creatures move only inches at a time, while others can run for miles without breathing hard? And what could give a being like Superman the ability to move so much faster than the average human being?

FASTER THAN FAST

To be fast is to use energy, and to have and to be able to use a lot of energy is to be strong. So the first factor in explaining Superman's speed is his vast strength. Without the power afforded him by his superstrength, superspeed would be impossible. Muscles that can drive his legs and arms at high rates and great force are essential. As we've seen, the strength within those muscles is partly genetic, stemming from Superman's Kryptonian origins, and partly environmental, arising from Earth's different gravity and especially Superman's capacity to use and store more of the energy in Earth's sunlight than Earth natives can.

Superspeed would also be of little use without endurance and the ability to withstand the wear and tear that speed entails. Runners, especially those who compete in marathons, know about both. In a race, there's little point in being faster than your opponents at the starting gun if you tire more quickly than they do, allowing them to outrun you. And if your knees, legs, and feet aren't used to the stress of running, you may not make it to the finish line even if you don't run out of breath.

Superman's greater lung capacity and efficiency in processing oxygen cover these requirements quite well, and his invulnerability prevents the usual physical consequences of rapid, prolonged movement, including muscle strains, ligament tears, or joint deterioration. Not that Superman wouldn't tire—eventually—while running at high speeds. In human beings, the fatigue and weakness you feel after physical exertion is due to the buildup of the byproducts of the metabolic processes by which the body manufactures energy. When more energy is needed than can be made with the amounts of oxygen being consumed, less efficient energy-producing processes kick in, creating waste products such as lactic acid, which gives us that tired, achy feeling. Superman's body chemistry and his metabolic processes are Kryptonian, not human, and on Earth they're even more efficient than in the Kryptonian environment; as we have seen, he can even convert some solar radiation directly to biological energy. But he still needs to breathe oxygen in order to make some energy from food, and when his solar energy stores are low and his great lungs have used up most of the oxygen within them, he's going to feel tired. Of course, this won't happen to Superman until long after it's already happened to whoever he's pursuing.

The final and perhaps most important element making superspeed possible would be a super-swift nervous system, perhaps one that was fully or even partially superconducting. Human nerve impulses travel at speeds up to about 500 feet per second, but those in a superconducting nervous system would be much faster. Superman would not only have much faster reflexes, but would literally be able to think faster and process more sensory information at once—attributes that are handy if you tend to go running at several hundred miles an hour and want to avoid nasty accidents!

Superman's body would also need a generous allowance of highly efficient neurotransmitters, which are complex chemicals that carry messages between nerve cells and from nerve cells to muscles. Deficiencies in various types of neurotransmitters are thought to be responsible for mental and emotional problems such as depression and manic-depressive illness, and phys-

Superspeed: No Limits?

A modest use of superspeed is usually enough for subduing common criminals.

ical disease such as Parkinson's disease and drug addiction, among many others. Too much of certain neurotransmitters can have other physical and mental effects as well. Superman's neurotransmitters would undoubtedly be similar to those of humans in some ways, radically different in others. But, at least during those times when he was using superspeed, a particular type or types of neurotransmitter would be required at a certain level. They would "supercharge" his already-fast system to an even higher peak for superspeed motion. This might also be accompanied by the release of certain hormones in Superman's body that increase his heart rate, respiration, and energy, as adrenaline does in human beings.

Superspeed, then, is a special function for Superman, one that would expend resources and capacities that aren't necessarily part of the everyday workings of his body. Why is speed important—not just for Superman, but in general?

WHAT'S THE HURRY?

Speed may be impressive, but what's the point? If it's so expensive in terms of energy, what are the advantages of being fast?

For animals, the answer is easy: survival. The ability to move and react quickly is a decided advantage. A rabbit fleeing a fox, a deer fleeing a bear, a fly fleeing your flyswatter: It is speed and reflexes that keep them alive. It works the other way around, too. The 65-mile-per-hour sprinting speed of the cheetah, the lightning-fast strike of the cobra, the swift diving flight of the Peregrine falcon make them deadly predators. Whether hunter or hunted, the fastest tend to live longer than the slowest. When a wolf pack targets a herd of moose, the wolves go for the slowest and weakest, not the fastest and strongest.

Fast animals are gifted with attributes their slower relatives lack, or have in lesser degrees. In general, they're leaner and lighter in weight, yet with great muscular strength. They may be streamlined to some extent, particularly in the case of birds and fish. They may have larger lung capacity and stronger hearts; the American pronghorn antelope, while not as fast as the cheetah, can run at speeds up to 45 miles an hour for long periods because its lungs and heart are three times larger than those of related animals. Speedy creatures also possess prodigious reflexes and reaction times. Try to get up close and personal to a rabbit, a deer, or other wild animals, and you'll witness the swift reactions that are imperative for survival in a dangerous and uncertain world.

If animals use speed to stay alive, why do we humans crave it so much? After all, we don't have to worry about being stalked by fierce predators (except, perhaps, those that are human); we're at the top of the food chain. For animals, speed is a means of escaping or capturing, but thanks to our tool-making capacities, humans have other means of getting food and avoiding potential threats. So what's our rush?

One reason we're so obsessed with speed is that we're cursed with something animals lack: an awareness of time and its passage. You'll never see a Kodiak bear rushing down the street, anxiously checking his watch, glancing about for a taxi, worrying about missing an important business meeting. But you can witness human beings doing precisely the same on the streets of any American city on any weekday.

Any discussion of speed in a human context must also involve time, because for us, they're inextricably bound together. We even measure speed in terms of time—miles per hour, seconds across the finish line. Human beings didn't invent time—it's as much a part of the universe as matter and energy—but we decided to divide it into segments, give those segments particular names, and build various devices to count off those segments.

Some of the units of time we use are based on real-world astronomical phenomena. A day is defined as the period it takes the Earth to rotate once on its axis; a month is based on the orbit of the Moon around the Earth; a year is the period in which the Earth completes one orbit around the sun. Seems simple enough, and we don't even need clocks to mark these intervals; it can be done just by watching the sky. Different cultures throughout history have devised various definitions of these units, based on different ways of observing and recording the real-world events they represent. A day, for example, can be defined based on the position of the sun or on the position of any other star in the sky. However they're conceived, commonly-agreed upon definitions are necessary to avoid the confusion and conflict that would result if one person's day or month was different from another's. But what about weeks, hours, minutes, or seconds? They don't coincide with anything in nature. Here we did *not* observe something happening in the real world and then come up with a term defining the time period involved. Hours, minutes, and seconds are strictly human inventions, a way of trying to impose a little more order on the universe for our own convenience. The idea of dividing up time into smaller units to be measured originated with ancient peoples, with different civilizations doing it in different ways. The Egyptians were probably the first to divide the day into twenty-four segments, twelve hours for daylight and twelve for nighttime. But because the length of daylight and nighttime periods varies with the seasons, the Egyptians literally had to shorten and lengthen their hours to compensate, i.e., each of the twelve daylight "hours" was longer in summer and shorter in winter. Later, the Babylonians adopted the system in which every hour is the same, regardless of whether the sun was up or not. This equal-hour system didn't catch on in Europe until as late as the 1300s. As to minutes and seconds, we have the Sumerians to thank for deciding that there are sixty seconds in a minute, and sixty minutes in an hour, since they used a number system based on 60. Using our now-fashionable base-10 number system, we could just as easily decree that there are 100 seconds in every minute, and 100 minutes in every hour, and 10 hours in a day. Weeks are simply a convenient way to divide up the month; we could have a five-day or ten-day week just as readily as the seven-day week we currently use.

The story of how various calendars and timekeeping schemes have been invented and changed over human history is a long and fascinating one—too complex to explore here. For our purposes it's enough to realize that, aside from certain units based on observable phenomena, such as days, months, and years, our notions of timekeeping are essentially arbitrary. A "week" is a completely human invention, unlike a galaxy or an asteroid. We can choose to define time units by linking them to something in nature; by international agreement, a second is precisely defined as 9,192,631,770 oscillations in the energy state of the cesium-133 atom. This is the standard upon which all clocks in the world are officially based, and is scrupulously kept by governmental agencies using hyperaccurate atomic clocks. Very impressive, yes—but still, based on arbitrary human decision. After all, why not 9,192,631,771 or 9,162,631,769 oscillations of the cesium-133 atom?

It doesn't have an hour or a minute hand, and there is no mainspring. The atomic clock keeps time by tracking the oscillations in an atom of cesium-133.

Also, we do not live in a clockwork universe as was believed several hundred years ago. Even natural time periods such as one orbit of the Earth around the sun, or one rotation of Earth on its axis, aren't eternal and unchanging constants. They vary over both short and long stretches of time because of gravitational perturbations, variations in orbital and rotational speeds, and so on. So occasionally we need to adjust our neat, orderly systems of timekeeping to compensate, adding or subtracting a day from the calendar every so often, or even adding a leap-second to the day once in a while.

Humans conceived the plan of dividing up time and counting its units as a means of organizing, coordinating, and regulating their activities, and without question, it has been one of our most important achievements. Civilization, much less our modern technological society, would be impossible without the structure that our system of time provides. But there's a downside to this great boon. As we devote more energy to thinking and worrying about time, it becomes more and more important to us. We become obsessed with it, engulfed by it, imprisoned by it, and we worry about "saving" it, using it, wasting it. We consider how much time is spent doing things we don't like doing, and struggle to find ways to alter the balance so we can spend less time on unpleasantness like work and more time on enjoyable pastimes like play.

And this is where speed comes into the equation. The faster one task can be accomplished—the less time it takes, in other words—the more time is left for other tasks or activities. The faster your Internet connection, the less time you spend waiting and doing nothing while an elaborate Web page loads. The faster you type, the more work you can finish in an hour. The faster you get home from work, the more time you have to go out with your friends in the evening. The faster you do everything, the more you can do in a day, a week, a month.

Speed can be a huge advantage, which is the reason we strive for it. But it has a cost. We're only human beings—we can only move so quickly, or do so many things at once. But that's okay, because we have technology to help us do more in less time, and hence become speedier.

Almost every technological innovation that radically changes our lives seems to involve speed, especially in the areas of transportation and communications. In the 18th century, it took months to travel across the United States, but with the advent of railroads in the 19th century, the time was reduced to weeks or days. In the 21st century, you can now cross the country in a matter of hours, so fast that you'll suffer physical and psychological disorientation from the shift in time (a problem so common, we've given it a name: "jet lag"). Through e-mail and instant messaging, you can send a letter to a friend in a matter of minutes or seconds, avoiding the old-fashioned "snail mail" that takes days or weeks. With cellular phones, people can make and receive calls anywhere, anytime, instead of waiting until they get home or finding a pay phone somewhere. With faster communications and faster travel comes more rapid and frequent interactions with others: more to do, more to plan, more opportunities, more choices, more problems. Life in general becomes faster and faster, until we feel overwhelmed, out of our depth, beyond our ability to cope. Scientist James Gleick examined this phenomenon in fascinating detail in his appropriately-titled book, *Faster: The Acceleration of Just About Everything.* First published in 1999, the book is ironically already outdated in some of the examples and anecdotes it provides.

Apart from its usefulness as a means of saving time, there's a more visceral aspect to our fascination with speed: it's exciting both to see and to experience. Who doesn't feel a delicious tingle of mixed exhilaration and fear when driving or riding in a high-performance sports car, riding a roller coaster, or looking out the window from a train moving at eighty miles an hour? The heart pumps harder and faster, adrenaline flows, breath shortens and quickens. It's mostly a fear response, because something in the ancient areas of the brain protests that *this is dangerous, human beings didn't evolve to move so fast!* But the higher, more developed, rational brain answers, *it's okay, everything's under control, we know what we're doing!* We enjoy the tension between the two opposing voices as the thrill of speed. This isn't merely a trivial diversion. Although they may not always admit it, the excitement of speed is a prime motivator for racing drivers, stunt and test pilots, motorcyclists—practically everyone who deals with speed routinely. Speed also provides a wide-open field for competition. No matter how fast an athlete runs, or how swift a car, airplane, or boat, the limits can always be pushed just a little farther, setting new records that can be broken by others.

Although it may be expensive in terms of energy and other resources, speed can have benefits that more than compensate for its costs and risks. Yet those benefits are not unlimited, and sooner or later the speeder hits a wall of diminishing returns—some kind of limits that either prevent going faster, or make it too costly to do so. Some of these limits can be avoided, altered, or at least lived with, but others are ironclad rules of nature with no appeal. Let's take a look at some limits to speed and how they affect animals, human beings—and Superman.

SOME SOUND PRINCIPLES

The whole notion of a speed limit is distasteful to most people. All drivers have occasionally chafed under the seemingly unfair restraints placed upon them by highway authorities, who inexplicably insist that 35 miles an hour is a perfectly reasonable speed despite the fact that 45 feels much more appropriate. What's more frustrating than being compelled to travel at 55 miles an hour on the open road in a car capable of doing about twice that speed? Frustrating or not, of course, highway speed limits are a fact of life, and they do have a good purpose—namely, saving lives. Still, as any state trooper will attest, such limits exist only legally, not physically, and are routinely broken every day.

But other limits to speed are more concrete. Even the fastest sports car has a top speed, determined by factors including the design, power, and efficiency of the engine, the type of fuel used, road conditions, and so on. It might be possible to exceed that top speed briefly, but only at the risk of substantial damage to the car, not to mention a fatal accident. These kinds of limits are easier to respect, because their consequences are more readily apparent and don't depend on the proximity of law enforcement officials. If you push your car too fast, you may escape a ticket, but not the destruction of your engine. Another example of this type of limit is simply running out of energy, whether biological or mechanical. A person eventually tires and stops; a vehicle runs out of fuel. But limits such as these are individual. Everything has its own limits, but they're not necessarily the same as those of something else.

Some speed limits, however, can't be argued with. They may vary according to environmental conditions, and may even be exceeded if certain strict factors are met, but otherwise they are consistent and implacable. These barriers to speed are determined not by legislation or by individual limitations, but by the physical laws of the universe. The speed of sound and the speed of light are the classic cases, and appropriately enough, are also the speed milestones that most concern Superman. We'll take the slower speed limit—that of sound—first.

The sound "barrier" wasn't even an issue until the 20th century and the advent of the airplane. Other supposed speed barriers were earlier thought to exist, coinciding with each new innovation in transportation. Some believed that human beings couldn't possibly withstand the blazing speeds of early locomotives, and that exceeding, say, thirty miles an hour would prove fatal. The same concerns were raised a century later with the invention of the automobile: how could people survive in a vehicle hurtling along at sixty miles an hour? These fears quickly proved groundless, and locomotive and automobile designers concentrated on overcoming the practical engineering constraints to greater speed.

The airplane opened up an entirely new realm in which to push the limits. Speed was an obvious tactical advantage for pilots in the skies of World War I, and after the war designers applied the lessons learned to building swift fighter aircraft and in the construction of powerful racing planes. World War II spurred the creation of even faster aircraft, including the first jets. Pilots flying hot fighter planes such as the P-51 Mustang reported that when they approached the speed of sound (which had been discovered by Austrian physicist Ernst Mach some years earlier), they experienced instability and violent buffeting and nearly lost control of the plane. In fact, many pilots died at such speeds when their controls "froze up" and they couldn't regain control before they crashed. Although the Mustang and other World War II aircraft weren't quite capable of reaching Mach 1 (as the speed of sound was called in Mach's honor), they could sometimes achieve the "transonic" speeds near Mach 1 at which these disturbing effects took hold, particularly in a screaming dive toward the ground. Noting that the dangerous instabilities became more and more violent as an aircraft drew closer to Mach 1, some engineers and scientists thought that an airplane would be inevitably torn apart if it achieved or exceeded the speed of sound, and the idea of the "sound barrier" became common coinage.

Others, especially most pilots, thought that the idea of a sound barrier was utter nonsense. After all, they already knew that objects could travel faster than sound—rifle bullets, for example. And they knew that because sound is simply a mechanical vibration transmitted through a conducting medium, its speed varies according to the temperature, density, and pressure of the medium—air, water, or solid matter. At sea level in air at normal temperatures, sounds travels at about 760 miles an hour. At higher altitudes, with their lower temperatures and pressures, its speed drops by some hundreds of miles per hour. In the thin, frigid air at an altitude of, say, 35,000 feet, the speed of sound drops to about 660 mph. And water and solids carry sound much farther and faster than air. So the speed of sound was not an impenetrable and deadly wall. The right aircraft with the right pilot at the controls would "break through" that nonexistent barrier with no problem.The right aircraft turned out to be the Bell *X-1*, a plane designed to do nothing else than fly faster than sound, and the right pilot to be Air Force Captain Chuck Yeager, a test pilot and WW II flying ace who had once shot down five German planes in a single day. On the morning of October 14, 1947, Yeager took the orange, razor-winged *X-1*—which was, not gratuitously, shaped like a .50 caliber bullet—to a speed of Mach 1.05 over the California desert. He found that rather than tearing his plane to pieces as some had predicted, the transonic instability vanished as he passed Mach 1. And as he broke the "barrier," observers on the ground far below heard a loud "sonic boom," the result of the

The historic craft that first broke the sound barrier, the Bell *X-1 Rocketplane*, now hangs on display in Washington's Smithsonian Museum.

shock wave caused when the *X-1* pierced through the front of compressed air before it.

Before long, test pilots were routinely flying past Mach 1 as new aircraft designs were devised and proven. Six years after Yeager's feat, his friendly test pilot rival Scott Crossfield took a plane called the Douglas *D-558-2 Skyrocket* just past Mach 2, setting a new world speed record. Shortly afterward, Yeager trumped Crossfield by breaking his record. At least in the skies over the test grounds of California, the notion of a sound barrier was ancient history. By the early 1960s, supersonic fighter planes were commonplace, and the test pilots were taking new experimental aircraft past supersonic speeds into the hypersonic region, Mach 5 and beyond, culminating in Major Pete Knight's October 1967 flight in the rocket-powered *X-15* to Mach 6.7—4,520 miles per hour.

Although the sound barrier proved to be a myth, moving at

such speeds does raise a few concerns that must be considered, even if you're Superman. One is aerodynamic heating. Friction creates heat, whether it's the friction of your hands rubbing together on a cold day or the friction of air against a rapidly moving object. For most airplanes, built of heat-resistant metals, this doesn't become much of a problem until approaching high supersonic or hypersonic speeds. The *SR-71* reconnaissance plane, which can fly faster than Mach 3 (just how much faster is top secret), is covered with special temperature-resistant paint and gets so hot at top speeds that its pilot can feel the heat on the canopy window through his heavily gloved hand.

A jet fighter goes "supersonic" by breaking through the sound barrier. Sound waves pile up and condense in front of the craft until it reaches the speed of sound. The craft then bursts through the waves, which, if the air contains enough water vapor, can become visible.

And that's at very high altitudes, where the air is much less dense than at ground level. For Superman, on or near the ground, aerodynamic heating would kick in at much lower speeds. Fortunately, Superman's invulnerability and tough skin would protect him from harm, and his bioelectric field would also work to shield him and perhaps direct heat away from him. He would have to worry about heat effects only if carrying something or someone vulnerable. And even in such a case, Superman's ability to extend his bioelectric field would probably provide enough protection, except at extreme speeds.

Sonic booms would be a bigger problem for Superman—or, more properly, for those around him. Powerful sonic booms created by supersonic aircraft can shatter windows and cause other damage from miles above the ground, and this, along with the general annoyance caused by such noise, is why supersonic flight is permitted only over certain designated areas that are sparsely populated. But imagine the effects of a sonic boom on a typical Metropolis street at ground level! Superman would have to take extreme care to run and fly at subsonic speeds in populated areas. But then, it's hard to imagine that a modest speed of a few hundred miles an hour wouldn't be sufficient to handle most any troublesome situation occurring near large groups of people or buildings.

Finally, Superman couldn't avoid the air buffeting and resistance of transonic speeds. This would be most difficult in his early years, as he learned to use and control his powers. No doubt he would find ways to compensate for and overcome this aerodynamic phenomenon with experience and as his strength increased with maturity.

Apart from these few matters, then, the speed of sound poses no problems to Superman. What about the other famous speed limit—that of light?

Superspeed: No Limits?

THE ULTIMATE SPEED LIMIT?

When we talk about speeds approaching that of light, we're discussing speeds that are truly huge. Yes, it's common knowledge that the speed of light is about 186,282 miles per second, or 300,000 kilometers per second (in a vacuum, that is—light travels somewhat slower through air and water). Sounds fast, but still not completely outrageous, right? 186,000 miles, well, it's a lot, but even the moon is farther away than that. Hardly sounds like any sort of ultimate speed.

But consider. The circumference of the Earth at the equator is about 25,000 miles. A beam of light, then, could circle the earth about seven and a half times in one second. Try to imagine what it would be like to travel that fast. Or consider that after you flip on the light switch in your darkened bedroom, the room remains dark for the merest infinitesimal fraction of a second—the time it takes for light to move from a light bulb, reflect off the walls and other surfaces, and enter your eyes. Could you move from the door to one end of the room before the darkness was gone, so someone already in the room would see you suddenly appear there? Of course not.

Light travels very fast, but not infinitely so. And if it has a finite speed that can be measured, it seems to makes sense that there must be speeds that are faster. History and experience seem to agree. The sound barrier proved to be nothing but an illusion. Speed records of all kinds are being set and broken all the time. Why should light, fast as it is, be any different? Who says it's the ultimate speed limit of the universe anyway? *Why should there be an ultimate limit?*

Alas, there *is* a universal speed limit, and the speed of light is it. The first hint came in a famous experiment in 1887 by A. A. Michelson and Edward Morley, who were attempting to detect the "ether," then believed to be the medium through which light and other electromagnetic radiation moved through space (because if sound waves needed something to travel through, then probably so did other types of waves). If the ether existed, they reasoned, then the speed of light should vary according to the motion of the observer through it—such as, for example, the motion of the Earth in its orbit. They measured the speed of light both in the direction of Earth's orbital motion and at an angle to it, and found absolutely no difference, implying not only the absence of any "ether," but also that something was special about light. In common experience, the measurement and perception of speed depend on the relative motions of the one doing the measuring and the object whose speed is being measured. A highway patrolman sitting still in his car on the side of the interstate with his trusty radar gun might calculate a passing car's speed at 80 mph—but to another car moving in the next lane at 75 mph, the speeder is moving at only 5 mph. (Trying this excuse on the next state trooper who pulls you over is *not* recommended, incidentally.)

But light doesn't work that way, and in 1905 Albert Einstein explained why in his special theory of relativity. Building on Michelson and Morley and other previous work, Einstein showed that the speed of light is constant: it's the same for all observers in all directions, whatever their motion with regard to the light source. But although the speed of light is unchanging, everything else changes when an object approaches that speed. It becomes shorter in the direction of travel, its mass increases, and time slows down. These aren't imaginary or apparent effects—they're absolutely real for the object, and become more pronounced the closer its speed grows to light speed.

This leads to some bizarre consequences. A classic example is called the "twin paradox." Suppose there are two identical twins, Brent and Stuart, both 25 years old. Brent joins the crew of an interstellar expedition to a star system twenty light years away, while Stuart stays on Earth. Brent's starship is quite sophisticated, and it travels the twenty light years to its destination at near the speed of light. Because time slows down for Brent and his crewmates, though, the journey takes only six years to them—while twenty-five years pass back on Earth for Stuart. If Stuart had a very powerful telescope and was able to catch a glimpse of Brent's starship on the way, the ship would look strange—shortened and highly compressed as if squeezed in a press, because of the length contraction effect. Assuming Brent doesn't stay too long and returns to Earth shortly after arrival at the alien star system, he'll experience another six years or so on the way home. He'll get back to Earth only about 37 years old—to find Stuart over 75 years old and a great-grandfather! Yet according to Earthly calendars, Brent and Stuart are still the same age.

In fact, time slows down for anything in motion. When you're flying in an airliner at 500 miles per hour, or speeding down the highway at 70 mph, you are actually aging at a slower rate than when you're standing still. (Again, this is not to be used as an excuse if you're caught speeding!) The Apollo astronauts who hurtled to the moon at 25,000 miles per hour arrived back on Earth just slightly younger than they would have been if they'd stayed home. Lest you think that this effect of special relativity, known as time dilation, is a fountain of youth, however, Einstein informs us that it occurs only at "relativistic" speeds, that is, near the speed of light. The effects of time dilation with the speeds we encounter in everyday life are so tiny as to be almost nonexistent. But they are real, and are routinely observed in the laboratory. As one example, short-lived subatomic particles, sped up to relativistic speeds by particle accelerators, exist longer than when moving at slower speeds. And when highly accurate atomic clocks are flown in swift aircraft, they slow down measurably compared to identical clocks left behind on the ground.

The particles also gain mass, which is another troublesome effect on anything moving at near-light speeds. This is where we run smack into the light-speed barrier. To move mass requires energy, the amount depending on the mass of the object—the more mass, the more energy. The reason is, as Einstein explained, that mass and energy are equivalent—that is, mass can be expressed as the amount of energy contained within an object. This is the principle Einstein expressed in his famous $E=mc^2$ equation, in which E is *energy*, m is *mass*, and c is the *speed of light*. So if the energy contained within an object is its mass multiplied by the speed of light squared, it's easy to see that even a small piece of matter contains a lot of energy. This, not incidentally, is why nuclear weapons are so powerful—some (not all) of the nuclear fuel they contain is converted into energy and released.

Conversely, it takes a lot of energy to move a lot of mass. For instance, as an object—say, a starship—approaches the speed of light, its mass also increases at a fantastic rate, and so does the energy needed to accelerate it further. At the speed of light, the ship's mass becomes infinite—meaning that, to go faster past the speed of light, infinite energy would be required. As if all this weren't enough trouble, the starship would shrink to a length of zero at light speed! Since infinite energy, infinite mass, and zero length aren't possible, nothing can travel at the speed of light.

At least, nothing with mass. Particles without mass, such as the photons that carry light and other electromagnetic energy, can and do travel at light speed—in fact, photons never stand still, *can't* stand still and are always moving at or near light speed. Otherwise they *would* have mass (or more properly, what's called "rest mass"—the mass of an object at rest) and would be subject to the same relativistic quandaries as other matter. And the universe would need some other particle to carry the electromagnetic force at the speed of light. Whatever his powers, Superman is still a part of the universe, and thus subject to the same physical laws as everyone and everything else. He might be able to bend some of those laws, as we've seen him do with gravity, but the light-speed barrier is non-negotiable.

But let's suppose for a moment that Superman *could* move at the speed of light. What would happen to him? What would he experience? We can speculate much as Einstein did in his "thought experiments," in which he imagined riding on a ray of light.

If Superman were running down a major street of Metropolis as he approached light speed, he would notice the entire world slowing down and receding before him. (We'll ignore the other problems such speed would cause in his surroundings, such as the vacuum he'd create behind him, the aerodynamic shock waves he'd make, and so on.) As he accelerated, he would feel progressively heavier, and it would be harder and harder to keep moving. At light speed, everything would appear to stop: the passage of time in the tiny speck of Metropolis before him, and time in his own frame of reference. He would feel frozen, unable to move—unable even to think, since time would be frozen for him. In short, he would be completely helpless, totally powerless. With his mighty heart and even his thoughts eternally frozen in limbo, he'd be trapped forever, unable to slow down, condemned in an eternity of light speed, just like a photon. He would, in effect, no longer be part of our universe, as far as human experience and perceptions were concerned.

Superman could avoid this fate as long as he didn't achieve light speed. If he moved at, for example, .9999999999 percent of light speed, he would certainly experience the slowing of time and the other relativistic side effects, but not the complete paralysis mentioned above. Not to worry, though. No matter how hard he tried, Superman simply couldn't reach light speed, because he doesn't have the infinite energy it would require.

So we, and Superman, have run headfirst into our universal speed limit. Pretty frustrating. But wait: There is a loophole, although it may be only theoretical. Relativity states only that nothing with mass can travel *at* light speed. Faster than light travel, then, isn't actually excluded. Hypothetical particles, called *tachyons*, have been proposed that are faster than light. The catch is that tachyons, if they do exist (none have been found yet), can *only* travel faster than light—they can never decelerate to light speed or slower. Since matter as we know it isn't made of and can't be converted into tachyons, that puts us out of the faster-than-light ballgame. And instant acceleration—jumping from sublight speed to hyperlight speed without any time in between—isn't possible either. Acceleration is a function of time, after all. You can't accelerate beyond light speed without moving at light speed, if just for the tiniest moment—but as we've seen, you *can't* move at light speed.

Naturally, all of this is only a problem for Superman if he wants to travel the immense distances of outer space. The light-speed limitation is hardly relevant on Earth, but if he wants to go to Alpha Centauri, a travel time of several years would be most inconvenient. He might avoid this annoyance by using "wormholes"—literally, shortcuts through space-time that might be created by the "warping" of space by gravity. The idea of a wormhole can be pictured quite simply with a tube of cardboard. Draw a dot on the tube, then roll it around and put another dot on the other side. If the surface of the tube represents curved space, and the dots are two points in space, then the only way to get from one to the other is by traveling across the surface of "space," i.e., the tube. But if you punch a pencil through at one dot, you can poke through to the other dot on the other side, avoiding the long way around the outside of the tube. You've just made a wormhole.

Such wormholes have yet to be detected, but many astrophysicists believe they may exist. There's nothing in Einstein's work or physics in general that prevents them. If they exist in nature, it's probably in conjunction with the intense gravity of black holes, gravity so strong that even light can't escape it. It's unlikely that such wormholes could actually be used for interstellar travel, because the gravitational and tidal effects of the black hole would rip apart any spaceship long before it could get near. Natural wormholes might also exist on a microscopic or even subatomic level, and in any case, they would probably be unstable and transitory. But if they could be created artificially, through generating extremely strong local gravitational fields, a sort of "warp drive" might someday be realized. The problems and complications of such an invention are immense, and beyond the scope of our discussion, but they make for fascinating speculations and cool science-fiction stories.

We've already postulated that Superman possesses some abilities to manipulate and control gravity, and that these powers help him to fly and move massive objects. It's not too much of a stretch to propose that he might also be able to create his own gravitational "wormhole," through which he could travel from one point in space to another far distant place. (This would be a power he would use only in outer space, far from Earth—it would be far too dangerous to open a wormhole on the surface of the Earth!) In this way, Superman would still be moving far slower than light, but over a considerably shorter distance than in "normal" space, so the trip takes much less time, just as you can get to the other side of a mountain faster by taking a tunnel through it rather than going all the way around it. So although Superman might still be subject to the light speed limit, it doesn't matter because his other powers make it irrelevant.

Superman's powers of flight, strength, and speed may be the most obvious manifestations of his "super" nature, but he has a few other interesting tricks up his Kryptonian sleeve. We'll examine those next.

CHAPTER SEVEN

SUPERHEARING: SOFT AS A WHISPER

A good case can be made for the proposition that hearing may be the one sense most critical for survival. Vision might seem much more important at first thought, and no doubt it's the sense that we as human beings consciously rely on most heavily. Yet vision is the one sense that we can turn off at will at any time, simply by closing our eyelids. We spend a good portion of every day without relying upon sight: when we're sleeping, of course, but also many other times when we close our eyes out of fatigue, concentration, playfulness, or other emotions, and when protecting them from wind, dust, and other dangers. So if the sense of vision is so vital, why did evolution give us the ability—in fact, the necessity—to shut it off completely so often?

Your sense of hearing, in contrast, never turns off. It's on twenty-four hours a day, no matter what, even during the times when, thanks to the noisy upstairs neighbor's stereo, you might wish it came with an off switch. You can only partially shut it off, and then only by the far-from-perfect technique of stuffing

something into your ears to block some of the sound. Also, unlike vision, hearing operates 360 degrees around you and in all directions above and below. You can't directly see what's happening behind you, but you can hear it easily. Nature obviously thought it was more important to be able to hear a predator sneaking up in the brush behind you than to see it. It's easier to hide from the eye than from the ear, and the ear never sleeps, not even when you do. A predator may be able to get close to a sleeping animal, but if the predator slips and makes a single sound, the prey is awake, alert, and fleeing.

However, hearing is more than simply a means of detecting danger. Coupled with the ability to create sounds, it allows communication, not only at close quarters but at great distances. That communication can be as basic as alerting others to approaching danger or wooing a potential mate, or as sophisticated as discussing the Jungian aspects of super-hero archetypes over cappuccino and crullers. And it can occur at frequencies so high that it can allow bats to "see" in utter darkness, and so low that two whales can communicate in the ocean across hundreds of miles.

Until fairly recently in our history, when technology literally expanded the palette of sounds we could detect, create, and use, humans tended to be largely unaware of the importance of sound in nature. Even today, most people take their hearing more or less for granted. Yet it's a vital part of our sensory apparatus and a crucial source of information about the world around us.

It's no less so for Superman. His superhearing is one of his less flashy abilities, yet also one of the most versatile. Before we go into specifics about the ears and hearing of animals, humans, and Superman, let's look more closely at the subject of their work: sound.

WAVING AND VIBRATING

Back in Chapter 2, electromagnetic waves were examined. There we saw the interesting relationship between frequency and wavelength: The higher the frequency, the shorter the wavelength, and vice versa. With electromagnetic radiation, different frequencies/wavelengths demonstrate different properties; with visible light, for example, red light is low in frequency and of long wavelengths, while blue light is high frequency and short wavelength. Frequency is generally measured in units called Hertz (Hz), after the German physicist Heinrich Rudolf Hertz, and wavelength is defined in metric units (millimeters, centimeters, and so on). We also saw a diagram of waves with the familiar up-and-down curve familiar to anyone who's ever seen

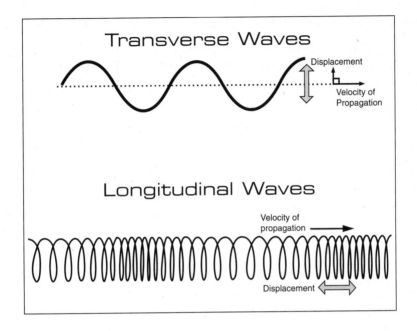

the opening titles of the original 1960s TV show "The Outer Limits." This sort of wave is called a transverse wave; it varies at right angles (as pictured, up and down, meaning higher and lower energies) to the direction of motion (left to right, meaning from one point to another in a straight line). Sound is simply a vibration in a solid, liquid, or gaseous medium and also travels in waves, but of a different sort. Sound waves are longitudinal waves, meaning that the variations of the wave are in the same direction in which it's traveling. With sound, this means that it moves through a medium—air, for example—as molecules of the medium are pushed together and move apart (compressed and rarefied). The speed at which the air molecules are disturbed by sound is the frequency, and the distance between the consecutive disturbances is the wavelength.

You may wonder why all this makes any difference. Waves are waves, aren't they? In a sense, yes; sound waves and electromagnetic waves follow many of the same principles, and we'll look at a particularly interesting and important example of this in a moment. Longitudinal waves are difficult to picture, and so for convenience they're often described as transverse waves. When we look at sound on an oscilloscope screen (such as in that "Outer Limits" opening), we're actually looking at an electromagnetic (transverse) wave that's been converted from a sound (longitudinal) wave. Or when you toss a pebble into a pond, the rings moving outward are transverse waves caused by the sound—but only on the surface, where the water can actually move up and down. Underneath the surface, the waves move longitudinally—the water can't move "up and down" in a transverse wave, because one part of the water can't "separate" from another.

If sound waves are longitudinal, however—traveling by pushing particles together, like dominoes falling against one another—then they must have something to travel *through*. Longitudinal waves are strictly mechanical waves, involving the movement of physical energy through a gas, liquid, or solid. Sound moves through air using air molecules, through water using water molecules, through solids using those molecules—but in a vacuum, there are no particles for it to push against and transmit itself. Electromagnetic waves, however, don't need to travel by pushing particles together, so for them, a vacuum poses no difficulty. (Electromagnetic waves sometimes *behave* as though they're made up of physical particles, but they're not.) The important point to realize is that, although it's common to speak of sound waves and electromagnetic waves in much the same way and using the same terminology, they're quite different in some important respects.

Despite these differences, the relationship between frequency and wavelength applies to sound just as with light, and it's the basis of a familiar phenomenon that we encounter nearly every day—with sound only, unless you're a scientist. It's called the Doppler effect, after the Austrian scientist who discovered it, Christian Johann Doppler. As sound travels outward from a moving source, say the siren on a speeding fire engine, the waves are compressed in the direction of motion and stretch out behind. The sound waves ahead of the truck are "squeezed" closer together, resulting in a shorter wavelength, while those behind spread out, giving them a longer wavelength. Since shorter wavelength equals higher frequency and longer equals lower, we hear the pitch of the siren change as the fire engine approaches, passes, and hurtles away down the street. The pitch of the siren doesn't change for the firemen aboard the engine, because they're moving with it; the siren keeps pumping out its wail at the same frequency until it's turned off. But for those the fire engine rushes past, the wavelength of the sound and its frequency literally do change because of its motion.

An inventive soul, Doppler found an effective way to convince skeptical colleagues of the reality of the effect: he hired a brass band, placed them on a flatbed railroad car, then had them play a single note as the train sped past the entourage. By report, his witnesses were most impressed and fully convinced.

The Doppler effect is seen with other waves as well. When you see your local TV weatherman waxing poetic about his station's powerful Doppler radar, he's talking about a system which uses precisely the same effect to measure and track the motion of weather systems by bouncing radio frequencies off of them. In astronomy, the light from stars that are receding from or moving toward us at great speeds is "red-shifted" or "blue-shifted" as its wavelength is expanded or compressed and its frequency consequently shifted. In the 1920s, astronomer Edwin Hubble used this phenomenon of red-shifted light from distant galaxies to prove that our universe is expanding.

Differences in various sounds are due to more than just variations in frequency, however. The shape of a wave can also vary, ranging from the elegant curves of the sine wave to the blocky-looking square wave, and all other shapes in between. (Again, remember that when we talk about the "shape" of a sound wave, we mean when represented as a transverse wave.) These differently shaped waves sound quite different from one another, and when occurring together, produce very complex sounds. Apart from the actual frequency of a given sound wave, called the *fundamental*, other weaker, softer waves can be generated, called *harmonics*, which are multiples of the fundamental wave. The musical note A, for example, used by all musicians as a tuning reference, has a frequency of 440 Hz. Generated by the pure vibration of a tuning fork, it's a simple colorless tone. But the same frequency played on a musical instrument that creates more complex vibrations (i.e., differently shaped waves and combinations of waves) also generates harmonics at other frequencies, such as 880 Hz and 220 Hz, which are lower in energy and volume than the fundamental but can still be perceived by the ear. These particular harmonics, multiples of 2 of the fundamental, are heard as a musical octave higher and lower from the A note. Other musical notes contained between the ends of the octave are at frequencies with a particular mathematical relationship to the fundamental that makes them sound "good" to the human ear, such as the note "E" five notes above A 440 (a musical "fifth") with a frequency of 660 Hz—blended together, they create musical harmony. The wave shape of the note varies depending on the instrument generating it, and also generates other complex harmonics at various frequencies and energies. These relationships between the shape of the fundamental wave and the particular harmonics created are why a cello, for instance, sounds very different from a French horn even when they're playing precisely the same note. For that matter, they're the reason a jackhammer sounds different from a freight train.

The speed at which sound travels depends on many qualities of the medium transmitting it: its temperature, elasticity, density, and so on. But sound absolutely requires something to move through. Although Stanley Kubrick in his classic film *2001: A Space Odyssey* seems to have been pretty much the only filmmaker to ever acknowledge it, sound is impossible in outer space. An object can vibrate so violently as to create a horrendous din on the Earth's surface, but without anything to transmit those vibrations, they're not going anywhere. Or, as the 1979 film *Alien* put it on its poster (but, alas, didn't demonstrate in the film itself): "In space, no one can hear you scream." Assuming you're screaming into a vacuum and not into the pressurized atmosphere of a spaceship, that's true.

As a physical phenomenon, sound has some other fascinating characteristics. Like other waves, sound can be reflected off of solid objects and refracted or "bent" as it passes from one medium to another of different density. Different sound waves can vary from one another in *phase*, the relationship between the peaks and valleys of their wave patterns, creating complex interference patterns or even canceling out one another. Sound carries energy and momentum and can cause other objects to *resonate*, or vibrate at the same frequency. All of these effects give sound the power to do things such as shatter glass and brick, burn paper, move solid objects, and even look inside the human body in real time. Because sound travels faster and farther in water than in air, ships and submarines use sonar (short for **s**ound **n**avigation **a**nd **r**anging) to find each other and underwater obstacles.

For humans (and even some animals), sound also holds immense psychological importance. It can soothe, annoy, enrage, and completely disrupt mental processes. In the form of music, sound can plumb the greatest depths and most expansive range of human emotion. The specific neurological and psychological mechanisms by which it does so are still not well understood. Why does the mournful moan of a Stradivarius cello playing a Bach suite bring tears to the eyes of one person and not another? Why does one person experience the soaring wails of a Jimi Hendrix guitar solo as the purest ecstasy, while another hears it only as noise? We don't really know. Through music's effects on the human mind and heart, the objective and the subjective blend together in subtle and mysterious ways.

If sound is caused by vibrations, how is it detected? How do we and other animals perceive it as sound?

LEND ME AN EAR (OR TWO)

When we think of them at all (except, perhaps, worrying that they look too big and stick out funny), we usually think of our ears as organs of hearing. In evolutionary terms, however, that's not how they started out. For the primitive fishes that are our distant aquatic ancestors, "ears" were concerned less with hearing than with maintaining balance and orientation in a three-dimensional environment. The same function is preserved today in modern fishes by the lateral line, a tube that runs the length of the fish's body just under the skin, with pores open to the outside. In some fishes, the lateral line is quite obvious, while in others it's harder to see. Either way, though, it contains myriad tiny hair-like cells that sense movement and pressure changes in the water, helping the fish keep track of its movements and possible threats.

Superhearing: Soft as a Whisper

Our own ears, and those of other advanced animals such as mammals and other vertebrates, are also critical for our sense of balance. We may not move through water like fishes, but we use a similar system to stay right-side up: the inner ear includes three semicircular canals, each oriented in a different plane, filled with fluid which moves against microscopic hairs lining the canals. The movement of the hairs is translated into nerve impulses which the brain decodes to provide information on orientation. Although the system is exquisitely sensitive, sudden movement or spinning of the body can cause the semicircular canal fluid to slosh about crazily, creating confused signals and resulting in dizziness. Once the fluid slows down and stops, the dizziness goes away.

A more sophisticated extension of this balancing mechanism gives us the ability to detect and hear sound. To see how, let's go back to the outside and work our way into the ear's structures. The visible outer part of the ear—what we're usually referring to when we're talking about it—is called the auricle or *pinna* (from the Latin word for feather or wing, which seems to imply that ancient peoples had *really* big ears), and is a structure of skin and cartilage shaped to collect sound waves and focus them into the ear canal. Interestingly, although the exact shape and contours of the pinnae vary greatly from one person to the next and are as individual as fingerprints, these variations don't seem to matter much as far as their sound-gathering capabilities are concerned. Moving through the canal, sound next encounters the tympanic membrane or eardrum, a thin barrier covering the width of the canal and separating the rest of the ear from the outside world. The vibrations of the tympanic membrane are picked up by three tiny connected bones called the *ossicles*, attached to the membrane in a horseshoe shape bridging the air-filled cavity of the middle ear. The middle ear cavity is also connected to the outside by the Eustachian tube leading to the back of the throat, which allows air pressure to be equalized on both sides of the eardrum to prevent it from rupturing; it's the sudden opening of this tube to release air pressure that causes that "popping" sensation in your ears when you fly on an airliner. From the eardrum inward, the ossicles are named the hammer, anvil, and stirrup, and their movements amplify the sound from outside by about twenty times. The stirrup is attached to another tiny membrane called the oval window, which covers the opening to the inner ear and the *cochlea*, a coiled, snail-shell-shaped organ filled with fluid. The vibration of the oval window is transmitted onward to a structure coiled within the cochlea called the *basilar membrane*, upon which is the *organ of Corti*, consisting of strips of about 16,000 minuscule hair-like fibers of different lengths and thicknesses, called *stereocilia* or hair cells. The vibrations of the basilar membrane cause the stereocilia to

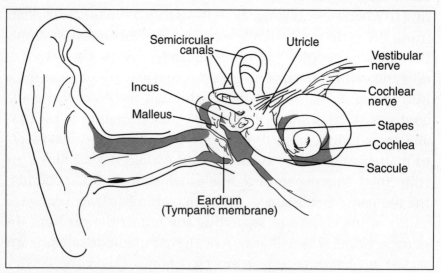

A schematic of the human ear shows outer ear, middle ear, and inner ear, which connects via nerve fibers to the brain.

vibrate in turn, generating electrical nerve impulses which are finally transmitted by the auditory nerve to the brain and interpreted as sound. Because the stereocilia resonate to different frequencies depending on their length and thickness, they respond to different pitches, intensities, and durations of sound. They're also incredibly sensitive—and delicate. Researchers attempting to study living stereocilia in the laboratory must use air-cushioned tables to dampen vibrations from the floor that could "deafen" the cell by making it move too violently. If the stereocilia responsible for a certain range of frequencies are damaged or destroyed by disease or injury, hearing in that range is reduced or lost.

The ears of other higher animals operate in much the same way. Some animals, such as birds and reptiles, have only one ossicle, or a shorter and straighter type of cochlea. Whatever its form, the ear is a device for converting sound vibrations to mechanical energy and then into nerve messages which can be read by the auditory regions of the brain. Differences in ear construction result in different frequency sensitivities. Ideally, human hearing ranges from about 20 Hz up to 20,000, while dogs can hear sound up to twice as high. Bats can hear (and produce) frequencies that are higher still, up to about 120,000 Hz, and use this ability to navigate in the dark (although they're sometimes credited with having "radar," bats use ultrasonics, not radio waves). Dolphins can hear sounds as high as 150,000 Hz, while whales and some other marine animals can hear and produce very low frequencies.

So while the ears of different creatures may work similarly, they're by no means created equal. Even with the same basic equipment, wide variations in hearing acuity can exist. We've all known people with extremely, almost aggravatingly sensitive hearing (or the opposite). An individual person's sense of hearing also changes inevitably over time, and can vary even between each ear. The 20-20,000 Hz range mentioned above is enjoyed by very few humans, but those who do are usually very young, and find that it narrows considerably as they age. If a person spends a lot of time in a loud environment, such as working with noisy machinery or going to a lot of heavy metal concerts, hearing will decline much faster.

Sometimes a brief exposure to high sound levels will cause a temporary and partial loss of hearing. You've probably experienced this if you've ever attended a rock concert. On the way out to the parking lot, your ears may ring, or sound may be muffled and indistinct; you can't quite make out everything your companions are saying. The loud music has overwhelmed the supercilia in your cochlea, blowing them over and "flattening" them like a strong wind tearing through a field of wheat. The supercilia soon recover and regain their normal sensitivity, just as the wheat returns to waving upright in the breeze. But if the supercilia are repeatedly subjected to the hurricane-like forces of loud and prolonged sound, they can be "blown over" permanently. Because the supercilia, like other nerve cells, don't regenerate or reproduce themselves, this results in irreversible hearing loss.

Sound levels are usually described in *decibels*, which measure relative intensity or loudness. The decibel (dB) scale is based on 10. This means that a sound at 20 dB is ten times louder than one at 10 dB; 30 dB is ten times louder than 20 dB but a hundred times louder than 10 dB; 40 dB is ten times 30 dB but a hundred times 20 dB and a thousand times 10 dB, and so on. You can see, then, that using such a scale, things get very loud very quickly. A whisper can be 10 to 30 dB, while normal conversation measures from about 30 to 60 dB. Loud traffic with impatient drivers honking and leaning on their horns comes in at about 90 dB—a thousand times or so louder than conversation! Although it varies from one person to another, the human pain threshold is generally considered to be about 120-130 dB (about the loudness of a jet plane taking off), but anything over about 90 dB, especially if prolonged, can cause hearing damage.

Fortunately, of course, we, like all other animals, have *two* ears, and we can get along with only one if we have to, or one which hears better than the other. Humans and animals with such an impairment are at a disadvantage, however, because there are excellent reasons for having two ears, and it's not so that we have a built-in spare. Recall our discussion of the lateral line in fishes, and how it and our ears evolved from organs whose purpose was to orient a water-dwelling animal in three dimensions and help it to maintain balance. For such a purpose, bilaterality—having two identical organs, one on each side of the body—is the most effective arrangement, particularly for a creature such as a fish with so distinct a two-sided, flat shape. Something dangerous could be happening on one side of the fish while all is calm on the other side, but if the lateral line happened to be only on the calm side, the fish could miss the threat entirely. Its own body would block it from detecting the danger.[1]

For land creatures with ears, who aren't shaped like fish and have moveable heads, this factor may not be so much of an issue, but two ears for maintaining balance and hearing instead of one are nevertheless a great benefit. Especially for larger animals, including humans, two inputs provide the brain with a much more sensitive capacity for detecting balance. The brain can combine and "average the data," so to speak, to create a

---

1. Obviously, we're disregarding the fish's eyes—but since we're discussing a creature that lacks bilaterality, it would either have only one eye, or two eyes on one side.

more precise picture of the body in space than would be possible with just one balance-sensing organ.

This process is called binaural fusion, and it allows you, and anything else with two ears, to locate a sound in space around you, and even to track its source as it (or you) move. The survival benefits for animals are obvious: enhanced ability to find, or keep yourself from becoming, food. In fact, some animals have such sophisticated sound-location abilities that they can find the source of an incredibly faint sound in total darkness—for example, a field mouse hiding inside a barn. In the 1970s, Caltech zoologist Masakazu Konishi studied one such animal, the barn owl, to learn more about how such feats are possible. He discovered an area in the owl's brain which is the equivalent of a three-dimensional sound map—upon hearing a sound, nerve cells fire in a specific location of the brain that corresponded with a particular location in space. Individual nerve cells respond to different combinations of frequency, duration, and timing, as detected by the stereocilia in the owl's ears. The brain puts it all together to tell the owl precisely where to find its dinner.

Our sound-location abilities aren't nearly as acute as those of the barn owl, but they're still most sensitive and useful. If you're walking down the street, minding your own business, and a friend suddenly yells out a greeting to you, your brain compares the relative intensity of the sound of your friend's voice from each of your ears, determines on which side the voice is louder and the difference in time between the sound entering each ear (which can be thousandths or even millionths of a second), and uses the information to compute where your friend is. It's your choice to turn your head in that direction and respond (maybe it's somebody you don't want to talk to!), but your ears and brain have already done their job.

And if you cross the street before you have a green light, still deciding whether or not to yell back, your ears and brain will also make it clear that a truck has just unleashed its air horn, perhaps with some choice obscenities from the driver, at you from your other side.

Sometimes this sound-location system can be fooled or confused if a sound is immediately above, below, before, or behind you, because the difference in intensity and the time lag of sound reaching both ears may be beneath the threshold of your ears to detect or your brain to discern. This doesn't happen too often, though. You might have to consciously focus on another sound occurring simultaneously and use that as a reference to distinguish the location of the first sound, but usually your brain will put the pieces together almost instantly, helped with the additional data from your eyes and other senses. As with sensitivity to different frequencies, this ability can also vary with individuals; some people are really good at finding the source of an odd noise, while others can hardly hear it at all.

But we're talking about human beings. What about Superman? Just how much would his hearing differ from ours? What would he be able to hear that humans can't?

SUPERMAN SONICS

It's likely that, because Kryptonians are basically humanoid in their general construction (although, as we've seen, wildly different from humans in other ways), Superman's ears would look much like ours internally. Certainly they would function under the same principle: converting sound into mechanical energy and then into nerve impulses. Superman's hearing would be "super" in two chief respects: the sensitivity of his ears to a wider range of frequencies and intensities, and the ability of his ears and brain to discern differences among sounds. The first is essentially a function of anatomy and, to an extent, his invulnerability and strength; the second also depends on these factors but is also based on Superman's faster neurological functioning. Let's take a look at both aspects of superhearing in turn.

The hair cells or stereocilia inside the cochlea of the ear are the bridge between the mechanical movement caused by sound and the electrical signals that the brain hears. As we've seen, the human ear only has about 16,000 of these hair cells, or roughly 32,000 in all—not that many, really, especially when we take into account that only some of them respond to any individual sound, and that even if we avoid damaging them permanently with noise, we lose a portion anyway as we grow older. It follows, then, that if an ear has many, many more stereocilia than a human cochlea, and if those cells are capable of responding to a much wider range of sound, that ear will hear with far greater acuity than ours. Such is the case with Superman's ears. The lower range of his hearing isn't much different—after all, the lowest frequency humans can hear is about 20 Hz, and there's not much lower to go under that (except for whales, which can hear underwater down into the single Hertz range)—but the high range would be well into the ultrasonic. In fact, the term ultrasonic would hardly apply here, because it refers to sound higher than we can hear, while Superman can hear such frequencies as easily as we hear a violin. His upper hearing range could be well beyond 150,000 or even 200,000 Hz.

Why would Superman's ears contain so many more hair cells? Most likely, because of the same evolutionary forces that gave him increased lung capacity and more efficient oxygen-processing ability—namely, a normally thinner Kryptonian atmosphere. Our Earthly air is actually a fairly poor conductor of sound compared to water or solid matter, and an atmosphere of lower density and pressure would propagate sound even less well. To hear and use sound at all in such conditions, animals would have to evolve with a vast number of extremely sensitive supercilia, along with the neurological capacity to receive and interpret the immense amount of information so many cells would generate. To some degree at least, just as Superman's tougher skin and ability to convert solar radiation for energy are natural for Kryptonians, his superhearing is less a "super-power" than simply an enhancement of his normal biological characteristics in Earth's environment.

But there's more to it than that. Superman's greater strength and invulnerability under Earth's sun aren't solely manifested in his muscles, but extend to other physiological systems, including his senses. For hearing, this means that the hair cells in his ears are tougher, more flexible, and more responsive than they would be on Krypton. Certain frequencies and very loud sounds of megadecibel intensity—a nuclear explosion at close range, maybe—might cause Superman pain and even destroy some of his supercilia. But he would also recover quickly, and losing a few hair cells out of so many would hardly make a difference to his hearing.

Wider frequency range and greater sensitivity of the sense of hearing raise other implications, and these bring us to the second major aspect of superhearing: how his brain handles and uses those enhanced abilities. Again, simply by evolving on Krypton, Superman's brain would have evolved the neurological capacities to deal with the auditory information coming from all those supercilia. On Earth, though, those same hair cells would be subjected to more sounds at greater intensities than they might ever encounter in the Kryptonian environment. In this regard, it's probably fortunate that Superman came to Earth as a fetus, before he was actually born and fully developed physiologically, because it gave his exquisitely sensitive sensory apparatus (including his eyes, as we'll find out in the next chapter) ample time to adjust to this alien environment. An adult Kryptonian suddenly subjected to the auditory world of Earth would probably find himself engulfed in an unbearably painful and relentless din. (Conversely, a human would find sounds to be curiously weak and muffled on Krypton.) Superman's brain was able to acclimatize and tune his sense of hearing to its keener edge on Earth. On a smaller scale of time and degree, you can become accustomed to an initially annoying sound or painful noise level until you barely notice it consciously. As we noted at the beginning of the chapter, you can't literally turn off your hearing, but your brain has some ways to compensate.

This is a necessary adaptation for a simple reason: our senses take in much more information than we can possibly attend to. Wherever you may be as you read these lines, there's a great deal going on all around you. Your eyes are reading, yes, but on the edges of your vision they're also seeing beyond the book to whatever's out there. Your ears may be collecting the sound of a subway train, a radio, a loved one's voice, an air conditioner, or even just a gentle autumn breeze rustling through leaves. The nerve cells in your skin and inside your body are transmitting a virtual encyclopedia to your brain about temperature, the pressure of your body on your seat, the dull ache in your back, the fullness or emptiness of your stomach, the taste of the iced tea you're drinking, the mosquito that's just alighted on your arm. All of this information is being collected simultaneously, yet you're conscious only of a small fraction of it, because your brain is devoting most of its attention to the fascinating book you're reading (we hope). Meanwhile, the brain discounts but still registers data that's not as important. Should a sudden change in the flood of incoming data require a brief shift in priorities, you'll drop the book and swat the mosquito.

In the same way, Superman would be able to discriminate in his hearing both consciously and subconsciously, but to a much finer degree. Subconsciously, this would prevent him from being distracted and overwhelmed by the sheer range of what he can hear; consciously, it would allow him to focus on a particular sound and to differentiate between sounds with laser-like precision, much like one of Dr. Konishi's barn owls. A superconducting nervous system with super-swift nerve impulses would make Superman's auditory system capable of detecting, interpreting, and responding to sound with such sensitivity, precision, and discrimination that, coupled with conscious cognitive abilities including great concentration and mental focus, he could not only hear a whisper in a windstorm, but also pick out a single voice in a crowd of thousands.

A pleasant side effect of Superman's superhearing would probably be a much richer experience of music. As we've seen, the complexity and expressiveness of musical sound is largely due to harmonic patterns that occur at frequencies far above or below those of the actual musical notes. Superman could detect musical overtones far higher and weaker than any human, adding color and depth to his perception of music.

As impressive as it may be compared to ours, Superman's hearing couldn't avoid some limitations—mainly, the speed of sound. His auditory perception and processing may be much faster than that of humans, but sound still reaches Superman's ears at the same speed as for everyone else. He may hear a cry for help in Metropolis from a hundred miles away, but even with his superspeed, he can't do anything until the sound gets to him first to tell him there's trouble back home. To hear some sounds at great distances, Superman might instead literally put his ear to the ground. There would still be a delay before the sound reached Superman, but a shorter one since the earth is a better sound transmitter than the air. Underwater in the ocean, Superman could probably hear trouble all the way on the other side of the globe.

Another difficulty with superhearing is the slight possibility that, temporarily at least, it might be overwhelmed and "overloaded" by a sudden, intense barrage of sound. Just as a human can be startled, disoriented or even frightened by an unexpected loud noise, a cunning adversary might be able to do the same to Superman. It would probably take more than a single sound to overwhelm Superman's auditory system and stun him, though—a carefully chosen burst of noise at various frequencies and amplitude might be necessary. Even then, the effect on Superman would be momentary at best, because his nervous system would recover almost instantly. And the unfortunate evildoer who unleashed the aural attack would find himself facing an extremely alert—and extremely angry—Superman.

Superhearing is one of Superman's more subtle abilities. In the course of his usual duties, it's a power he may not even need to use on an everyday basis, and one that many people, both friends and enemies, no doubt often forget he possesses. But when it *is* needed to save a life or to run down a criminal, it's an invaluable asset and complement to the rest of his super powers—including his supervision, which we'll explore next.

CHAPTER EIGHT

SUPERVISION: ALL-SEEING EYES

Of the five physical senses, vision is the one that always seems to get the most press. Literature, songs, and our everyday language are replete with references and metaphors that directly or indirectly involve seeing and eyes. The eyes are the windows of the soul and the traitors of the heart. They're dark liquid pools of emotion, the source of tears of both despair and joy. We insist that someone look us in the eye, confident that they can't do so without telling us the absolute truth; if another person can't meet our gaze, we think of them as evasive. Every hurricane has an eye, you can see for yourself with your own two eyes, and the night has a thousand eyes. We say that we understand something not with the words "I touch" or "I smell," but "I see." Those who don't understand don't see; we may even consider them to be "blind," because we don't see eye to eye with them. At least until they come around to our point of view, because then they've seen the light. Two sets of eyes meet across a crowded room and love blossoms at first sight. We dress to look good—to appeal to the sight of others. Criminals are convicted by eyewitnesses, rarely if ever by earwitnesses. We store memories and chronicle our lives in photos and videotape, sights frozen in time that allow us to relive the past by seeing it again. Those in the public eye strive to escape the unblinking eyes of the cameras that follow them, hoping to see through their image and catch an eyeful. Meanwhile, we flirt by making eyes at each other, monitor suspicious types by keeping an eye on them, and watch how things develop.

You get the idea. It's apparent even in a quick look at our culture that seeing is of supreme importance to human beings. It's definitely the sense on which we most rely, at least consciously. And because of this, humans have a tendency to define sight in strictly human terms: we speak of the visible light portion of the electromagnetic spectrum as if it's the same for all sighted creatures. Animals whose eyes work differently somehow aren't really "seeing."

Naturally, this is human chauvinism, pure and simple. Eyes and vision work in marvelous ways, but those ways can be quite different depending on whether we're considering the sight of humans, animals, or Superman. Before discussing the differences, let's examine the similarities, starting with the characteristic all eyes share: sensing some form of light.

LET THERE BE LIGHT (ONE KIND OR ANOTHER)

Earlier, we looked at the spectrum of electromagnetic radiation and a certain range of frequencies that are called light. Why is one relatively small slice of the EM spectrum called "light," while others are named microwaves or X-rays? What's special about it?

Frankly, nothing—except that, for whatever reason, it's the part of the EM spectrum that our eyes happened to evolve the ability to detect. There's nothing magical about it. If by evolutionary chance, we developed eyes that detected different wavelengths of EM radiation, we would refer to another slice of the spectrum—the infrared or ultraviolet, perhaps—as "visible" light. Given our size and the scale of our world, however, it's logical—and fortunate—that we evolved to see light as we do. Visible light has a wavelength range of about 400 nanometers (billionths of a meter) at the high-frequency/short-wavelength violet end of the spectrum to about 770 nanometers at the low-frequency/long-wavelength red end. Anything larger than this, then, is going to reflect or scatter light, while light waves will pass around anything much smaller than 400 nm. With molecules around 400 nm in size, though, more of the shorter, blue/violet light waves are going to hit the molecules and be scattered by them, while the longer reddish waves simply miss them altogether. This is why the sky is blue: air molecules scatter the shorter, bluer wavelengths of light much more than the longer, reddish wavelengths. Near sunset or sunrise, when the lower angle of the sun means that its light passes through more air than when it's directly overhead, the shorter light wavelengths tend to be absorbed by air (not to mention haze and pollution), and the longer wavelengths pass through more easily, making the sun look red.

Suppose, however, that we could only see in radio frequencies. Radio waves range in wavelength from several yards to miles in length. Think of how difficult it would be to walk down the street, dress yourself, or brush your teeth if you couldn't see anything smaller than, say, thirty yards wide! In fact, you and everyone else would be invisible, because we're transparent to radio waves. For immense creatures with a lot of room around them—those that lived not on the surface of a planet but in open space, perhaps—such vision might make sense, because such beings would rarely if ever have to see anything small. Animals living on a planet, though, where many important objects are inches or up to several feet in size, wouldn't last long with "radiowave" vision.

The range of wavelengths that any particular species perceives as visible light generally depends on the environment that spawned it and the characteristics it evolved in order to live in that world. Most animals on Earth that see in any important way do so more or less in the visible light range. Some creatures have a visual range that's somewhat different; some insects, for example, can see ultraviolet light. For beings that evolved on a different planet, under a star with a different spectrum of light, the visual range is also bound to be different from ours.

To our Earthly eyes, Krypton's sun, Rao, would appear obviously red. Rao emits most of its visible light to human eyes in the red. What would it look like to a Kryptonian, whose eyes had evolved under its glare?

Our sun is indeed yellow, but to us its unfiltered, normal light is "natural" white light—an equally balanced blend of all the visible wavelengths it emits. Rao would likely appear similar to Superman, with eyes and a visual system evolved to handle its light. To Superman, with our sun's shorter visible light wavelengths compared to Rao, our "white" light may appear bluer, because for him it's shifted more toward that end of the visible spectrum. This is not to say that Superman would see everything on Earth as if he were wearing blue sunglasses. The effect might only be mild, similar to the perceptible difference between incandescent (redder) and fluorescent (bluer) artificial light to our own eyes. Also, just as Superman's naturally sharper hearing adapted from his birth into our "noisier" environment, his vision would also adapt. After all, Superman first opened his eyes to Earthly sunlight, and over the years his visual cortex would learn to "normalize" the initially alien light spectrum.

This adjustment of Superman's visual system to our solar spectrum could actually be more than a simple compensatory effect and could give him some abilities that are quite remarkable, as we'll see shortly. First, it's time for another brief anatomy lesson. Let's take a look (to use another visual metaphor) at how eyes see.

THE EYES HAVE IT

Humans may make a big deal out of their eyes and the importance of vision, but it's justified. Of all the animals on our planet possessing organs that can be defined as "eyes," our particular equipment is nothing short of amazing. The human eye, coupled with the visual cortex of the brain, is a sophisticated and extremely sensitive instrument, so much so that its complexity used to be considered as an incontrovertible proof against Darwin and his pesky theory of evolution (and still is, in some stubborn quarters). How could such an organ, so exquisitely designed and constructed, have arisen by mere random chance? Some antievolutionists extended this argument to insist that because the eye was so perfectly designed for its function, it was simply too incredible to believe that it developed step by step from a simpler plan, because the eye can't work in anything other than its current form. If the eye evolved, then there must have been intermediate steps before it reached its current pinnacle of perfection—but what use is half an eye?

Yet the human eye, and all others, did evolve, and the many types of visual equipment we see in other creatures provide an answer to that question. The notion that the eye of a human being (or cat, dog, or any other animal) is useful only in its present form is a flawed all-or-nothing analogy, and is another example of that unfortunate human chauvinism noted earlier. True, a more rudimentary eye can't see as much or as well as one that's more complex—but it's far from useless. For survival purposes, "half an eye" is far better than none at all.

Eyes come in different varieties, and not all feature a lens and an eyeball. Many invertebrate animals, especially those that dwell in the ocean such as jellyfish, have *photoreceptors*, nerve cells that react to light. These photoreceptors are incapable of forming an image, but they can tell the difference between light and dark, an ability of great usefulness to an animal that feeds on other creatures that are found in well-lit areas such as the surface of the sea. Such organs also allow the perception of movement, which not only helps to find food but also to avoid predators.

We're all familiar with the multifaceted eyes of insects, crustaceans, and other multilegged critters. These are compound eyes, and just like it sounds, are composed of many individual units (up to thousands in large creatures), each with its own lens and light receptors. These create a mosaic image that, while not as detailed as those produced by vertebrate eyes, is more than adequate. In fact, compound eyes tend to be more sensitive to movement than vertebrate eyes (one reason it's so hard to catch a fly) and to have greater light-gathering capacity—sometimes beyond our visual range.

Whether equipped with photoreceptors or compound eyes, animals with such organs would be helpless without them. Both the compound eye and the more complex and sophisticated vertebrate eye owe their origins to the humble, primitive photoreceptors that arose in the early ancestors of life on this planet. Although they followed different evolutionary paths to their present forms, both the compound eye and the vertebrate eye are indispensable and vital to their owners. Neither arose overnight, of course. But each type of eye increased its capacities as it developed through intermediate stages, becoming more refined over a vast span of time, and both are fine examples of the power of evolutionary specialization at work.

To keep things simple, we'll use the human eye as our example of vertebrate version. Some differences exist among the eyes of birds, reptiles, and other mammals, but the same basic arrangement is common to all—simple in principle and practice, exceedingly complex in detail.

Hitching a ride on a ray of light into the eye, we would first enter the *cornea*, the curved forward surface of the eyeball. Why is the eye round? First, in most animals, the eye is moveable, attached to muscles along its surface that contract or relax to point it in various directions. A flat eye inside a bony skull couldn't move; an animal would have to turn its entire head to look in a different direction. A round eye fits neatly into a spherical bony chamber inside of which it can be turned in any direction. Also, if the eye were flat like a window, light entering it from different angles couldn't be focused properly at various points on the back of the eye. Even with a curved lens to bend or refract it, light would travel slightly different distances through the eye, making a sharp image impossible.

After the cornea, light passes through the *pupil*, the opening in the *iris*, a circular, colored curtain of muscular fibers that opens and closes the pupil to control the amount of light entering the eye. Behind the pupil is the *lens*, a curved piece of tissue that focuses the light just like the lens of a camera or telescope. Suspended in liquid material, the *aqueous humor* in front and the thicker *vitreous humor* behind, the lens is held in place by muscles and ligaments that can change the shape of the lens and therefore adjust its focus. Refracted and focused by the

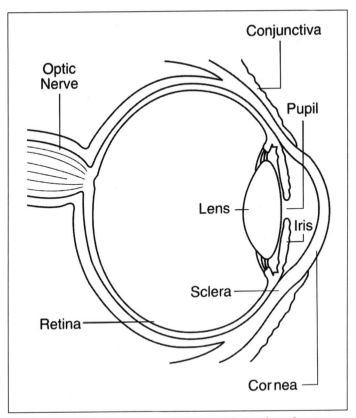

A schematic of the human eye. Light-receiving rods and cones line the retina.

lens, light passes through the vitreous humor to a point on the *retina*, the multi-layered membrane that lines the inside surface of the back of the eyeball.

Up to this point, the process has been all optical: the transmission and bending of light, angles of refraction, basic geometry. As soon as light strikes the retina, however, matters become much more complicated. The retina consists of millions of light receptor cells of two types, *rods* and *cones*, named for their shape. While the roughly 100 million rods are extremely sensitive to light and motion—a single rod can detect a single photon of light—they're unable to distinguish color. That's the job of the 5 million cones of the eye, each one of which responds only to red, blue, or green light. Through extraordinarily complicated reactions that are still not fully understood, the activation of the rods and cones of the retina by light releases neurochemicals that create nerve impulses carried by the optic nerve to the brain. The information is processed by different areas of the visual cortex to interpret motion, color, shape, and the other characteristics of the subject of the eyes' gaze. Because the cones need bright light in order to be activated, and we have far more rods than cones, we can't see color very well, if at all, in dim light. Colored lights are readily visible at night, because they're generating strong light. Other colored objects, their image reflected to your eyes by weaker light, are hard to distinguish or invisible. Try looking at a vividly colored picture under moonlight, or guessing the colors in a friend's shirt under starlight. In low light levels, you're seeing in black and white, not color. At night, it's more important to detect movement and distinguish light from dark than to see colors—at least, from an evolutionary perspective.

Not all of the retina is covered by rods and cones. The spot where the retina connects to the optic nerve has no rods and cells, and appropriately enough, is called the blind spot. You're usually not aware of it, but many optical illusions rely on its presence. Another area on the retina, called the *fovea*, is a tiny depression with an especially dense concentration of rods and cones. Sometimes you can see an especially dim point of light, such as a faint star, by not looking directly at it but by slightly averting your gaze. You can thank the rod cells in your fovea for the pleasure. (Not out loud, preferably, lest your fellow stargazers give you odd looks.)

Supervision: All-Seeing Eyes

Some animals have more rod and cone cells, faster focusing or better light-gathering capacities than humans. By and large, however, humans have nothing to complain about when it comes to vision. With our large brains and nervous systems to assimilate and interpret visual information, along with our technology to expand and deepen the range of our sight, we can see more and see better than any other animal on Earth. Even without our glasses, binoculars, telescopes, microscopes, X-ray tubes, ultrasound scanners, and magnetic resonance imagers, we can see much that's invisible to other creatures.

There's also little that's invisible to Superman. The difference is that while humans require clever instruments to make the invisible visible by translating it into something we can see, Superman needs only his own eyes. Unlike humans, who can see, for example, an infrared image only by its representation on a screen in visible light, Superman can see in a wide range of wavelengths at will and in real-time. How does he do it?

TO SEE BEYOND

In the same way Superman's hearing would operate essentially in the same way as that of humans but to a greatly enhanced degree, his vision uses the same principles as ours or any other sighted creature. He has eyes that collect and focus light and convert it into nerve impulses. Structurally, his eyes would enjoy the same advantages as his other senses: invulnerability, sensitivity, faster neurological response. It's likely that his iris would be capable of opening to a wider diameter than that of humans, with the increased light-gathering power this would provide. Just as his ears contain more hair cells for sound detection, his retinas would feature more rod and cone cells, and they would respond to a wider range of light wavelengths and intensities than terrestrial eyes. As a result, Superman's eyeballs themselves might be somewhat larger than those of humans to accommodate more light-sensitive cells. Despite all this, Superman's eyes would look pretty much like those of anyone else, at least to a casual inspection.

With supervision, as with other superpowers, the real difference is in the details. We mentioned above that because they evolved under the solar spectrum of a red sun, Kryptonian eyes would see a normal range of "visible light" that would be somewhat different than ours. But even with his Kryptonian eyes, Superman is a being who grew up never having seen the red sun of home, maturing under Earth's yellow star. The adaptation of his natural Kryptonian visual system, meaning not only his eyes but also the brain areas that control them and handle their input, is the key to his power of supervision. The infant Superman on Earth may not have been a very happy baby at times, assaulted both aurally and visually by sensory stimuli he hadn't evolved to handle. With time, and fortified by the extra energy he was able to absorb from our sunlight, his brain and senses found an accommodation. As Superman's body matured, he was able to exert more control and conscious will over the adaptations that began as nothing more than an instinctive response to a strange world.

Humans and other animals basically see whatever light comes at them, as long as it falls within the visual range of the eyes. We can't choose to see only red or blue light, for example; if we want to alter our perceptions, we have to do so mechanically through special lenses or other equipment. In other words, we don't have the biological ability to "tune" our vision. To see the world with a rosy tint, we have to don rose-colored glasses that filter out all other wavelengths.

On the other hand, Superman's visual system, in adapting

Having heard someone in distress, Superman uses his supervision to locate her.

itself to sunlight with a different set of wavelengths, has developed a tuning ability. You may recall that before the age of digital tuners, radios were equipped with dials. Sometimes the dial looked like a ruler on which was marked a range of radio frequencies, with a needle that moved back and forth as you turned a knob to select a station. Other smaller radios had the frequencies marked right on the tuning knob itself. Whatever the arrangement, the principle was the same: as you adjusted the tuning knob, the radio tuner picked up different frequencies. You spun the dial up and down the range until you found your favorite station. (Modern digital tuners actually do exactly the same thing, but without the more graphic representation of the old tuners.)

This is precisely how Superman's vision works. Normally, he sees much as we do, thanks to the acclimatization of his visual system to Earth's solar spectrum. As mentioned, his Kryptonian eyes may see our sunlight as slightly "bluer" than we do, but he would hardly notice this after so many years on Earth. More than this, however, Superman can consciously "slide" the range of his vision up and down the electromagnetic spectrum. To see at night, for example, he tunes his sight toward the infrared. To find the source of a specific frequency of EM radiation—perhaps a crook's cell phone—he would "slide the needle" on his visual tuning dial until he hit the right frequency, and then could actually *see* the transmission.

Much like a musician's ability to distinguish tones and tuning, this power would improve dramatically with practice. When Superman was very young, he may have stumbled upon it quite unexpectedly—suddenly he was seeing the world in a completely different way! But he quickly recovered from this startling experience and learned to control the workings of his vision. As he became more aware of its range and limits, his conscious control would have become more precise, until he could tune his sight to narrower frequency bands. Superman's fast and efficient neurological functioning would expedite this process. He would also learn to ignore extraneous visual "noise"—a brief strong burst of a radio signal from a passing police car, for instance, or a bright source of EM radiation in his surroundings. The brain does this as a matter of course. Consider that the tip of your nose is always present in the visual field of each eye, but you're not generally aware of it unless you consciously look for it. (See, there it is!) Your brain still sees it, but disregards it in favor of more interesting and important things.

This visual tuning ability also clears up a common misunderstanding regarding Superman's vision, particularly his X-ray vision. Contrary to popular belief, Superman doesn't generate and project X-rays from his eyes. Rather, his eyes gather and focus the X-rays already present in his environment. (As we'll see shortly, this is only a partial explanation of how Superman can see through some solid objects, and in fact, the term "X-ray vision" is a rather inaccurate description.) Superman must also deal with the natural characteristics of whatever EM radiation he sees, and these impose certain limitations on supervision. X-rays and some other forms of high-energy radiation can't penetrate lead, for example, so at those frequencies, lead is opaque to his vision. EM waves can be refracted and reflected, become distorted and interfered with, and be opaque to other materials, and Superman would have to take such effects into account. He would be subject to "optical illusions" that humans could never experience, and he'd have to be aware of these.

Naturally, the speed of light is another limitation, especially in space. Superman can see the universe in many ways, but electromagnetic energy can't reach him faster than light speed. The range of Superman's visual "tuning dial" must also have limits, which would change somewhat depending on conditions. For example, his ability to see extremely short wavelength radiation such as ultraviolet would be much greater in space than in an atmosphere, since air tends to absorb such radiation. We can guess that Superman's absolute upper visual limit would fall somewhere within the X-ray region, while his lower limit would be in the radio frequencies. Radiation outside of these boundaries would be either much too weak and long in wavelength or energetic and high in wavelength to be detected by an organ constructed like an eye.

The visual tuning ability would be largely a neurological phenomenon. Individual rod and cone cells in Superman's retinas would be activated only by specific frequencies of radiation, and the signals from the appropriate cells would be passed on to the higher brain areas for processing only when they corresponded with the light range in which Superman had chosen to focus. The visual areas of Superman's brain would be highly sophisticated, permitting the firing of certain sets of neurons that responded to the light Superman wanted to see and suppressing the activity of other nerve cells to avoid their unneeded response.

Some anatomical qualities of Superman's eyes would not only supplement his visual tuning but also grant him other enhancements of sight. The muscles and ligaments that control the focusing of the lens of his eye are tough, strong, and capable of extremely fine movements. By changing the shape of the lens in various ways, they could adjust both focus and magnification. In tandem with other muscles and ligaments that could alter the spherical shape of the eyeball, this could give Superman a degree of telescopic and microscopic vision. Used in conjunction with his visual tuning, these would be powerful assets. For telescopic vision, Superman could optically magnify and tune to whatever wavelengths were strongest at the distance he was viewing; for microscopic seeing, he could concentrate on the radiation best emitted or reflected in the tiny field of view.

Supervision: All-Seeing Eyes

From our discussion thus far, you may have the impression that Superman's vision, like ours, is essentially passive in nature. It may be far more sensitive to a much wider range of light, and tunable at will, perhaps, but like hearing, it can only work with whatever goes into it. Vision, like the other senses, receives information about the world; it doesn't act upon it directly. In Superman's case, however, there is a notable exception: his heat vision, which involves more than simple passive reception. He also has the ability to see through objects that are opaque to the rest of us: his "X-ray" vision. How do these powers manifest themselves through Superman's eyes?

HOT LOOKS AND SEE-THROUGH CLOTHING

The common misperception is that Superman's X-ray vision consists of the ability to project X-rays from his eyes. What's wrong with this idea? Why couldn't Superman generate X-rays? To find out, let's take a closer look at what X-rays are and how they allow us to see through solid objects.

In 1895, the German scientist Wilhelm Roentgen was experimenting with cathode ray tubes—vacuum tubes that shoot electrons as cathode rays from one end to a chemically-coated inner surface or screen at the other end, causing the screen to glow. When you watch television, you're staring at a cathode ray tube; the picture is created by electrons hitting the inside of the screen and causing the release of photons. Roentgen noticed that when he turned on his cathode ray tube, in another part of the lab a piece of paper coated with a fluorescent material was glowing in the dark, even though it was far away and shielded from the cathode rays that would normally make it glow. He realized that a different sort of radiation was emanating from the tube and making the paper glow, and with further experiments discovered that this radiation possessed such energy that it could penetrate a sealed box. He named this new type of radiation the X-ray—X for unknown.

Roentgen and other scientists experimented further with X-rays, and it wasn't long before their power to penetrate the human body was discovered. For the first time, doctors could see inside the body, and a priceless new diagnostic tool was born. Physicians busied themselves with developing the medical applications of X-rays, while physicists continued to investigate the nature of this strange energy. They found that X-rays are created when speeding electrons are abruptly slowed down, such as when they strike matter. Soon the X-ray tube was invented, in which beams of electrons are directed onto a material such as tungsten to generate X-rays at various wavelengths.

In order to artificially create X-rays, then, we have to first generate a stream of fast electrons, and then make them strike something else. Sounds simple, but these requirements cause a fair number of problems if we're trying to find a way to do it organically in a biological creature. First, we need huge amounts of electrical power—easy to find in the lab or hospital, but not so easy in the body, even that of Superman. We've seen that he has a bioelectric field and that he can generate and manipulate electromagnetic energy to a degree, but not at the voltages required to create X-rays.

A natural X-ray tube would also have to contain a perfect or near-perfect vacuum, so that the electron beam could travel unencumbered. Vacuums are already difficult to create and maintain artificially; it's hard to imagine how one could be created and maintained inside a body that required oxygen and atmospheric pressure in order to live.

X-rays are an extremely powerful form of electromagnetic energy, which is what gives them their penetrative power—and

what makes them dangerous. In large quantities and high intensities, X-rays slice through living cells and destroy them. Even in small doses, damage can build up over time. (This explains the lead aprons at the dentist's office.) Superman's cells, though near-invulnerable, would find it impossible to withstand such concentrated X-ray radiation generated so close by.

Finally, because concentrated X-rays are so harmful to living tissue, it's hard to imagine how such a highly specialized organ dedicated to the generation of X-rays would evolve naturally. It's possible that it might arise as a random mutation, but highly unlikely that it would be passed on to future generations—its unfortunate bearer would simply irradiate itself to death.

All right, then. If the idea of Superman generating his own X-rays is impractical and unworkable, what about the possibility mentioned earlier—simply seeing X-rays that are already there? Is that enough to see through walls? Possibly, but probably not enough. Because of their extremely short wavelength, stray X-rays tend to be scattered and absorbed by the atmosphere. Fortunately for us, there just isn't much random X-ray radiation bouncing around us most of the time, which means that there wouldn't be a lot around for Superman to see. When he tuned his vision to the X-ray range, the everyday world would appear pretty dark, unless he happened to be visiting the radiology department of a large hospital and standing next to an operating X-ray machine. Superman might enhance his X-ray sight by using his bioelectric field to project an intense stream of electrons in a particular direction, but this would probably work only at relatively short distances, again because of air scattering.

What about other "see-through" possibilities? As that radiology department could demonstrate, plain old X-rays are not the only way to see inside of things. CT (computed tomography), also known as CAT (computed axial tomography), uses a narrow beam of radiation to visualize "slices" of the body in different planes that are then put together by computer to form images, but it's still based on X-rays. Another powerful and useful imaging technique to see inside the body is ultrasound scanning, which takes advantage of the reflection or absorption of ultrasonic sound by different soft tissue densities to create real-time images. Ultrasonic waves can also image blood flow by using the Doppler effect to measure motion. Still, Superman *hears* ultrasonic sound—he doesn't see it.

A highly sophisticated medical imaging technology is MRI (magnetic resonance imaging), based on an interesting natural phenomenon called nuclear magnetic resonance. In basic terms, an MRI scanner creates an intense magnetic field (using superconductor technology), causing the atomic nuclei of the matter inside it (such as a patient's body) to line up in the same direction. Radio pulses of certain frequencies are then applied to the field, causing the nuclei to briefly reorient themselves to the radio pulse, and then readjust themselves to the magnetic field. The changes in orientation of the nuclei (their resonance) cause them to generate radio energy at frequencies that vary according to the types of nuclei. Each type of atom—each element—resonates at a specific radio frequency. All the various frequencies detected are processed by a computer to produce incredibly detailed images.

Could nuclear magnetic resonance provide a mechanism for Superman's "X-ray vision"? Unfortunately, not really. As its name implies, MRI requires a high intensity magnetic field—very high. Although it's true that Superman possesses a bioelectrical field, and a superconducting nervous system related to the superconducting technology used by MRI scanners, the magnetic field needed for MRI is so intense that it affects anything inside of it or around it that's magnetic. Those who work around a hospital MRI scanner have to be extremely careful to keep all magnetic objects away from it when it's in operation; the scanner is strong enough to yank metal across the room at great speed, and woe to anyone who happens to be in its path. Even if Superman were able to generate such a field, he would wreak magnetic havoc all around him: hurling metal objects about, crashing computers and wiping out their memories, interfering with electrical equipment, and generally making a nuisance of himself.

If X-rays aren't abundant enough around us to account for "X-ray vision," and Superman can't see through things in the same way we do with technology, how does he do it? The key to the power lies in the enormous range of wavelengths he *can* see, and how his brain's visual cortex has learned to process that torrent of data. We've seen how Superman can "tune" his vision at will to focus on particular wavelengths across his visual range. Across that range, some wavelengths, such as X-rays, pass through most solid objects—these objects are transparent to EM radiation at those frequencies. Other wavelengths, such as those in the visible light range of humans, can't penetrate most solid matter—objects are opaque to such radiation. Still, at any given moment, an entire spectrum of EM radiation, from radio and microwaves to gamma rays, is bouncing about—more at some wavelengths than others, of course, but all visible to Superman. As he tunes his vision, his brain concentrates on one type of light while filtering out the perception of other types.

Seeing through solid objects, then, is a matter of selectively receiving those wavelengths that are passing through whatever objects Superman is gazing upon. These wavelengths might vary sometimes depending on atmospheric conditions and other factors; if his vision was blocked by haze or smoke at one set of frequencies, for example, thus preventing him from seeing into a building, he can shift to another visual range at which the building was also transparent but unaffected by the haze. Superman can also see at widely separated wavelengths as necessary: one range in the microwave and another in the X-ray region, for example, "skipping over" the frequencies in between. Separate areas of his retina tune to the different wavelengths simultaneously, automatically adjusting to whatever radiation was least affected by the intervening walls or other objects. Superman's visual cortex, already accustomed to dealing with and interpreting a much wider range of information than that of a human (or

Superman using his heat vision.

even a normal Kryptonian on his home planet), analyzes and integrates the palette of visual data collected by his eyes and builds up a complete picture that he sees. This is similar to the manner in which a computer collects and processes the various bits and pieces of images collected from a multitude of angles and planes by an MRI or CT scanner, and reconstructs them to create a single dimensional image.

Essentially, then, Superman's "X-ray" vision is a product less of his eyes than of his brain, a sophisticated refinement of his visual tuning abilities. This sort of "penetrative vision" is actually superior to true X-ray vision. Superman can not only see through walls and solid objects, but he can tell a great deal more about what's behind and inside them than he could with only X-rays. With Superman's ability to see in other wavelengths, some of which penetrate walls, it's not easy to hide from him.

One form of radiation invisible to our eyes but capable of penetrating many solid objects is infrared, which brings us to Superman's heat vision. Infrared radiation is longer in wavelength and lower in frequency than visible light, hence the term infrared—below red. It's sometimes considered to be equivalent to heat, although this is technically inaccurate. Heat is simply the mechanical motion or oscillation of molecules, while infrared radiation is a form of electromagnetic energy. Heat produces infrared radiation and infrared radiation can be said to transmit heat (it's converted to heat when it encounters matter), however, so for practical and informal purposes we can consider them interchangeable.

We know that Superman can see in the infrared, and even lower into the radio bands. And there's a lot to see in infrared, especially with the sensitivity of Superman's vision. It's common knowledge that infrared radiation is present even at night, and sniper scopes and infrared film take advantage of this fact. What's not so well known is that anything that generates heat can leave its infrared signature behind long after it's gone. Your car shines brightly in infrared while it's running because the engine creates heat—but even after you've parked the car, turned it off, and gone to bed, the engine continues to glow in the infrared. As it cools, the infrared image becomes dimmer and dimmer, but if we keep looking at it in different infrared wavelengths (longer and longer, corresponding to cooler temperature), as Superman can do by tuning his vision, the warm engine can be seen for some time.

What about heat vision? How can Superman create "heat beams" with his eyes? The most likely mechanism involves the concentration and focusing of infrared radiation that's already entering Superman's eyes. The same retinal cells that allow him to see infrared light may also be able to draw on Superman's great energy stores to intensify and reflect infrared rays on command from the brain, focusing them on the lens of the eye, which would then project them outward in a directed beam. The phenomenon would be similar to the manner in which the eyes of a cat seem to "glow" or shine back at you if light from a flashlight strikes them at the proper angle. With heat vision, the difference is that the infrared light is not only being reflected but also greatly intensified. To enhance the effect, Superman could use his bioelectric field to focus the infrared beam further. His control of heat vision would be as precise and definite as his visual tuning ability, since it would be generated by the same basic eye-brain interface. He could vary its strength from barely warm to super-hot, from hundreds to possibly thousands of degrees for a short burst.

Heat vision wouldn't be perfect or usable in all situations. First, the term "heat vision" is quite accurate: while using it, Superman could only see in the infrared. Fortunately, since infrared radiation pervades our environment, this isn't too much of a problem. Superman might run into trouble under certain atmospheric conditions, however. Fog or smoke might dissipate the intensity of his heat vision, and at worst almost block it entirely. These are minor difficulties, though, and hardly alter the importance of heat vision as another powerful tool in Superman's arsenal of powers.

We've examined the major elements of that arsenal in great detail, acknowledging that some of Superman's powers may have some small limitations placed on them, sometimes because of physical laws such as the speed of light, other times because their use may cause harmful side effects. However, we've also seen that Superman can often sidestep or accommodate the limitations of one power by supplementing it with another, or by using it in a particular way. Practice makes perfect with super powers just as with everything else, and as Superman has learned through years of experience how best to use his powers and how to compensate for their limits, he's become steadily more powerful. Anyone can pick up a sword, but the person who learns how to handle it well and use it to best advantage is much more formidable than an amateur, even though they're both holding the same weapon—the same "power."

Take that sword away from the master, however, and suddenly his power is gone and he's at the mercy of the novice swordsman. For the master, it might be a lucky blow by the novice or a rare mistake that costs him his weapon. For Superman, only one thing can "disarm" him in the same way: the radioactive ashes of his own world, the element of kryptonite.

CHAPTER NINE

KRYPTONITE: THE ACHILLES' HEEL

Perhaps the greatest irony of Superman's existence, especially considering his status as Krypton's only son and sole survivor, is that the greatest threat to that existence comes from the shattered remains of his own planet. Those remnants, transformed atomically into radioactive kryptonite, are rare on Earth. This is fortunate for both Superman and for human beings, because while kryptonite affects Superman in a different way than humans, it's also a definite threat to our form of life, simply due to its highly radioactive nature.

Radiation has been explored at great length in previous chapters, but mostly of the electromagnetic variety. EM radiation can certainly be hazardous or even deadly at some wavelengths and intensities, and these dangers are not to be ignored. The radiation emitted by naturally radioactive elements is different from the electromagnetic variety in important ways, however, both in how it's created and in its effects on living creatures. These differences were mentioned briefly in Chapter 2, but to fully understand the dangers of kryptonite and other radioactive elements, we'll now look at them in more detail.

Kryptonite: The Achilles' Heel

A LACK OF STABILITY

Natural radioactivity was discovered by French scientist Henri Becquerel in 1896, just about a year after Roentgen found X-rays. In fact, Becquerel was also studying the phenomenon of fluorescence and whether X-rays might be somehow related. One of the fluorescent compounds he used in his experiments contained uranium, and Becquerel found that not only did this substance fluoresce when exposed to light, but it could fog a photographic plate long after it had stopped fluorescing. Instead of simply absorbing energy and then re-radiating it as light, the uranium compound was somehow generating radiation on its own. Shortly, Becquerel and other scientists, including Pierre and Marie Curie, found that all forms of uranium and closely related elements create this radiation, which is highly penetrating and powerful. It was named radioactivity.

Soon scientists noticed that this radiation didn't behave uniformly, but split into different types defined by how much they were deflected in a magnetic field. A physicist from New Zealand working in England, Ernest Rutherford, named them for the first three letters of the Greek alphabet: *alpha*, *beta*, and *gamma*. Experiments demonstrated that each type of radiation has unique characteristics: alpha radiation is positively charged; beta radiation is negative; and gamma radiation carries no electrical charge, but is the most powerful in its penetrative ability and travels at the speed of light, while alpha and beta are somewhat slower.

Radioactivity apparently had something to do with the disintegration of atoms, but early experimenters were in the dark about the exact process, particularly since the inner structure of the atom was still a mystery. Rutherford cleared up the mystery in 1911 with experiments that showed the presence of a nucleus in the atom and gave us the familiar "solar system" atomic model of negative electrons orbiting a nucleus made of positive protons. Rutherford's picture has since been refined, and we now know that atoms don't actually look like solar systems or the common "atom symbol" seen in old science fiction films, but it's still a handy way to think of things. And in general, Rutherford had it right: a nucleus surrounded by electrons.

The discovery of the nucleus, along with the later revelation of the neutron by James Chadwick, provided the missing pieces to the radioactivity problem. Alpha, beta, and gamma rays are created by activity in the nucleus, and for this reason are called *nuclear radiation* to distinguish them from the electromagnetic varieties. Alpha rays are the slowest (relatively speaking—they move at a good fraction of light speed) and heaviest particles, made of two protons and two neutrons (equivalent to a helium nucleus), while beta rays are electrons, much lighter and faster than alpha particles and with a negative charge. Both are literally pieces of atoms, the leftovers when nuclei break apart or otherwise change. Gamma rays are the most powerful form of electromagnetic radiation, even more so than X-rays, of extremely short wavelength and super-high frequency. Not much can stop gamma radiation except thick, heavy lead or concrete shielding, making it the most dangerous of the three.

To find out why some atoms spontaneously emit nuclear radiation, we have to take a closer look at the atom, specifically what makes one different from another. It's the number of protons in the nucleus, also known as the *atomic number*, that determines the characteristics of that atom. In other words, the only real difference between the helium in a balloon and the silicon in a rock is the number of protons in each of their respective individual atoms. When, like most atoms, an atom has the same number of electrons as protons, it's electrically neutral; if electrons are stripped away from or added to the atom, it becomes positively or negatively charged. Elements are also characterized by their *mass number*, which is the total number of both protons and neutrons in its nucleus. Atoms with the same number of protons but different numbers of neutrons are *isotopes* of the element; they're chemically the same but may differ in some physical qualities. Both uranium-235 and uranium-238 have an atomic number of 92, for instance—92 protons in the nucleus—but U-238 has three more neutrons.

Why is this important? Unlike their much lighter elemental cousins ("lighter" meaning fewer protons), many heavy elements have unstable nuclei. To become more stable, a nucleus can break apart, sending out alpha particles and thus losing protons and neutrons in a process called *alpha decay*; or a neutron in the nucleus can convert into a proton, also shooting out an electron (beta particle) in *beta decay*. These processes can also create gamma radiation. As the number of protons and/or neutrons in the unstable nucleus changes, the atom becomes another isotope of the same element, or sometimes even transforms into a different element altogether. This process of radioactive decay is defined as an element's *half-life*, which refers to the amount of time half of the atoms in a given sample change to another isotope or element. It varies with different elements; some atoms decay in fractions of a second, others can take thousands or millions of years. The reason that the *half* rather than "whole" life of an element's decay is measured is that the process never really ends; there will theoretically always be a few atoms left to decay, and waiting for every single one to do so would simply take too long!

Elements, then, can change into other elements. Change the atomic number of lead in the right way and you have gold. At least, academically speaking. As we've seen, although all the elements that make up Earth, all its life, and everything else in the universe were created from simpler elements, the processes that work such magic consist of more than just mixing together and boiling a few chemicals. In 1934, Irene Joliot-Curie (Marie Curie's daughter) and her husband Frederic Joliot-Curie found another way: artificial radioactivity. By bombarding certain atoms with alpha particles, they were able to create radioactive elements. The same techniques devised by the Joliet-Curies are used today to create radioactive isotopes for medical applications and scientific research.

SOMETHING IN THE AIR

Despite the scientific wizardry that allows us to create artificial radioactivity, natural radioactivity occurs all around us. The Earth's crust contains uranium and other radioactive elements, constantly decaying to produce a small amount of background radiation. Another source of environmental radiation is outer space. Aside from that produced by our own sun, high-energy cosmic rays of various kinds continually fall on Earth. The atmosphere shields us from most direct cosmic radiation, but particles can strike and interact with atoms in the upper atmosphere, generating showers of secondary particles that reach the ground. There's little point in worrying much about natural background radiation, though. For one thing, we can't escape it; it's part of the world in which we live. Also, the levels of such radiation are generally far too low to harm us. We evolved in this environment, after all, and we've developed a natural resistance to such threats. Some biologists even believe that Earth's natural background radiation has been essential for creating the occasional genetic mutations that spur evolutionary change. It may be true that a certain number of cancers and other diseases are caused each year by the cumulative effects of background radiation on a few unlucky individuals, but aside from living in a lead-lined bunker, there's little to be done about it. In fact, a person living surrounded by lead wouldn't necessarily be safe, because more than likely there would be an occasional stray particle of radiation from the lead itself. He would also have to observe a strict no-smoking policy: smoke from a burning cigarette usually contains a certain number of radioactive isotopes, mostly alpha emitters such as radon, polonium, and bismuth. Aside from providing another source for background radiation (although this type generally affects only the smoker and whoever else inhales the secondary smoke), this interesting fact can serve as yet another good reason for the reluctant to kick the habit.

Another variety of background radiation on Earth exists, but unlike the others, it's not exactly "natural." Humans created it themselves by detonating hundreds of nuclear weapons in Earth's atmosphere. The relatively small fission weapons that began the atomic age, such as those dropped on Hiroshima and Nagasaki, had only local atmospheric effects, and their fallout affected a small area of the planet. As the United States and the Soviet Union began enthusiastic testing of atomic weapons in the 1950s, they downplayed the hazards of fallout, although the ranchers and farmers of downwind communities noticed definite ominous effects on their livestock and crops. Eventually, the downwinders themselves appeared to be suffering higher rates of radiation-related illnesses, including various leukemias and cancers. In fact, there are few areas of the United States that weren't sprinkled with fallout from the atomic explosions at the Nevada Test Site in the 1950s.

With the advent of huge thermonuclear fusion weapons (hydrogen bombs) in 1952, however, fallout became an even greater problem. Now tons of radioactive material were being routinely lofted far into the stratosphere, where high wind currents carried it all over the globe. Most of the fusion byproducts produced by such explosions, radioactive isotopes of various elements, have a short half-life and so decayed rapidly into harmless forms long before they could gradually fall back to Earth, but some remained hazardous long enough to reach the ground—and human beings. When high levels of longer-lived radioactive isotopes such as iodine-131 (a half-life of eight days), strontium-90 (28 years), and cesium-137 (30 years) began to show up in milk and vegetables, from which they could be taken inside and stored within the body, scientists and the public became concerned—almost panicked, in some quarters. Some unfortunate incidents highlighted the potential nastiness of fallout. In 1954, a Japanese fishing trawler (ironically named the *Fortunate Dragon*) near the site of an H-bomb test in the Pacific was doused with fallout in white particles that looked like snowflakes. The crew came down with radiation sickness, their catch was contaminated, and one crewman later died. Eventually a worldwide movement against atomic testing arose, leading President John F. Kennedy and Soviet leader Nikita Khrushchev to sign the Limited Test Ban Treaty in 1963, prohibiting nuclear tests in the atmosphere and driving them underground. Unfortunately, the treaty formally applied only to the two superpowers and their allies, and other nuclear-armed countries such as France and China chose to ignore the dangers of atmospheric testing for several more years, until international public and political pressure also forced them to take their bombs underground.

Nevertheless, no one alive on Earth during or after the years of atmospheric testing has escaped its legacy. Some of the nuclear remnants of those tests still drift in our atmosphere, and much more of it has reached the Earth. There's no way of accurately gauging its ultimate effects, of calculating how much or how little disease and genetic damage it has created since the first atomic weapon was detonated. Still, there's a good chance that somewhere within your body, possibly your bones or your thyroid gland, is a radioactive atom or two created in the heart of a nuclear bomb. You'll probably never know it because it will never do much damage, but it's there nonetheless as a souvenir of a dangerous age.

The three varieties of radiation from the unstable nuclei of radioactive elements are all hazardous to living creatures, but not all equally so. Now that we've seen how alpha, beta, and gamma radiation are created, it's time to find out what each can do after it leaves the quivering nucleus.

FROM BAD TO WORSE

The biological effects of any sort of radiation, electromagnetic or nuclear, are largely dependent on how much energy it packs. In the electromagnetic spectrum, energy travels in waves or photons oscillating at frequencies ranging from radio all the way up to X-ray and gamma radiation. The most damaging is at the high end of the scale, the X-rays and gamma rays. Because of its high frequencies and short wavelengths, a ray of this radiation can penetrate almost anything, and isn't stopped or diverted by much less than a direct hit on an atom. That's why thick shields of dense material are needed to stop X-rays and gamma rays—a wide area of tightly-packed atoms increases the chances that a penetrating ray will be stopped.

Radiation of whatever variety can be classified by whether it's ionizing or nonionizing. Nonionizing electromagnetic radiation, such as radio waves and visible light, is of lower frequency and energy and longer wavelength than the ionizing variety,

225

which begins in the ultraviolet range. As far as living cells are concerned, it's the ionizing variety that creates the most trouble (although some nonionizing radiation, if it's intense enough, can cause damage—strong microwaves can create heat, for example). Ionizing radiation knocks electrons from the outer reaches of atoms or pushes in new electrons, both of which change the atom into an ion, an atom with a positive or negative electromagnetic charge. It can also knock the atom's existing electrons into different orbits, disturbing the atom.

The formation of ions—ionization—is a phenomenon that can be handy in many ways. In another form it's the basis of chemistry, because exchanging or sharing electrons is how atoms join together to form molecules. When dealing with living tissues, however, random ionization can disrupt the delicate chemical processes of life. It can break existing chemical bonds and prevent other vital bonds from forming, and creates free radicals—those pesky molecular fragments that glom onto other reluctant molecules and disturb their functions.

Alpha particles, which are actually helium nuclei, and beta particles, which are fast-moving electrons, are both highly ionizing. Because they're so large and heavy (subatomically speaking, of course), alpha particles in particular can wreak havoc on the unfortunate atoms in their path. Alpha radiation faces some big hurdles, though. Their positive charge means that they can be deflected by another positively charged object. Then there's their size and weight. If a gamma ray moving at light speed is a rocket, then an alpha particle is a big, lumbering truck. When the alpha particle hits, it hits hard, but it doesn't keep going. A piece of paper, or for that matter, your own skin, is thick enough to stop it cold. Even in air, alpha particles don't get very far before colliding with air molecules—a few inches at most.

Kryptonite: The Achilles' Heel

This doesn't mean that alpha radiation is to be ignored, however. It may be relatively benign at a distance, but when alpha particles get inside the body, in close proximity to the cells of your lungs or digestive tract, they can cause massive damage. The inhalation or ingestion of alpha particles lets them bypass the normal barriers that protect the body. Once inside, they tear apart DNA and other organic molecules, possibly leading to various cancers.

Beta radiation is similar in its effects, although its particles are faster and more penetrating. On the outside of the body, beta radiation can get through the outer skin layers and cause a nasty sunburn-like lesion called a beta burn. Again, though, beta radiation does most of its dirty work from the inside out, when beta particles find their way inside the body and their ionizing effects damage or destroy organic molecules.

Gamma radiation, as mentioned, is the most threatening of the three, although somewhat less ionizing than alpha or beta. But it can travel great distances—some cosmic gamma rays originate light-years away—and penetrates living tissue as if made of glass. Matter (in the form of heavy lead or concrete shielding) will slow down and stop gamma rays, but not at first. It's the vast energy coupled with the light speed of gamma rays that gives them such penetrative power and makes them so dangerous. When a nuclear weapon is detonated, gamma and X-rays are immediately released and cause the most initial radiation damage; alpha and beta radiation are seen later, in what's left over in fallout and debris. Intense gamma rays are sometimes detected emanating from distant deep-space objects called "gamma ray bursters." If such an event occurred within several light-years of Earth, the results could be disastrous for life.

If small amounts of ionizing radiation can cause cellular damage that leads to cancer or genetic defects, what happens to a person subjected to an intense dose—for example, near a nuclear explosion? The result would be acute radiation syndrome, more commonly called radiation sickness. The effects on any individual can vary greatly depending on his or her general health, age, sex, how large a radiation dose was received, and other factors. Generally, though, the effects are felt throughout the body and involve many systems. A massive dose of radiation damages or kills millions of cells at once: in blood, muscle, the stomach and intestines, bones, nerves. This causes vomiting, diarrhea, hair loss, internal and external bleeding, extensive burns, mental confusion, and other neurological dysfunctions, and decreased immunity and greater susceptibility to disease and infection. Bluntly, the body falls apart.

Since the body has the ability to repair and replace damaged cells, it can recover from radiation sickness—if enough undamaged cells remain, and if the effects caused by the damaged cells on bodily systems aren't too severe. If too much damage has been done, though, the body will succumb before it can adequately repair itself, and the person dies. Even if the victim recovers, lingering effects such as sterility can remain, or show up years later in the form of cancer or leukemia. Years before the atomic bomb existed, many scientists died from continued exposure to radiation over many years, including Marie Curie. Although only a large dose in a short time causes acute radiation sickness, lower doses of ionizing radiation sustained over many years can still prove fatal.

Because of the long time period that can elapse before the effects to a low-level exposure to radiation show up, it can be difficult to prove a definite connection. If, for example, a soldier who participated in maneuvers during a bomb test in 1955 develops cancer or leukemia fifty years later, there's no definite way to prove that it's because he caught a dose of radiation while in uniform. The disease might have been caused by other environmental factors, a genetic defect he was born with, or even a stray cosmic ray. And even if the bomb test was indeed responsible, the different effects of radiation on various individuals might mean that the guy standing in the trench next to our soldier is still perfectly healthy. Thousands of soldiers who witnessed A-bomb blasts during the years of atmospheric test-

A rare kryptonite crystal.

ing have faced just such a dilemma when trying to convince the government to pay them damages and treat their illnesses.

Although exact causes and effects can be endlessly disputed in individual cases, the dangers of radiation to living creatures are well-established fact. Despite his powers, Superman is not immune, because kryptonite has the ability to cut through his natural defenses, just as gamma rays can pierce human skin. What makes kryptonite so special?

PIECES OF HOME

Kryptonite is more than simply a rock left over from the planet Krypton. It's the metallic ore of a new radioactive element, kryptonium, formed under an unusual and special set of circumstances, namely, the destruction of a planet. Krypton wasn't made of kryptonium; although its specific composition was undoubtedly different from that of Earth or any other planet, it was most likely made up of various proportions of the common elements that occur throughout the universe, such as silicon, iron, oxygen, carbon, magnesium, and so on. If we extrapolate from our one example of a Kryptonian life form—Superman— we might infer that the crust of the planet Krypton contained a somewhat higher proportion of radioactive elements, which impelled the evolution of life with a naturally high resistance to environmental radiation, as we see in Superman. The presence of a large amount of radioactive elements deeper in the planet could also be responsible for producing heat, which many geologists believe is a contributing factor to the tectonic forces on our own planet. We've seen that Krypton probably lacked plate tectonics, but intense heat in its interior could lead to stresses that created earthquakes and volcanoes—and possibly, its ultimate destruction.

Kryptonite: The Achilles' Heel

We'll examine the destruction of Krypton in more detail in the next chapter.

For now, it's enough to realize that the process was violent and powerful enough to create an array of radioactive isotopes, in much the same way as does a nuclear explosion or the bombardment of elements by subatomic particles in the laboratory. Like most exotic radioactive isotopes, the majority of these substances decayed rapidly to other, more stable elements, but those with longer half-lives remained. Kryptonium, in the form of kryptonite, is one of these. It may have resulted from a number of processes. It's possible that a different isotope of kryptonium existed earlier on Krypton, and that the planet's destruction created a new isotope. It may have been born in the energies and chaos of the explosion itself in its present state. Kryptonium could also be a more stable "daughter" element that remains from the decay of another element.

Whatever the case, we're left with an extremely rare, possibly unique element that probably exists nowhere else in the universe, and may not be capable of being formed under other natural conditions. This might sound bizarre—how can an "unnatural element" exist? Yet such elements are created all the time in particle accelerators, as physicists cause atoms of lighter elements to collide. Most such artificially created elements don't last long and exist only in the form of several atoms, but while they're around they are just as real as iron or hydrogen. Some, in fact, don't disappear overnight. The radioactive element plutonium, first created in 1940 in the cyclotron at the University of California at Berkeley, has a half-life of over 24,000 years.

As we've seen, an element can have different isotopes, and kryptonium need not be an exception. Other forms might exist or might be artificially created in the laboratory. Like other isotopes, these would have the same chemical characteristics but might vary in other qualities, such as color or the type of radiation they emitted. By the same token, it's theoretically conceivable that "synthetic" kryptonite could be made. The equipment and expense required for such a trick might be prohibitive, though. The effects of synthetic kryptonite or other isotopes of kryptonium on Superman might be similar to those of natural kryptonium or quite different.

Because the synthesis of artificial kryptonite is unlikely, Superman would be most likely to encounter the natural form created by Krypton's death throes. The first bits of the element arrived on Earth with Superman himself, embedded in the tail section of his spacecraft as Krypton exploded behind him. Such fragments couldn't amount to much in size or weight, or they would have destroyed the craft upon impact. How would other pieces of kryptonite have reached the Earth's surface?

The obvious answer, of course, is that they would arrive as meteors, plunging through our atmosphere and surviving to reach the ground. Pieces of Mars and the Moon have reached the Earth as meteors, so this is hardly an outlandish idea. If this is true of kryptonite, however, the fragments in our solar system couldn't have simply drifted through space to us. The planet Krypton was light-years away; even if the force of its explosion was violent enough to send pieces of the planet hurtling at a decent fraction of light speed (which is unlikely), they would take thousands of years to reach Earth. This could mean that Krypton actually exploded thousands or millions of years ago and that the unborn Superman spent all that time in flight while the fragments of Krypton followed. More likely, however, is that, if Kal-El's ship was equipped with a stardrive capable of opening up and traveling through a space-time wormhole to reach Earth, some amount of kryptonite was dragged along in his gravitational wake. As his small ship fled the dying Krypton, fragments of the planet would be all around. When the stardrive activated, nearby chunks could have been pulled into the local space-time surrounding the ship and into the wormhole created by the drive. When Kal-El's ship re-entered normal space-time in our solar system, so did these "stowaway" fragments of kryptonite. As they drifted through space in nearly the same solar orbit as Earth, a piece would occasionally cross our path and find itself yanked toward our planet by gravity, and another kryptonite meteor would fall to Earth.

A BREACH OF DEFENSES

If Kryptonians evolved to resist high levels of radiation, and if Superman himself is resistant to the normal radiation of Earth's environment, why does kryptonite affect him? What does it do to him, and how?

In Chapter 2, we saw that Superman has a three-part defense against dangerous ionizing radiation, a system vastly enhanced by the energy he absorbs from the sun. He has a bioelectric field for warding off charged particles; tough, dense, resistant skin layers; and a highly efficient and effective cellular repair system. Weak radiation would be stopped or deflected by the bioelectric field, while stronger, more powerful rays would be hindered by the skin. Some of the most energetic radiation, such as gamma rays, might get through the first two lines of defense, in which case any damage would be rapidly reversed by his body's powers of cellular repair. To cause serious damage, then, one or more of these defenses would have to be seriously impaired in a way that would prevent the other radiation countermeasures from compensating.

This is just what kryptonite does to Superman. By emitting

high-powered electromagnetic radiation at frequencies that interfere with and cancel out his bioelectric field, it completely removes one line of radiation defense. Without this field, more penetrating nuclear radiation is able to get through even his super-dense skin, affecting his nervous system and further weakening his ability to create and maintain his bioelectric field. Superman's cells begin to wilt under the barrage, causing pain and disrupting his body's capacities to use energy. His powers diminish and his skin layers begin to break down under the nuclear assault, allowing yet more radiation to enter his body and do still more damage. As the exposure to kryptonite radiation continues, his body is unable to recoup its normal energy stores to rapidly heal the cellular damage, and the process spirals downward. In effect, the disruption of Superman's bioelectric field is the first domino to fall in a sequence that allows enough radiation through his skin to weaken him and sap his powers until his body can't heal itself fast enough to avoid damage—or death, if the exposure is long enough.

If the kryptonite radiation ceases before that fatal point is reached, however, Superman's weakened body immediately begins the cellular repair process, first by tapping whatever physical energy reserves are left, then by taking in more solar energy at a greatly accelerated rate, like a nearly drowned person gasping for air. Depending on the length of the exposure, it may take anywhere from several minutes to several days for Superman to regain his full capacities, but as long as the fatal exposure threshold hasn't been crossed, he will recover completely.

For humans, kryptonite is just as deadly—more so, in fact, because human beings don't possess Superman's cellular recuperative abilities. We have no bioelectric field to speak of, so the interference of such a defense by kryptonite radiation isn't a factor. The gamma rays emitted by kryptonite are more than enough to destroy human cells, especially with prolonged exposure. Kryptonite also generates alpha and beta particles, just as dangerous as those from any other radioactive material at close range or if taken into the body. The radiation sickness that kryptonite radiation induces in humans at high levels is identical to that caused by more Earthly phenomena.

Basically, kryptonite radioactivity is the same as that from uranium or other radioactive elements. Its energy levels and EM wavelengths distinguish it from other elements in some ways, but it still consists of the alpha, beta, and gamma rays already examined. Because kryptonite was formed from the raw materials of Krypton, its radiation is more naturally "tuned" to affect living creatures from that planet—such as Superman. Had it existed before the planet's destruction, it would have been just as lethal to the average, non-super-powered Kryptonian.

For us, kryptonite is merely a deadly danger, but for Superman, last son of the world that spawned it, the element is a bitter reminder of the truth of the old saying: you can't go home again. Yet, even though Superman can't return to Krypton, let's do so ourselves, for a closer look at some other aspects of that doomed but magnificent world.

The Science of Superman

CHAPTER TEN

THE SCIENCE OF KRYPTON: JOR-EL'S LEGACY

At the beginning of this investigation into the powers of Superman, we took a detailed look at the physical characteristics of Krypton: its geography, structure, environment, and its relationship to its sun, a red dwarf star named Rao about fifty light years from Earth. We also speculated about the evolutionary pathways life might take on such a world, and how such life would fare in our own environment on Earth. It was seen that, partly from chance and partly because of geographical and other factors, Krypton probably developed a more unified and homogeneous civilization than Earth, and as a result, its people reached a more advanced technological level earlier than present-day humans.

We can extrapolate and infer with confidence on a scientific basis regarding Krypton itself, because the universe works in the same way everywhere, and there's much to be gleaned even from the fairly limited data available on the planet and its shattered remains. When discussing the civilization of Krypton and its people, however, there's little to go on. It took archaeologists many painstaking years to construct accurate pictures of past Earth civilizations such as the Babylonians or Egyptians, despite the fact that their people left behind clues of their way of life in ruins and remnants. The evidence of past empires usually comes to us in a piecemeal and haphazard way, almost randomly at first, but over time scholars and scientists find the patterns and logic behind the artifacts and the overall reality of the lost world emerges, even if a few tantalizing missing pieces of the puzzle remain.

In attempting to reconstruct the past of Krypton, we're far from being so lucky. Even when the city of Pompeii was destroyed and all its people killed by the eruption of Mount Vesuvius in 79 A.D., much of the city remained for archaeologists to unearth and study. The people of Krypton, however, were annihilated as thoroughly and totally as possible: their very world tore itself apart underneath them. If an archaeological space mission is ever mounted to the Rao solar system, they'll find that their trip was in vain. There will be no Kryptonian artifacts to find adrift in the cloud of kryptonite that marks the planet's grave. No books, statues, buildings, recordings, paintings, photographs, tools, vehicles, clothing, or any other signs of the existence of a Kryptonian civilization survived the cataclysmic explosion that destroyed the world. All that remains are the radioactive ashes of kryptonite, drifting around a molten mass of kryptonium, its dangerous radiation serving as a warning to curious star travelers or grave robbers to stay away and let the memory of Krypton rest in peace.

With one exception, however. One son of Krypton, Kal-El, escaped Krypton's death and became the being we know as Superman. He brought with him to our planet the only surviving example of Kryptonian technology, the experimental miniature starship created by his father, the scientist Jor-El. Thanks to Jor-El's prescience and wisdom, the craft contained some historical and family records so that Kal-El could later learn of his true origins and heritage. While certainly an incomplete picture—Jor-El hardly had the time to assemble and prepare a comprehensive, encyclopedic database in the chaotic last days of Krypton— these records, and the technological artifact of the ship itself, are all we have to tell us of the glories and tragic end of Krypton. It seems a fitting way to close our study of Superman's powers, then, with a brief examination of how he came to our planet, and the science that made his journey possible.

DESPERATE MEASURES

Like so many visionary scientists tend to be, Jor-El was something of a spiritual renegade, ahead of his time and misunderstood by his more orthodox contemporaries. We know that the Krypton of his time, while peaceful and highly advanced, had become a rather sterile and soulless society, in response to past political and social upheavals that had threatened to drag its civilization into darkness and total collapse. Kryptonian people tended to be isolated from one another physically, particularly in the higher strata of society, and many intellectuals and other prominent citizens lived an almost-literal ivory tower sort of existence. Sophisticated communications and virtual-reality technology removed any need for in-person interactions to the point where such contact was almost distasteful to many Kryptonians. Because medical and technological advances had extended the life span to centuries, population levels were strictly controlled, with the birth of new citizens permitted only on the rare occasions when others died of natural causes or were killed in accidents. To preserve genetic integrity and quality, parents were carefully chosen and children were born by advanced in vitro techniques in a planetary gestation chamber, their biological parents never actually meeting in person.

Unlike most Kryptonians, however, Jor-El was dissatisfied

Jor-El launches the spacecraft carrying his son's birthing matrix.

with the restrictions of his society. Although he understood and sympathized with the goals of preserving order and avoiding undue passions and strife, he found many of his world's customs to be cold and heartless in practice. As a young man studying science, he refused to limit himself to the traditional practice of simply studying Krypton's vast central data banks, and instead set out on field trips to see the wonders of his planet for himself. He became fascinated not only with his own world but the entire universe, especially the existence of other planets and the possibility of life beyond Krypton. His work in the realms of astronomy, astrophysics, and nuclear physics was seminal and quickly earned him a reputation as a scientist of the highest order—although his colleagues sometimes questioned his unconventional methods.

When he was chosen to father a child, matched with the aristocratic historian Lara, Jor-El wasn't content to simply contribute his genetic material and continue with his own life. He wanted more of a connection to the woman with whom he was paired, and insisted on seeing an image of Lara and learning more about her. In doing so, he found himself succumbing to an affliction that was almost unknown on the Krypton of that time—he fell in love, despite the fact that the physical meeting of couples chosen for reproduction not only wasn't necessary but was actively discouraged.

Other circumstances doomed any possible happy ending for Jor-El and Lara, however. Geological upheavals were beginning to rock the planet from pole to pole. Earthquakes, previously fairly rare on Krypton, broke out in widely scattered areas with violent intensity. Some of Krypton's volcanic mountains, which had lain dormant for uncounted millennia, erupted into deadly activity. Accompanying these phenomena in many places was a strange release of unknown radiation, apparently originating somewhere inside the planet. Millions died from the geological violence and mysterious radiation, as the unknown processes generating the planetary crises seemed to accelerate and intensify.

Jor-El devoted all his energies to learning what was happening to his world. The earthquakes and volcanoes by themselves were unusual in their frequency and strength, but certainly not unknown in Kryptonian history and easily explainable by well understood geological processes. However, Jor-El was mystified by the concurrent radiation. The presence of natural radioactivity in Krypton's crust was well established, yet the intensity and nature of this new radiation were inexplicable by any known geological phenomenon. Jor-El hypothesized that the radiation, and consequently the geological disturbances, might therefore have an artificial cause. Few of his scientific colleagues took him seriously: how would such a thing be possible? And who would be insane enough to set such catastrophes into motion?

Jor-El ignored such criticisms, however, and pursued his ideas by returning to the great Kryptonian central data banks he had studied—and then partly spurned—in his youth. Devising an ingenious computer algorithm that could simultaneously examine, cross-reference and collate millions of data points from nearly every branch of scientific, historical, and cultural knowledge, he uncovered details of a dark period in Krypton's past. Ancient Kryptonian society had used a system of cloning to extend the lives of its citizens, and over time many Kryptonians began to protest this arrangement and demand civil rights for clones, threatening the foundations of the established government and culture. A civil breakdown ensued, spawning both noble resistance groups dedicated to freedom and peace, and violent extremist cells sworn to terrorism and chaos. One of the worst terrorist groups, named Black Zero, actually destroyed the city of Kandor with a hydrogen weapon, sparking the only world war in Kryptonian history. The war ended after millions were killed, and civilization was ultimately restored after an interlude of barbarity.

Through his computer program, Jor-El was able to locate and examine hundreds of surviving documents and artifacts from those years—many of which had never been thoroughly, or even briefly, studied before by scholars. His researches revealed chilling but inescapable evidence that before it was wiped out by its enemies, the Black Zero group had managed to construct a doomsday device—and, by commandeering an advanced tunneling apparatus used to study Krypton's interior, planted the device deep near the planet's core. For the members of Black Zero, it was a desperate, fanatical gesture of cosmic fatalism, a means of ultimately attaining their insane dream of "purifying" an "evil" Krypton by destroying it, even if it happened when they and their group were long dead.

The Black Zero device was ingenious in its lethal simplicity. It was merely a large device designed to emit massive levels of nuclear and electromagnetic radiation of extremely high energies through a huge, sustained fusion reaction. In effect, it was an enormous fusion reactor, as if a small piece of sun had been lowered into the planet. The hope was that the radioactive and heat reactions induced by the device in Krypton's core would intensify and increase natural geological stresses to the point at which the planet would literally tear itself apart. The creators of this nefarious invention had no idea how long the process would take, or even if it would happen at all. In their minds, however, there was nothing to lose.

Jor-El calculated that the doomsday device itself had in fact been destroyed by the forces of the planet's core only several hundred years after its placement, but its purpose had already been fulfilled. It had caused a sharp increase in the heat of Krypton's core, leading inevitably to a buildup in internal pressure and stress. Without natural plate-tectonic activity to help relieve internal pressures, Krypton's death sentence was assured: it was only a matter of time. Meanwhile, far above on the surface of the planet, Kryptonian civilization continued to advance and mature, unaware that it was inexorably doomed.

Tragically, Jor-El's discoveries proved that the doomsday process was irreversible. Krypton was in its death throes, and the science of its inhabitants couldn't reverse its slide to oblivion even if the cause had been discovered earlier. Resigned to his own fate, Jor-El decided that his and Lara's yet-unborn child, who was to be a boy named Kal-El, would survive. A rebel to the end, Jor-El retrieved Kal-El's birthing matrix—the self-contained biocapsule inside of which Kal-El was being formed with exacting genetic control—from the gestation chambers of Krypton. Before Jor-El placed the matrix into the small experimental hyperdrive spacecraft he had developed, Lara found and confronted him. Meeting the woman he loved for the first time, Jor-El explained his plan to send their son safely to another inhabited world he had discovered and observed—Earth—on which Kal-El could not only survive but might also develop greater strength and other physical abilities. Lara agreed, and she and Jor-El watched as the star craft lifted Kal-El away from his dying home. After leaving the atmosphere and reaching outer space, the self-controlled ship activated Jor-El's stardrive and set course for Earth—just as Krypton blasted itself into eternity behind it. Even before he was actually born, Kal-El had become an orphan twice over, losing not only his parents but his home world.

REMNANTS

This tale of Krypton's end makes it clear that, even thousands of years before the planet exploded, the scientific knowledge of its people was far in advance of anything known on Earth. Ironically, this same advancement was the ultimate cause of their demise: it provided them with the knowledge and technology to invent a device that could destroy an entire planet before they had acquired the maturity to deal with that knowledge, and to set it in motion to doom the future generations who would attain the maturity that could have prevented the tragedy. Even humans, with our thousands of nuclear weapons, are far from controlling such power—fortunately. True, we may be able to essentially destroy the ecosystem of our world and a good portion of the living creatures it sustains in a spasm of thermonuclear rage if we choose, but the planet itself would hardly notice. Earth has suffered much worse in its more than four billion years of existence.

In a more positive realm, we're also as yet unable to build a spacecraft capable of carrying a living being, even if only in its fetal stages, across light years of space in a short time.[1] Jor-El, however, not only created such a craft, but he made it so small and lightweight that the human beings who found it, Jonathan and Martha Kent, could move it and hide it in their barn. How was Jor-El's amazing engineering achievement possible? In short, what does Kal-El's ship tell us about the state of Kryptonian science and technology?

We've assumed that the vessel was equipped with some kind of stardrive, hyperdrive, or similar propulsion that gave it the ability to reach Earth's solar system nearly instantaneously. Without such a drive system, the light-speed limit of the universe would prevent a trip from Krypton to Earth in any reasonable length of time. After arriving at a point in our solar system, the ship may have switched to a more conventional propulsion system to travel the remaining distance to Earth

1. However, we have sent four spacecraft into interstellar space: *Pioneer 10* and *11*, and *Voyager 1* and *2*. But after thirty years, none of them are even close to a light-year away, and none will pass near another star for thousands of years.

and to land, taking several days to several months.

Any drive capable of creating a "wormhole" in space-time would require the generation and manipulation of truly enormous energies. These would be far beyond anything currently possible with our technology—perhaps ever. To even approach such an accomplishment, however, large and complex equipment would be needed. Assuming that we're someday able to build a true starship, it's likely to be immense and very, very expensive—unless, through some currently unknown technique, we discover a means to create the energies needed to "warp" space-time around a large spacecraft with a power source smaller than several nuclear plants joined together.

The Kryptonians were apparently old hands at such feats. At the time of their planet's death, they'd had nuclear technology for both power generation and weapons for many thousands of years. They would have learned and developed ways to create and control nuclear power without the bulky auxiliary systems for cooling, transmission, and so on that we use. This might involve anything from the synthesis of new radioactive elements that lend themselves to such applications to the creation of "mini-black holes" that produce massive energy from a near-microscopic source. The ship's energy generator would also be the key to its stardrive. Whatever its form, a detailed examination of the power source and propulsion system of Kal-El's vessel would no doubt revolutionize Earthly physics. Although Jor-El's design was apparently only a prototype, and therefore undoubtedly not perfected, it worked at least once. Jor-El may even have known that the design was impractical or might not work at all, but desperation led him to conduct one last experiment that, if it succeeded, would mean the survival of his son.

The size of Kal-El's escape craft also implies advanced miniaturization technology of other kinds. The ship obviously required some kind of guidance system, life support for Kal-El's biocapsule, and a highly sophisticated computer system to control the various subsystems. We have no idea what sort of computer might be necessary to compute a course through hyperspace, but it's likely to be blazingly fast and of prodigious capacities, much like one of our present-day supercomputers. For all of the secondary systems packed into the ship to support the computer and the guidance and life support functions, Jor-El may also have made use of a technology that is still cutting-edge and largely speculative for humans: nanotechnology. This involves the construction and use of "machines" at literally the molecular level, which can build millions of copies of themselves at great speed to perform tasks formerly possible only with much larger devices. On Earth, the science is in its infancy, and not everyone agrees that it can be made to work on a practical level. Kryptonian scientists, however, may have learned to apply and control nanotechnology to great sophistication. It might also have come in handy when dealing with emergencies during Kal-El's journey to Earth. Under control of the ship's computer, the "nanomachines" could repair or modify the ship as needed to handle unforeseen contingencies—building thicker shielding around Kal-El's capsule to protect him from an intense radiation source, for instance.

Of the technologies aboard Kal-El's craft, the example that's probably closest to the present level of Earthly science is the birthing matrix. We might not yet be capable of constructing a device that could protect a fetal human being from the hazards of space travel, but *in vitro* fertilization, genetic engineering, and cloning are well within our technology, as anyone who's followed news developments in recent years is aware. The major impediments to the development of such techniques have been ethical and political, not technological. The abilities of human beings to alter their genetic makeup, modify traits, and even "design" their children will only increase and become more sophisticated in the near future, and we'll have to face the hard questions that arise from such powers. On Krypton, however, these reproductive and genetic practices were routine, so moral quandaries didn't affect the development of the technology. For good or ill, though, it would not be too great a practical step for humans to adopt similar techniques if we chose. It will be one of the most important decisions humans face in the 21st century.

No matter how wondrous the technology of Kal-El's spaceship, perhaps the most important message it would contain for Earth is embodied in its passenger: the first definite example of extraterrestrial life ever seen by humanity. More than that, Kal-El and the starship itself would prove the existence of *intelligent* life elsewhere in the universe: beings that could construct such a craft and send it on its journey, beings that understood and could wield the secrets of life. Kal-El's very existence would demonstrate that the emergence of advanced, sentient life forms wasn't a cosmic fluke that occurred only once, on our dust speck of a planet, in one dim corner of the universe. We would know that intelligence can arise elsewhere, and also that it can survive its beginnings to achieve levels of knowledge we can yet only imagine.

A comparison of Kryptonian science to ours, and also of Superman to human beings, leads to an interesting question: Is it possible that, one day, science may grant us super powers ourselves? And not merely by extending our human abilities through technology, as we already do in many ways, but by literally changing and improving the human body itself?

A SUPER FUTURE?

Our understanding of ourselves as biological creatures has expanded immensely in the last half-century, beginning with the unlocking of the structure of DNA by the team of Francis Crick, James Watson, Maurice Wilkins, and Rosalind Franklin in the 1950s. With the birth of the science of molecular biology that followed, and the development of new techniques to study, alter, and redesign the genetic structures of life itself, humankind has rapidly acquired abilities and knowledge that to previous generations would seem almost godlike. Life is no longer a mysterious, transcendental "force" whose secrets are forever locked inside the walls of cells; we've penetrated to its deepest heart and seen its workings at its most infinitesimal and basic levels. We may not yet have breathed life into inanimate dust like a mythical god, but we can routinely construct its building blocks, change its composition, and adjust its development.

At least in a rough first-draft form, we've already mapped the human genome, the complete genetic blueprint of what we are and how we function. Many years of work lie ahead in interpreting the picture this work has given us, but those years will bring startling—perhaps frightening—discoveries. The 21st century will undoubtedly see the advent of the human capacity to heal and perhaps banish many formerly intractable chronic and acute diseases by the precise alteration and repair of the genome—and the ability to choose and change nearly every other human characteristic. This ability will extend from the trivial, such as changing our hair or eye color, to the most profound aspects of human nature, such as intellectual capacity and our large-scale physical form and functions.

It's too early to tell the specifics. We can't say yet how we might, for example, give ourselves six fingers or four arms for added dexterity, create super-geniuses in the womb, or alter astronauts to survive in space without a protective suit. And as we delve still deeper into the human genome, we may encounter roadblocks to such modifications—side effects or added consequences that will make such radical changes impossible. Theoretically, however, the horizon appears almost limitless so far. We may be at the threshold of the first age in which the definition of "human being" becomes something that's not set in biological stone, but something almost infinitely changeable and flexible.

All of this means that *yes*, it's quite possible that we will be able to become "super" ourselves, in whatever way we choose to define the term. Flying may be out of the question until we learn a lot more about gravity, and even then the physical modifications necessary might be more than we'd want to accept (unless we go the old-fashioned route and grow wings for ourselves). Superman's other powers, though, are well within our reach. We can already achieve a sort of temporary super-strength, for example, by flooding our bodies with steroids and other special chemicals. With the genetic modification of muscles and joints and the body's metabolic functions, we could increase physical strength and stamina permanently, as has already been done with the University of Pennsylvania mice. The structure of the eye, ear, and other sensory mechanisms could be enhanced or changed to become more sensitive to sights and sounds to which we're presently blind and deaf. By bolstering the body's own immune system, its healing and recuperative powers, and strengthening the skin and the body in general, we might achieve virtual invulnerability.

And imagine what it might mean if human beings were able to run off of solar energy directly, as Superman does. "Coupling human cellular metabolism with light just as plants do is really not so far-fetched," says Jeff Livingstone, a biochemist and vice-president of Signet Laboratories, a Massachusetts biotech company. "We could have soldiers who could go forever . . . solar-powered people. Someday, someone's going to do it."

The history of the past century, however, demonstrates that what we may someday be *able* to do and what we *should* do can be worlds apart. Fifty years ago, the invention of nuclear weapons made this gulf between theory and practice sharply clear. Some scientists saw it earlier than anyone else. The Hungarian genius Leo Szilard, who first conceived the idea of a nuclear chain reaction while crossing a London street one day and soon after helped to set the Manhattan Project in motion, later pleaded for international controls on atomic weapons and had second thoughts about using the bomb in World War II, even as the Los Alamos scientists tested the first atomic bomb in New Mexico and prepared it for use against Japan. In much the same way, some scientists today are calling for caution and introspection as humankind's ability to manipulate life continually grows more complete. Other people demand that all research and work devoted to understanding and possibly improving the human genome be abandoned.

Banning such technology and completely discarding its great promise to ease human suffering would be foolish and short-sighted. Yet the ethical and moral questions raised by its use, or more properly, its misuse, must be seriously considered, not only by the scientists involved but by everyone, because ultimately everyone will be affected by them. To fairly and fully consider the questions, it's necessary to understand something about the science behind them, yet many of the politicians and policymakers who decide the issues know little or nothing about science. A populace educated in the basics of science and scientific reasoning—even just a little—will provide the best insurance that present and future generations don't carelessly throw away valuable knowledge, but are able to use it wisely.

Superhumans may someday live among us. Some of us may even choose to become "super" ourselves. If we make the right choices and consider all the possible consequences now, the superhumans, the old-fashioned "normal" humans, and whatever other varieties we may create will all consider themselves and each other as part of the human race. Or we could plunge forward thoughtlessly and in the process unravel and corrupt the exquisite handiwork of millions of years of human evolution. The choice is ours.

CONCLUSIONS

Kal-El came to our planet as a refugee, an orphan, a lost soul, launched on his journey as the last act of a brilliant, desperate man trying to ensure that one small fragment of his planet's long-lived civilization and advanced culture would survive. Jor-El succeeded to a degree far beyond what he could only vaguely have imagined. As the heroic Superman, Kal-El is more than a representative of a lost world, or evidence of the possibility of life beyond our planet; he's a testament to the noblest achievements and aspirations of the people of Krypton.

From his observations of Earth and his knowledge of Kryptonian biology, Jor-El was aware that his son would likely develop strength and abilities beyond those of the Earth's inhabitants, but he had no way of knowing whether those physical augmentations would amount merely to slight enhancements of natural capacity—a biological compensation to aid Kal-El in surviving on an alien world—or powers that would make him vastly superior to the people of Earth. Yet Jor-El was confident that, if Kal-El literally became superhuman, he wouldn't abuse

The end of Krypton . . . and the beginning of Superman.

his powers by using them to dominate the weaker beings around him. Although he would never live to personally impart his own values and morals to Kal-El, Jor-El had faith in the Kryptonian heritage and instinctive goodness that, despite some grievous failures, had led his people to great heights. A superbeing could easily become a dictator on a planet of lesser beings, but Jor-El knew that a Kryptonian would never dream of such an ambition.

Fortunately for Earth and its people, Jor-El was correct. His son became not a ruthless despot, but a symbol of freedom and justice, a champion not of darkness but of light. He uses his powers not as weapons to subjugate the weak, but as tools to save and preserve life. Yet Kal-El made this choice consciously, not simply as a result of his Kryptonian origins, but because of the very human influence of his foster parents, Jonathan and Martha Kent. Although it's unlikely that Kal-El would have used his powers for evil purposes as he grew into manhood, he might have been content to live out his life on Earth as an average individual, hiding his great abilities or using them only occasionally for minor purposes. Without the guidance and the humanistic values inculcated in him by the Kents, young Kal-El would probably not have realized that his abilities were more than a curiosity, but could be used as a powerful force for good. More than any other single influence, even that of Kal-El's noble Kryptonian heritage, it was the example of Jonathan and Martha Kent—their basic decency, their compassion, their concern and abiding respect for others, and their firm belief in the essential goodness of humanity—that created Superman, the defender of Earth and its people.

An old proverb states that absolute power corrupts absolutely, and no individual on Earth has had such near-absolute power in his hands as Superman. He could, in fact, impose his will on Earth in an almost godlike manner if he chose. Superman has the same emotions as any human being, and no doubt he sometimes grows impatient with the overwhelming imperfections of this world and feels tempted to do more than merely right its wrongs on an individual scale, saving a life here, stopping a crime there. But he realizes that the responsibility to literally decide the fate of the world is too great for any one person to accept, no matter how vast his or her power. The histories of both Earth and Krypton show conclusively that neither humans at their present level of development, nor Kryptonians at the peak of their achievements, are or were wise enough to bear such a burden.

Superman is more than a product of the glories of Krypton. In him, the best of humanity is present as well: the drive to use one's talents in the service of others, to lessen suffering and create peace, to make the world a more just and less cruel place. Awesome as his powers may be, the most impressive quality of Superman is how he's chosen to employ those powers. As a super hero, as a survivor of a lost world, and as an intelligent being, Superman has much to teach us.

And in the story of how Kal-El came to Earth and why his world died, we can learn something else. The end of Krypton provides a tragic example of the follies of unbridled war, unreasoning hatreds, and the misuse of science and technology for evil ends—an example we can't ignore because it comes from another world as objective fact untainted by any human agendas or prejudices. In the final analysis, even if Kal-El had not grown into the champion of Earth as Superman, this message, more than anything else, more than all the good he has done through his super powers, might be his most precious gift to humanity.